Praise for Christo
PURE OF

"An Extraordinary Creative Fantasy. Highly recommend for adults and it's also suitable for young adults to enjoy."
— *Nancy Silk, Author*

"A Connecticut Yankee meets Lord of the Rings."
— *Kevin Dunlap, GoodReads*

"A wonder. A clean heart, a clear head. A message to us all."
— *Douglas A. Stephens, Amazon Reader*

"Written with imagination and skill this is a tale for those who like Tolkien, and similar writers of Sword and Sorcery stories. It may well become a classic in that Genre." — *Michael Muir*

"Dean could become the new Harry Potter or Harry Dresden, if those are your authors try Christopher Greyson you won't be disappointed." — *David Russell, GoodReads*

"This was a great adventure, with vivid, memorable characters. Great book! I highly recommend it!!" — *Bruce Irik, GoodReads*

"This book was funny, exciting, scary, and just pure fun!"
— *Tala S. Gilbert, Amazon Reader*

"If you loved Tolkien but want something like it but less wordy, this is the book for you." — *Susan P. Spurgeon*

Also by Christopher Greyson:

PURE OF HEART

A FANTASY ADVENTURE

CHRISTOPHER GREYSON

GREYSON MEDIA

Pure of Heart

Copyright © 2015 Greyson Media

Find out more about the author and upcoming books online at www.ChristopherGreyson.com.

This book is dedicated in loving memory to
Theodore Ricci and Mark Geodecke.
Two men whose teaching shaped my life
and showed me the qualities a true man should have.

Pure of Heart

Evil spreads across the land
Silently into the spirit of man

Touch it, you can't
Feel it, you can
Buy it, you may
Control it, nay

Spear, bow, ax, and sword
Search to destroy the Dark Lord

A sword cannot win the fight
Money cannot buy the light
A king cannot rule the night

Only one can save the land
He's the one who's yet a man
He's the one from another part
The only one Pure of Heart

1

ALONE

A cold rain fell from the midnight-blue sky and washed over his shoulders. Soaked through to his socks, he let his old sneakers fall heavily on the broken sidewalk, the sound swallowed by the storm. The rain matted his dark hair before flowing over his cheeks, erasing any sign of bitter tears. He flipped up the collar of his worn, black leather jacket to protect himself against the chill—but still he shivered.

Dean was used to being alone; orphaned as a child, he'd made his way through life relying on himself. Tossed from one temporary home to the next, he'd never felt he belonged anywhere. Now, at seventeen, he'd had enough—and he'd struck out on his own.

A lone car drove slowly past him. Its headlights sparkled against the raindrops; the puddles shimmered and the sidewalk glistened. When the taillights disappeared around the corner, the darkness seemed even deeper than before. Dean thrust his hands into his pockets and tried to forget his troubles.

As he passed yet another dark, littered alley, he saw three figures huddled over a man lying face down on the ground. Dean stopped. He knew the man didn't stand a chance; it was three against one.

The wounded man raised his head. He was old, with a thin, pale face. His steely gray eyes locked on Dean's. There was something odd in those eyes: a glimmer of hope.

Dean's shoulders slumped. He knew he was no one's savior. He turned to leave, and the light in the old man's eyes faded.

"You should have given us your wallet, old man," the tall punk snarled. "Now we have to take it the hard way. Get it, Bobby."

"Shut up, Randy. I'm getting it." Bobby stepped closer, an iron pipe in his hand. He wore a twisted smile.

Dean backed away, the scene burned into his heart, but he shut his eyes and disappeared back into the darkness, swallowed by the rain once more.

"Waste him!" cried the fat one.

"Hit him!" Randy yelled, goading his friend on.

Bobby raised the rusted pipe over the old man's head.

Dean stood tall, silhouetted beneath the streetlight, the pouring rain washing over him. "Let him go," he said, defiant.

The three figures stiffened and turned.

"Get lost." Bobby pointed the pipe at Dean.

Dean held up his hands. "Why don't you just let the old guy go? He probably doesn't have any money."

"Old people always have something," the fat one sneered.

"He doesn't." Dean shrugged. "If he had any, he would have taken a cab out of this crummy neighborhood, or he would have given it to you already."

"What did you just say?" Randy poked himself in the chest with his thumb. "This is my hood."

Dean sighed. "During the day, when the sun's out and it's not raining, I'm sure it's really nice. Come on. Just let the guy go."

Bobby glared down at the old man. "He's holding out on me. No." He lifted the pipe over his head again, and his lips curled into a snarl.

Dean charged.

Before Bobby could react, Dean lowered his shoulder and

carried him right through some trash cans and into a brick wall. Bobby crumpled to the ground. He rolled over and groaned in pain.

The other two punks circled behind Dean. The fat one picked up the pipe and swung it menacingly in front of him.

"I'm gonna kill him," Randy spat as he pulled out a long knife. "This little hero's mine."

Dean stepped back, looked around, and realized he was cornered. Behind him, the alley was blocked by a chain-link fence.

"You're dead now," growled the fat one.

Behind the two punks, the old man rose to his feet, his face set and determined. In his hands was a discarded broom. As he raised the broom over his head, his eyes blazed.

Dean's mouth fell open.

"What? Are you gonna tell us the cops are behind us?" scoffed the guy with the pipe.

Dean smiled. "Nope."

The old man slammed the broom down on the back of the fat guy's head. The guy tumbled to the ground, the pipe skittering across the pavement.

Randy slashed at the old man with the knife. Dean was about to intervene, but the old man deftly sprang backward out of the way. Randy surged forward, wildly slashing again and again, trying to hack the old man. But the old man easily deflected all of the strikes with the broom handle, and the corner of his mouth curled impishly upward.

Then the broom cracked down against Randy's forearm, and the knife fell from his hand. Randy opened his mouth to scream in pain, but before any sound came out, the old man swung sideways and struck him in the chest. The force of the blow sent the punk flying backward into the wall. Randy whimpered as he slid down the bricks into a heap.

Dean just stared. "How did you—?"

A scream pierced the air. "Police! Police!"

Dean turned to see a large woman at the entrance of the alley waving her arms and pointing at him.

"We must leave," the old man warned, and he ran away from the woman, down the alley toward the fence.

Dean hesitated, but the sound of sirens sent him racing after the old man. "Wait!"

The old man expertly hopped over the chain-link fence without even slowing.

Dean tried to do the same, but his feet slid on the wet metal as he climbed. As he made it to the top and awkwardly kicked his legs to the other side, he looked back up the alley. A police car screeched to a stop; its blue and red lights flickered on the faces of the three men on the ground.

Dean's heart pounded in his chest. He slipped, fell backward, and landed hard on his back. With a groan, he picked himself up and continued to sprint down the alley.

The old man was waiting at the end of the alley, looking irritated. "Can you run faster, or do you wish to go to jail?" And he took off again.

Dean took a deep breath and charged after him, his feet splashing in the puddles. The alley turned a corner, and he came around it to see the old man leaping gracefully over a jumble of crates that blocked the way. Dean attempted the same leap, but his feet crashed into the crates, and for the second time in the last minute he found himself sprawled on the asphalt.

"Come." The old man yanked him to his feet.

Dean was amazed at the old man's speed and ability. He had a feeling the old man was holding back so as not to outdistance him.

They exited the alley, then sprinted down the street and into another alley. The old man suddenly yanked Dean sideways into some garbage cans.

"What the—?"

The old man's hand clamped down on Dean's mouth, and his other hand pointed. A police car was slowly prowling down the street behind them, its spotlight sweeping the shadows. They both waited until it turned a corner, out of sight.

Dean caught his breath. "Thanks. What's your name?"

The old man pulled Dean to his feet. "Don't talk. Run."

They sprinted into the obscurity of a park. Dean's lungs burned and his heart pounded in his ears as he ran alongside the old man. They passed a fountain that sprayed water high into the air; it settled down on Dean like a mist.

Dean stumbled to a stop and panted for breath. "My legs can't take this."

But the old man just grabbed him by the collar and pulled him forward, and Dean muttered, "I know. Don't talk, run."

The old man smiled.

It wasn't long before they reached the other side of the park. The road there was lit by streetlights that showed it was deserted. Mercifully, the old man came to an abrupt stop.

Dean put his hands on his knees and panted for breath, but when the old man put his thumb out like he was hitchhiking, Dean scoffed, "Like we're gonna get a ride that way."

The words had barely left his mouth when a rusted red pickup truck came to a screeching halt right before them. A heavyset man in his forties with a thick beard leaned out the window. "You fellas need a lift?"

The old man nodded. To Dean he said, "Get in the back and stay down."

Dean hesitated, unsure what to make of all this. But he figured he had few options, so he climbed in the back.

"Hide under that." The old man pointed to an army-green tarp. Dean obediently lay down underneath it while the old man went to sit up front.

The truck started moving, and Dean wondered where they were going. Not that he really cared; he just didn't want to get caught and spend another night in jail. He knew this time the police might never let him out.

The truck drove for a long time, and they left the city far behind. Feeling safe in the warm darkness under the tarp, he let the gentle rocking of the truck lull him to sleep.

***

The sound of the passenger-side door slamming shut woke Dean with a jolt. He pulled off the tarp, and saw the old man standing beside the truck, gesturing for him to get down. He hopped out, and immediately the truck pulled away.

Only then did Dean really look around. He realized they weren't just out of the city, they were way outside the city, somewhere high in the mountains. The lights from the city were barely visible in the distance.

"Wait! Wait!" Dean called as the truck disappeared from sight. "Oh, crud! Where am I?"

"You're far enough away from the danger of the city and only a short distance from my home." The old man gave him a friendly smile.

"Well, it was real interesting meeting you, but I think this is where we part ways." Dean turned away and started walking back down the mountain road toward the city lights.

"Where are you going to go, my young friend?" the old man called, as if he knew the answer.

Dean kept walking.

"The police will be looking for you," the old man added.

Dean stopped and spun to face the old man. "Why are the police going to be looking for me? I didn't do anything. You're the one who kicked their butts."

"I know that and you know that, but that woman who saw you doesn't know that."

"Well then, you can come with me and tell them what really happened. That I was saving you, and you beat them up in self-defense."

"I don't think they'll believe an old man like me beat up those three young men. Do you?"

Dean clenched his hands in frustration. He looked down to the city and then back to the old man.

"You know, I am looking for someone to work on my small farm," said the old man. "Since you seem to be in a predicament, I think a safe place to stay with free room and board is an offer too good for you to pass up."

The old man was right; Dean already knew he would accept the offer. Back in the city, he was wanted by the police for shoplifting food. That was a minor offense, but Dean had taken off, and the store manager slipped on some ice and fell while giving chase, injuring his arm. Of course, the manager told the police Dean had assaulted him. So now Dean was looking at both robbery and assault charges. And after tonight, they would probably charge him with more.

"What kind of work and how much?" he asked.

"Feed horses. Mend fences. And I can also teach you how to defend yourself."

"Defend myself? I saved your neck in that alley back there."

"You rushed headfirst into one assailant, leaving your backside completely unprotected. That was stupid. Not the mark of a skilled warrior."

"I guess it's a good thing your opinion doesn't matter to me," Dean said.

A smile crossed the old man's worn face, and a mischievous gleam appeared in his eyes. "But you did demonstrate courage.

Thank you for your assistance."

Dean was thrown off balance by the old man's sudden change in tone. "Um…you're welcome."

"I seem to have forgotten my manners. Panadur Theradine, at your service." The old man gave a regal bow.

"Dean Walker."

"Well, Dean, would you like to see where you'll be staying?"

Dean looked the old man over again. It was a risk to trust this stranger, but at this moment, it was a risk he was willing to take. "How much?"

"Enough. Plus room and board. That means meals included."

Dean's stomach growled at the mention of food. It had been two days since he'd eaten anything, and that was only half a hamburger he'd picked out of the garbage.

"Come. Look at the farm, and we can discuss it." Without waiting for an answer, Panadur turned and started walking away.

Dean debated only a moment more before following.

They took a narrow path that led up the side of the mountain. They had trudged along for almost half an hour when the trees faded away and Dean found himself standing in a wide clearing. In the moonlight he could see a little wooden cottage that looked like something out of a dream. It was made of worn, dark wooden planks covered in green moss. The faded roof was hidden underneath a labyrinth of vines. A brick chimney poked out from the back.

Beside the cottage was a small barn that smelled of farm animals, and next to that was a huge oak tree.

Panadur walked up the three steps of the cottage's small porch. "Welcome to my home, Dean."

Dean followed and stopped in the doorway. Panadur took a lantern from the wall and lit it. It bathed the cottage's interior in a warm glow.

Centered in the room was a table and chairs. Another, smaller, table sat next to the door, and a counter and sink rested against the far wall. On the right-hand side, a wood stove, flanked by cabinets, stood in front of a red-brick chimney. Three little windows looked out into the darkness.

Panadur disappeared into another room and reappeared almost at once with a bundle under his arm. He went to the corner of the room and laid it down. Dean realized it was a sleeping bedroll with some clothes. "The clothes may be rather large, but they're dry. You can sleep here."

"Thanks." Dean took the clothes.

"You can start work in the morning. If you need anything during the night, I'll be in the next room."

Panadur walked over to the cabinets next to the stove. He rummaged around for a moment before turning back with a plate of bread and a hunk of cheese.

Dean's stomach growled.

Panadur set the plate at the table and gestured for Dean to eat.

Dean rushed over and picked up the bread. It was homemade. He took a huge bite.

"Slow down. Your stomach needs time to adjust." Panadur moved back to the sink. "And sit down." He picked up a cup and started filling it from a hand-operated pump.

Dean sat down. "You've got no electricity?" He mumbled with his mouth half full.

"I don't need it." Panadur set the cup before Dean. "Like most things in life, if need be, you can do without."

Dean nodded.

"Well, I'll see you in the morning. Pleasant dreams." Panadur walked off into the other room and closed the door.

Dean broke off a hunk of cheese. He never had pleasant dreams—they were always nightmares.

He finished the last of the bread and washed it down with the cool spring water. Always wary, he couldn't believe he was trusting this guy. But what choice did he have? It was too dark to trek back down the hillside. He looked at the closed door for a while before he made up his mind. He decided that if the old man meant him harm, he would've hurt him already.

Dean walked over and collapsed onto the sleeping bag. He'd spent the last week sleeping in a doorway near the docks. Compared to that, this little cottage was a world-class resort.

As he dozed off, the sound of a thunderstorm rumbled closer.

2

HOW TO TRAIN A WARRIOR

Dean jumped when someone shook him awake.

"Good morning." The old man stood over him, smiling. "Breakfast is ready for you, and I suggest you eat heartily, for we have a long day ahead of us."

"Okay, great. Thanks."

"I'll return in a few minutes. I have a few things I must take care of outside first." As Panadur walked out the door, he was grinning from ear to ear.

Dean sat up slowly, the events of last night coming back to him. He looked around the darkened room. "The sun isn't even up yet," he grumbled to himself.

Wearily, he rose—and then he saw that the table was heaped with eggs, ham, and biscuits. He'd never seen so much food in one place. He sat down and dug in hungrily.

He had just scraped his plate clean when Panadur came back. "We will start your training now. Follow me."

Dean wiped his mouth with the back of his hand and hurried after the old man. They walked across the dirt yard to the oak tree next to the barn.

"Hey," Dean said. "Before I start working, I want to know how much I'll get paid."

Panadur took three one-hundred-dollar bills from his pocket.

Dean's mouth fell open. "Uh . . . Why so much?"

Panadur grinned. "I wasn't entirely honest with you, Dean."

The hair on the back of Dean's neck rose. He got ready to run. "What's that for?"

Panadur laughed. "Nothing bad."

"Yeah, I've heard that before."

"If at any time you want to leave, you can take the money and go."

Dean eyed him suspiciously.

"But for now, although I don't like it, I aim to buy your trust."

"If that's all you're looking for, then three hundred is a good start." Dean reached for the money.

Panadur tore the bills in half.

"What're you doing?" Dean cried.

"You get half now." Panadur handed him the ripped bills. "You get the other half at the end of the week."

Dean's smile faded. "Everyone has an angle," he grumbled.

"The chores will come second. Training comes first."

"Training? What kind of training?"

"It's my intent to train you to be a warrior."

Dean laughed.

Panadur didn't.

"Excuse me? A what? A warrior? You're crazy, old man."

"Was it not enough money?" Panadur tilted his head. "Or do you not think you are up to the task?"

"No . . . but I didn't know it was for training to become some sort of bodyguard. I figure for that you should pay me ... at least twice as much."

"No."

"I'll take—"

"No. My offer stands as is. You get room, board, and three hundred every week. Decide."

Dean's full stomach was all the answer he really needed. He

remembered the cold and hunger of the streets. A meal like he'd just had was worth any amount of work. And he knew three hundred dollars could last him a month.

He nodded.

"Good," said Panadur. "Now, first, you have to train your mind. A warrior is more than just a fighter. A fighter knows how to use physical weapons, but a warrior knows how to use the most important weapon of all: his mind. Now. Sit beneath this tree and reflect on what has happened to you, what is happening to you right now, and what will happen to you. I'll return later."

"Uh, sure." Dean plopped down against the tree, all too eager to close his eyes again. Rising early, and then filling his stomach, had made him tired. He stretched his legs out. He could hear Panadur going from here to there, whistling or humming as he worked.

He nodded off.

Sometime later, icy water splashed him in the face.

"Hello, sleepy one." Panadur glared down at him with an empty pail in his hands. "If training your mind doesn't keep you awake, maybe training your body will. Come with me," he ordered before turning and marching away.

Dean rose, surprised at the old man's ire. "Come off it," he called after him. "You get me up before dawn, then expect me to stay awake meditating?"

"Yes, I did," Panadur called back over his shoulder.

As Dean followed the old man behind the cottage, he saw a series of walls and various other obstacles that stretched off into the woods. "You have your own obstacle course?" he asked in disbelief.

The old man just smiled.

"Are you like a survivalist, or is this one of those games where at the end you hunt me down and try to kill me?"

Panadur laughed. "It is an obstacle course. They've been used for training for centuries. They even have these in your Army."

"My Army?"

"Just get ready."

Dean raised an eyebrow. "You want me to run an obstacle course?"

"You didn't run too well last night, my friend, so I think it's best if you start to learn how to run faster than an ox."

Dean snorted and rolled his shoulders. "If I do this good, do I get more money?" he asked.

"If you do this well . . . and the answer is no. Run!"

Dean sprinted down a little path to the first wooden wall. He scrambled over it, but fell as he tried to lower himself, landing solidly on his back with a loud groan, just as he had the night before when climbing down from the chain-link fence. Embarrassed, he quickly jumped to his feet and continued on.

The next obstacle was a stream that cut across the trail. A very round log spanned the water. Dean's first cautious step onto the moss-covered log pitched him directly into the cold stream. Sputtering and cursing, he climbed to his feet and waded across. Determination and pride drove him onward.

He ran up a steep hill. After stopping to gasp for breath at the top, he continued down the other side—but his legs started to move too quickly underneath him, and he pitched forward. He thrust his hands out and twisted so he'd land on his shoulder and not his face. Arms and legs flying, he tumbled down the hill and rolled to a stop in a big cloud of dust.

"Man, this moans. Gym class wasn't this bad," he muttered to himself. But he rose to his feet and knocked the dirt off.

With a snarl, he decided to plow through the next obstacle: a row of tall bushes that blocked the path. He leaped right into them—and yelped in pain as long briars scratched his skin. But, pushing forward, he tore himself from the thorns and raced ahead.

He did better on the next section. It was a mostly open stretch, and he jumped over deep holes and rolled under fallen trees.

The path led directly into a vertical cliff face. Dean stopped and looked up at the rock towering above him, then looked down at his body, now covered in mud. "Do you have insurance?" he yelled up the hill. He heard only the echo of his own voice in reply.

With a huff, he began to climb. Loose bits of rock pulled free from his handholds here and there; he struggled just to hold on. But he kept at it. And finally, scratched and bruised, he pulled himself to the top and collapsed, panting.

When he raised his head, he saw that from here the path descended gently—but it was covered with chest-high briars.

"Crazy old man . . ."

As he got to his feet, he saw that a low tunnel had been cut through the briar patch—but to pass through it, he'd have to crawl through practically on his stomach. So he dropped down, lowering his belly as much as he could, and edged forward into the tunnel. As he wriggled along, he was forced to stop repeatedly to free his snagged clothes or his tangled hair from the long thorns.

Finally, the tunnel ended, and he stood once more. From here, he could see that the rest of the path was clear, and would circle him back to Panadur's cottage.

He ran again. By the time he came to the final straightaway, his legs felt like stone. But when he saw Panadur waiting at the end of the path, pride made him quicken his pace. He smiled in relief as he approached the finish.

He almost didn't see the flash streaking at his legs. He tried to leap out of the way, but the swinging tree limb knocked him off his feet. He landed hard on his chest, right in front of the old man.

"Ugh." He was exhausted, frustrated, and humiliated.

"A very nice first attempt, Dean. Very nice!" The old man leaned down. "But you'll have to do much better if you ever want to escape a Krulg."

"Escape a what?" Dean panted.

"A Krulg. Nasty things."

"What the heck is a Krulg?"

Panadur thought for a moment. "Krulgs are about your size but rather heavy, with greenish skin and little black eyes. They have two tusks that protrude from their bottom jaw. They're strong, fast, and intelligent—in a wicked way. If they catch you, they eat you. Even though you wouldn't be a pleasant meal for them. They don't like gristle." Panadur smiled.

"I think I'd taste just fine," Dean snapped as he rose to his feet.

Panadur laughed, and Dean scowled; this guy was crazier then he'd thought.

After he'd caught his breath, Dean said, "So, I completed your obstacle course. Not bad, huh?"

"You tried very hard, but you have to learn to do it faster. Much, much faster. I wasn't kidding when I said a Krulg would catch and eat you. I once escaped from a Krulg of the Blood Moon clan, and he'd have caught you before you even reached the first wall."

Dean rubbed the back of his head and looked at his feet. He didn't want to insult his new boss, but he had to ask. "Do you really believe in these . . . Krulgs?"

"I do. In another world. But anyway, time for the next step before lunch." Panadur turned and headed back toward the cottage; Dean limped behind him.

When they arrived at the front porch, Panadur picked up two long, smooth sticks, and tossed one to Dean.

"What're we going to do with these?" Dean asked.

"You're going to learn how to use a sword."

"With a stick? Why can't we use real swords?"

"When you're ready for a sword, you'll use one. But right now I don't want you poking your eyes out—or mine, for that matter. Now, prepare to fight." Panadur lifted his stick until it was level with Dean's chest.

"I can't fight you." Dean lowered his stick.

"You've just broken the two most important rules of combat. First rule: don't underestimate your opponent."

"Great. What's the second?"

"Those who hesitate, die." Panadur's stick shot out and struck Dean firmly on the arm.

"Ow! That hurt!" Dean backed away.

"If a light blow like that hurt, this one will be very painful." The old man's stick struck Dean's ribs.

"Hey! What're you doing?" Dean lashed out at Panadur with his own stick, but the old man easily sidestepped the blow and smacked Dean in the back.

"My nanny used to hit harder than you," Panadur said. He hit Dean again.

"I'll show you who's a nanny," Dean growled, and he swung his stick fast and hard. Panadur once again dodged, then jabbed Dean in the stomach.

"Hmm. Maybe you can hit harder than my nanny," Panadur said. "But I do not think I'll ever find out." He laughed as he struck Dean again.

With his stick raised over his head, Dean ran at Panadur. Panadur ducked low, caught Dean in the stomach with his shoulder, then flung him over his back. Dean landed with a loud groan but quickly jumped to his feet. He wasn't giving up until he landed at least one good hit on this crazy old man.

Again and again the two lashed out at each other. But Dean never landed a strike. And his whole body ached; he'd been struck dozens of times, and not lightly, either.

After a solid hour of this, Panadur held up his hand. "Enough."

Dean tried to look like he wasn't bruised and beaten. "Oh, had enough, old man?"

Panadur shook his head and walked back to the porch. "Why don't you take a break?" he said. "I'll get you some water."

Dean felt as if his whole body had turned to lead. Every step he took caused him pain. He slumped down on the steps. "Thanks." He lay back on the worn wood and wondered how much more of this he could take. Then he thought of the three hundred dollars and all the things he wanted to buy. He let his arms stretch out at his sides.

Too soon, Panadur returned, taking a seat next to Dean on the steps. He held out a tall glass of water.

Dean groaned as he sat up. He drained the entire glass before speaking. "How am I doing so far, boss?"

Panadur chuckled. "Just fine. Better than I thought."

"Thanks." Dean's lips pressed together.

"I mean no offense. It's how you move."

"How I move?"

"Like an angry elephant."

"And you didn't mean any offense by that?"

"Don't be so sensitive. Everywhere you go, you stomp around. Like Stampy the elephant."

"Sensitive? Stampy? I'm light on my feet."

Panadur laughed. "No. You're not. But don't worry, we'll fix that. First, let's get you some lunch."

***

After they had eaten, Panadur went into the barn. When he came back out, he was carrying a long pole with a large ball of padding on one end. "Come with me, Stampy," he called.

With a loud groan, Dean said, "No way I'm getting stuck with a nickname like that. Knock it off."

Panadur smiled.

Dean didn't. "Seriously."

Panadur nodded. "I'll refrain from using that name"—he looked Dean up and down—"if you don't have an issue standing up for yourself."

Dean straightened up. "I don't. If I don't stand up for myself, who's going to?"

The two walked around the cottage, and Panadur led Dean down to an area where the little stream was much wider and deeper. Three flat wooden pillars rose just above water level near the bank.

"Now you're going to train your reactions and footing," Panadur said.

Dean took a step back and shook his head. "You're out of your mind if you think I'm going to let you hit me in the head with a giant cotton swab while I stand on some slippery logs."

"Okay." Panadur smirked. "How about this? First I get to hit you—and then I'll let you try to hit me."

"Really?" Dean eyed him suspiciously.

"Yes, really."

"All right then." Dean grinned as he took off his sneakers and shirt. He waded to the waist-deep logs, shivering in the cold water, then pulled himself up onto the first log. He wobbled as he tried to turn around and face Panadur. "Hang on, I'll tell you when I'm read—"

Panadur struck him smartly in the forehead. Dean fell backward into the water. Sputtering and wiping the water from his face, he shouted, "I said I'd tell you when I was ready!"

"You should always be ready. Get back on the log."

Dean huffed, but he climbed back on. He brushed back his

hair and spread his feet as far apart as he could on the log—which wasn't far. This time when Panadur's pole shot forward, Dean ducked, bending at the waist. But the padding hit him on the top of the head, and he almost flipped completely over as he splashed back into the water.

"Don't take your eyes off the pole," Panadur barked.

"How do I duck and not take my eyes off the pole?" Dean snapped back.

"If you're going to duck, bend your knees and don't tip forward like a goony bird." Panadur bent down and kept his back straight, demonstrating. "Like this. Bend your knees, not your back. That way you can still see what's coming at you."

"It's kind of hard when I have to stay on this stump." Dean climbed back onto the log.

"Who said you have to stay on one log?"

"Seriously? You can't keep changing the rules."

"There was never a rule."

The pole shot forward, and Dean sprang sideways toward the second log. "Missed me!" he yelled as the pole passed his head. Then he groaned as his feet overshot the log he was jumping to, and he landed in the water with a big splash.

"I know. I know," Dean grumbled as he climbed back up. "Don't take your eyes off the pole or where you're trying to land. But I didn't get hit—" The pole smacked him in the back of his head and sent him flying once more into the water.

"Don't be so cocky."

Dean muttered under his breath.

"What did you forget?" Panadur asked cheerfully.

"Always be ready." Dean brushed back his hair.

***

After what felt like hours—and probably was—of dodging and

ducking and splashing and sputtering, Dean stood waist-deep in the water and asked, "When am I going to be able to hit you?"

"Now's a good time." Panadur gave a sly grin, then held up his hand as Dean waded toward the bank. "Oh, stay where you are," he said. "You can strike at me from on the logs."

"That's not fair," Dean protested.

"Neither am I." Panadur's voice was low and serious.

Dean straightened, and both men climbed up on logs. Panadur handed the pole to Dean, who tested its weight by swinging it back and forth. A slight smirk crossed his face, and without warning, he thrust the pole forward.

Panadur stepped to the side, grabbed the pole, and pushed. Dean flew backward and into the stream.

"You didn't say I could do that!" Dean bellowed as his head broke the surface.

"And I never said you couldn't. Try again."

Dean was fuming when he climbed back up on the tiny platform. This time he swung the pole sideways with all his strength. Panadur ducked low, and the pole whizzed over his head. Dean groaned as the weight of the pole carried him with it into the water.

"You could have let go of it," Panadur said, shaking his head.

"But what if you were a Krulg? If I let go of it, I wouldn't have a weapon," Dean teased.

"You'd also be on your feet and in a far better position to get your weapon back," Panadur said.

Dean got back up on the log. He cracked his neck and exhaled. With the pole in both hands, he thrust it forward. Panadur stepped to the side and grabbed it once again. With a large smile, Dean released his grip.

"Ha! I let go of—"

Panadur flipped the pole around and smacked Dean in the stomach—and into the water.

"Know when to hold on and when to let go." Panadur grinned.

"Great. How do I know when to do which?"

"Trust your instincts and use your brain. Think. There's a time to let go and a time to hold on. That applies to everything in life."

"And if you mess up on which one, life cracks you in the head and sends you into a cold stream? Sounds like a bad fortune cookie." Dean laughed as he climbed back onto the log. "Lighten up—"

Panadur hit him again.

For the next hour, Dean thrust and swung from every angle and even jumped from log to log, but not once did he manage to knock Panadur into the water.

Finally, Panadur held up his hand. "Enough. I need a break, and then I'll get you some supper."

"You need a break?" Dean grumbled as he waded toward the bank. "Yeah, it must be hard work smacking me into the water."

Panadur laughed as they headed back to the cottage.

While Dean changed his clothes, Panadur cooked, whistling the whole time. He set a pot on the stove, and Dean lay down on his sleeping mat. He was looking forward to a good meal and then a better night's rest. His body had never ached this much.

But when dinner was done, Panadur went to the barn and saddled two horses. Dean cringed; apparently his day wasn't yet over.

It took him a few attempts, but soon Dean was atop his horse and riding next to Panadur through the land around his home. They went at a slow pace, Panadur letting Dean get accustomed to the horse. And as they rode, Panadur spoke to Dean of Krulgs, Varlugs, and other wicked things. He also spoke of good things like Elves, Dwarves, and Elvanas. He talked about a place that was filled with great beauty. He spoke of heroes and villains, and he sang songs. Even after they'd finished their ride and returned to the cottage, Panadur continued to talk of these things.

As dusk fell and Panadur still talked, Dean's eyelids grew heavy. They were sitting at Panadur's table, but even in this position he was falling asleep.

"What're you doing, Dean? You have to complete one more part of your training before you can sleep."

"Are you kidding me? It's night. I'm tired. There's no—"

Panadur rose and walked to the front door. "Now," he commanded in such a low, even voice that Dean stood and moved after him, almost without thinking.

"What am I going to have to do now?" he asked, but Panadur was already walking off into the trees.

Dean sighed and followed.

They arrived at the center of a large field. Somehow, Panadur had come up with a bow and two quivers of arrows.

"You're going to teach me how to shoot a bow now? It's dark out." Dean raised an eyebrow.

"I am going to try to teach you stealth. How to move like a shadow. How long this training will take is up to you. You can start anywhere at the edge of this field. I'll remain in the center. All you have to do is move up on me without me seeing or hearing you."

"No problem." Dean grinned as he jogged to the side of the field, all too eager to hurry up and complete this task so he could go to bed. Suddenly, he spun back around. "What's the bow for then?"

"If I do hear you or see you, I'll shoot you."

"Are you out of your mind?"

"The arrows are padded, like the pole I used today. They'll not hurt . . . much."

Dean stared at the old man. "I'm out of my mind," he

muttered to himself as he turned and continued toward the edge of the field.

When he arrived at the edge, he ducked down and tiptoed along the border. His mouth ticked up in a smile as he started to flank Panadur. When he thought he was almost at Panadur's back, he lay on his stomach and crawled through the tall grass.

But after traveling for only a few feet, he heard a faint whoosh and an arrow struck him soundly in the leg.

"Ow!" he cried.

Another arrow hit him in the side.

"Ow!"

A third arrow smacked him in the arm.

"Stop!" he yelled as he rose to his knees.

A fourth arrow hit him in the middle of his chest and knocked him backward.

"Cut it out! Knock it off! I give up!" Dean waved his arms frantically.

"When you get hit, don't yell, or you'll get hit again. If I were with a band of Krulgs and one shot you and you yelled like that, you'd look like a pincushion," Panadur warned from somewhere in the darkness.

"Oka—ow!" he screamed as a fifth arrow caught him in the stomach.

But when the sixth shot struck him squarely in the ribs, he merely gritted his teeth in silence.

Dean's hopes of being able to sneak up on Panadur and quickly go to bed soon faded. Whether he crawled fast or slowly, on his knees or his stomach, arrows flew through the air to strike him. At least he'd learned one thing: no matter where he was hit or how much it hurt, he never made a sound.

Finally, Panadur ran out of arrows. Dean dejectedly rose to his feet, and his whole body seemed to groan.

"I tried to be quiet but you kept hearing me." Dean kicked

the ground.

"I didn't hear you for some time." Panadur put his arm around Dean's shoulders. "I kept hitting you because of your white undershirt. I saw you the whole time."

"And you didn't tell me?" Dean pulled away and glared.

"Dean." Panadur's voice turned very serious. "I don't have as much time to train you as you need or I wish. Don't ask why. You have to learn quickly. If I seem harsh, it's for your own good. In time, you'll understand. For right now, though, please just try."

Dean stood silently for a moment, then mumbled, "All right."

Panadur's arm came back around Dean's shoulders as he helped him to the house. As they walked, Panadur again told him stories of this other world that he seemed to care so much for. He talked to Dean as he lay down on his mat and continued talking until Dean fell asleep.

3

THE RED FLAG

D ean spent many days training. Each day he woke before the sun rose to sharpen his mind. Next, he improved his speed and agility, then he moved on to one-on-one combat with Panadur, worked on his footing and reactions at the stream, practiced riding, and, finally, improved his stealth. And all the while, Panadur told him tales of this other world he believed in.

As the days passed, Dean became stronger and more agile. He could now run the obstacle course with no difficulty and at great speed. He stayed dry on the logs and could surprise Panadur in the field. He could ride a horse and meditate for hours. He thought that he was indeed becoming a warrior.

One night when he was lying down to sleep, Panadur came to him with a small red flag in his hand.

"Tomorrow this flag will be on the top of the mountain to the north. You'll have until midnight tomorrow to bring it back down."

"Until midnight? To get to that mountain and back?"

"Yes, to get the flag and bring it back. Now I suggest you get some sleep."

"Yeah, okay." Dean grinned. "If you're going to get that flag to the top of that mountain by tomorrow, I'll get it back before lunch," he murmured before he fell asleep.

But when Dean awoke, the sun was already shining brightly.

He leaped from his bedroll and dashed out the front door, where Panadur was reclining in a chair.

"It's almost ten!" Dean cried in disbelief.

"Yes, it is. You'd better be on your way. You've already lost valuable time." Panadur put his hands behind his head and closed his eyes.

Without worrying about breakfast, Dean immediately started to jog toward the faraway peak.

He moved at a slow trot through the woods, and in a relatively straight line, now being used to traveling in the forest. He listened to the birds and enjoyed the warm fresh air.

After about three hours, the peak of the mountain was still far away.

"There's no way Panadur got that flag up to the top of that mountain and then came all the way back that fast. I bet it's not even up there."

Despite his words, Dean ran faster. He knew Panadur must have put the flag at the top, and that thought drove him on.

Soon he ran up a mountain path, the incline at last increasing. Every once in a while, he would step on a rock he thought was stable and it would give way, pitching him forward, so Dean had to concentrate on his footing as well as his breathing. On he raced up the slope as the hours ticked away and the sun dipped low in the sky.

When he finally reached the top of the mountain, he found the flag on the end of a stake. But the sun had already set, and the flag was lit by the newly risen moon.

How did Panadur get it up here so fast? And how am I supposed to get back before midnight?

Dean grabbed the flag and raced back down the mountain.

Angry with himself for being so nonchalant about the race —and wanting to show Panadur he was capable—he pushed himself even harder than before. Stones skipped and fell before him as he half-slid and half-ran sideways down the steep, rocky slope.

When he reached the bottom, he sprinted through the woods. His lungs burned as he jumped over fallen logs and ran through brush. Sweat soaked his hair and clothes, stung his eyes; his muscles ached, but still they pumped to the rhythmic beating of his heart.

As the moon rose to its zenith, Dean knew he was close to the cottage, but his whole body felt as if it were about to burst into flames. Still he pressed on.

Finally, he broke through the bushes at the edge of the cottage's clearing. He saw Panadur on the little porch, leaning back in the same chair. With one last push, he drove forward and leaped the three steps to stand before his trainer, the sweat-soaked red flag in his outstretched hand.

As Panadur took the flag, a broad smile crossed his face.

Dean collapsed on the top step. He lay there panting, trying to regain his breath.

"I did it," Dean finally gasped.

"Yes, and I knew you would." Panadur laid his hand on Dean's shoulder. "Let me get you something to eat before you go to bed. You should wash up first, though."

Humming, Panadur went into the cottage, and Dean wearily rose and trotted down to the stream to wash. When he returned, the smell of dinner drifted through the mountain air. Dean sat down on his bedroll and watched Panadur set the table. The two ate a quiet meal, not because neither felt like talking, but because they both were thinking of the other.

"Panadur, where did you learn all these things?" Dean asked while he cleared the table.

Panadur looked startled by the question. "Another place," he said with a lopsided grin.

"Tell me another story about this 'other place.'" Dean felt

childish and blushed at his request of a bedtime story as he lay down on his bedroll.

Panadur smiled and sat back in his chair. "There once was a wizard named Lorious. His power was great, but it was evil. He was malevolent. He wanted to rule the lands, to rule everyone and everything. In the beginning, nothing stood in his way. He either enslaved the people in the lands he conquered or he killed them. He thought nothing could stop him. However, in this one land were three brothers. They, too, were wizards. They decided to go to Lorious's stronghold and kill him—"

A faint snore interrupted him. Dean was already asleep.

Panadur gazed down at Dean, and his smile faded. "I hope you're ready. I think you are, but I don't know. But you have to be, Dean. There's no more time. I can hold it off no longer. Soon we'll both know if I'm right, and you're the one."

As he turned to put out the light, he looked very old . . . and very tired.

4

THE MIDDLE STONE

The next morning, Dean found Panadur waiting for him on the porch.

"Good morning, Panadur. And what dreaded task do you have in mind for me today? A jog through a lion park while covered in barbecue sauce? A walk over some hot coals with gas cans strapped to my butt?" Dean laughed. He was surprised that he wasn't sorer from his ordeal the day before.

"Oh, nothing that easy. I want you to hunt a bear." Panadur smiled.

"Is that all?" Dean shrugged.

"With a fork." Panadur's smile vanished.

Dean's laughter faded. "Seriously?"

Panadur roared with laughter.

"Ha ha." Dean wobbled his head back and forth. "Knowing you, that's something you could ask me to do."

"What I really thought we'd do today is pack a lunch and ride the horses to a little pond I know. Do you want to go fishing?"

"That sounds great." Dean leaped from the porch and raced toward the barn. He slid to a stop and looked back at Panadur. "Really? Just fish? No bears?"

"No bears. You saddle the horses, and I'll get the rest of the things." Panadur went into the cottage, humming a little tune.

They rode away from the cottage and down a little trail. At the end was a wide, flat field with a huge stone at its center. The stone was about five feet wide and twelve feet high. It loomed above them, even on horseback.

"That's a weird-looking rock," Dean said. "How'd such a huge rock end up smack in the middle of an open field?"

"It's a Middle Stone," said Panadur.

"That's an original name." Dean chuckled. "Good thing it wasn't over a little bit. Then it'd be a slightly-to-the-right stone."

Panadur sighed.

The horses trotted forward. They stopped at a sunlit pond with deep, clear blue water; not a ripple marred its smooth surface. Panadur showed Dean how to cut a small sapling for his pole. Panadur picked one that was not so large it wouldn't bend, nor so small that it would snap. He showed Dean how to use the ring from a knot of hardwood as a hook and how to split the branches of a willow tree to use for the line. Then, with their bait in the water, the two sat back against a large elm tree, its branches bathing them in shade.

They spent the day fishing quietly, telling each other stories, and enjoying each other's company.

***

The next morning, Dean rolled over and felt something cold and hard next to his hand. As he opened his eyes, he saw an old sword lying next to him. "A sword?" he asked. "Am I ready to fight with a sword?" He picked up the weapon and swung it around.

"Yes. The time has come for you to use a real sword." Panadur stood in the doorway, twirling a silver sword of his own. "Let us begin."

They walked into the morning sun and turned to face each other. Dean realized the weight of the real sword was very close to the weight of the stick he'd been using.

"The first thing you should know about a real sword is that you must always take care of it. A sword becomes part of a warrior. The two are forged together in the fires of battle until they're inseparable."

They circled each other, testing blows. Their swords rang like struck crystal in the crisp morning air. Then they moved in. Each time one swung, the other's sword seemed to be already there to fend off the blow.

Long they fought, neither seeming to get the upper hand, until Dean parried a blow from Panadur and followed through by flinging Panadur's sword from his hand.

"Very good!" Panadur burst into a broad grin. "You've learned very well."

"Hey . . . like they say, I had a great teacher." Dean smiled awkwardly.

Panadur patted Dean on the back. "I think it's because I had a lot to work with. You're an excellent student."

Dean grinned from ear to ear.

As Panadur walked back toward the cottage, Dean retrieved Panadur's sword and wiped it down. He held the sword at arm's length and looked down the blade. A shadow swept over him. His skin ran cold, and he trembled.

He looked up at the clear blue sky and raised an eyebrow. "That's weird."

Just then, Panadur pitched forward onto the porch.

"Panadur!" Dean rushed to his side.

"I'm all right, Dean." Panadur tried to rise but fell back.

"It's okay. I'll take you inside." Dean helped Panadur to his feet.

"I think I'd better lie down for a little while," Panadur whispered.

Dean helped him into the cottage, led him to his room, and assisted him into his bed in the corner.

"Do you need a doctor or something?" Dean searched Panadur's pale face.

"No. A doctor will not help me, Dean. I'm dying."

"You're not dying. You're just sick, that's all. Old people get sick, then they get better," Dean said. "Hey, you didn't even yell at me for calling you old." Tears welled up in his eyes.

"Dean, I must tell you some things before I die."

"You're not dying!"

"Dean, listen," Panadur demanded. His voice was weak but stern. "That other world I talked about is real. The evil there has spread to this world, and I'm too weak to stop it. My power is fading. Your time has arrived."

"Panadur . . . sure. It's okay." Dean didn't believe it, but he wanted to comfort the old man.

"Don't try to humor me . . . listen," Panadur snapped, half rising. "I'm sorry, but please, listen. I have one last story to tell you. A story that's true. In that other world, there were three brothers. All of them became wizards. They were Carimus, Volsur, and Panadur. Yes, Dean, me." A faint smile crossed his lips.

"We were bonded by more than kinship. We fought evil. We were very good at it, too. For a time our world was more or less peaceful. The wicked things still existed, but they were driven to hide in the dark places or fled to the Barren Lands.

"The people chose a king. He was a good man and he ruled fairly so we decided to settle down—except Volsur. Volsur had always loved adventure. Carimus and I both thought he loved the thrill of adventure itself, as we did—but no. He loved the spoils it brought. He soon came to love money, fame, and power, becoming greedy and always wanting more. And without my brother and me with him, Volsur went unchecked. He now fought both good and evil, favoring whichever would give the greatest spoils. This lust quickly blackened his heart and twisted his power for evil. My brother and I banished him to the Barren Lands, but we didn't have the heart to kill him.

"We knew nothing of him for years, but during that time his power grew quickly, and people rushed to join him. Others gave in to his will. His evil started to spread throughout my world until it had crept into the hearts of all. My love for Volsur had blinded me to the truth until it was too late. Volsur killed the king and all of his line. Volsur is pure evil now. Only someone pure will be able to destroy him. So Carimus and I started our quest to find someone who is pure of heart.

"My brother and I searched our whole world. But Volsur's evil had crept so far and so deep, it lived in everyone's heart. There are still good people in my world, but not pure ones. They're slowly being twisted by this evil. It was then that I traveled to this world, your world, to continue my search. Long have I searched here, too, through many lands, but I could find no one truly pure of heart. The evil one's power has spread into your world as well.

"But my search is now over. I found you. You're the one who's pure of heart."

"Me? I'm not pure of heart," Dean whispered.

"You are." Panadur grabbed Dean's hand. "Now that you know me, do you think those three men in the alley could have really bested me in a fight? I was testing you. You passed. You knew you couldn't win, but you were willing to fight to try to help an old man you didn't know. You must believe in yourself. You must believe me. Dean, you have to go to my world and defeat Volsur. Find Carimus. He will aid you. Go to the stone in the field before the house. The Middle Stone. It's a gateway to my world."

He groaned, and his eyes flickered.

"A gateway? How do I use it?"

"Believe. Run straight into it. I've set it up. It'll open for you and you alone. Use all your training, Dean. I wish I could teach you more, but there's no time. What I've taught you, you must use to survive. You have to live. You must kill Volsur, or all is lost. You must believe."

Dean held Panadur's hand and fought back tears.

After a few moments, Panadur continued. "The horses—let them go free. I want you to have my sword, for you're like my son. I'm very proud of you, my son. I love you."

"Panadur . . . you're going to be okay." Dean leaned over to hold the formerly powerful man who now looked so frail. "I love you, too."

As Dean held him, the old man's eyes closed and a smile crossed his face. A final tear rolled down his cheek.

Dean laid Panadur back on his bed. He folded the old man's arms across his chest and laid a sheet over Panadur's body. Then he bowed his head, tears flowing freely down his face. Finally, he could take it no more; he walked outside and stood next to the tree, where he wept silently for a long time.

By the time he returned to the house, the sun had started to set and had turned the sky golden. He gathered his few things and straightened the house, then walked out onto the porch and locked the door behind him.

He would not be returning.

He sat down on the steps and put his head in his hands. Now what do I do? Now I really have no place to go.

A whinny sounded from the stable, and Dean remembered the old man's instructions. He went to the barn, tied open the gates to the horses' stables, and filled their troughs.

Then he stood in the yard, trying to take everything in. He wanted to remember everything as it was right now. Somehow, he knew he would.

He walked down the little path and looked back one last time. A sad smile crossed his lips. He was leaving the first place that had ever felt like a home.

He traveled down the path until he came to the field with the large stone in its center—the Middle Stone. He walked across the grass in the darkening day. The stone loomed above him, more than twice his height. He stood and glared at the rock. Slowly, he walked forward and placed his hand against the cold, hard surface.

"Panadur, I wish that other world of yours wasn't a dream. I wish I could go there. I'm sorry."

Then he turned and walked back to the path. The sun became a golden red, and streams of amber pierced the darkening clouds. *Believe in me.* Panadur's words echoed in Dean's ears. *Believe in me.*

Dean stopped. All his life, he had wanted someone who would value him. Someone who cared. He had found that. And as he stared at the dirt at his feet, he felt guilty. He realized he wasn't even trying to believe in the old man who'd had faith in him.

"I owe him more than that," Dean whispered. "If I can do anything for him, I can do this. I can believe in him."

He turned and marched back to the stone. He stopped and stood before the rock, Panadur's sword clutched in his hand.

He pressed against the rock. It stood as motionless as before. He rapped firmly on the stone with the hilt of the sword. Nothing happened.

He sheathed his sword and backed away to the edge of the field. He rolled his shoulders and exhaled as he remembered what Panadur said. Run straight into it.

"I'm out of my mind. This is going to kill me."

With a battle cry that rang through the field, Dean ran at the stone as fast as he could. His sneakers pushed into the ground, and his arms pulled at the air. He gritted his teeth, and then he jumped straight into the stone's face.

Darkness swept over him, and he fell into the void . . .

5

FROM THE HEAVENS

As the sun rose, Han walked out the door of his small cottage with a wooden rake in his hands. He was in his teens, thin, with the sharp, distinct features of the Elves, and at just under four feet he was of average height for an Elvana. His pointed ears poked up through his dark-brown hair which was in sharp contrast to his clear blue eyes. Han gazed upon a morning that seemed to have become a shadow of the night. Gray clouds swirled overhead, but the air was completely still.

As he walked, he looked out over his dead crops. All the plants were yellow or brown, if they had not already turned black and crumpled. The ground was dry and cracked; it crunched as he walked over the arid field.

"Curse this year and everything to do with it," Han yelled at the sky. He raised his rake and shook it in defiance. "How can I hope to grow so much as a weed this year? First the late frosts, then the heavy rains washed all the seeds away. Now, nothing but dry." He kicked the ground and a cloud of dust swirled up.

He leaned his rake against the split-rail fence and rubbed his face. The neighborhood calico cat darted out of the bushes, rushed over to him and rubbed against his legs.

"I don't have anything for you today, Lilly. Besides"—he reached down and scratched behind her neck—"you've probably eaten better than I have."

He put his chin in his hands and looked across his ruined field. "It's all Volsur's fault. I don't care what they say about him, I know he's evil to the core. I'd give anything to go and grab his big neck and make him stop this." He chuckled darkly. "Ha, that's rich. Me go and kill the Dark Lord. An Elvana. It's hopeless. Now I'm going to have to go work for the seller."

Lilly meowed loudly.

"What other choice do I have—besides dying here?" Han looked up at the sky once more. "Why?" he screamed at the gray clouds. "Why will no one even try?"

A great crash sounded behind him, and Han spun around. There was an enormous hole in his roof where none had been before.

***

As Dean spun through the darkness, he could see light ahead—and then, without warning, a roof rushed up to meet him. He closed his eyes and flung his hands over his face. He slammed through the roof and landed—hard.

Dust and pieces of wood covered him. He sat up, coughed twice, and shook his head.

A small door across from him swung open, and an elvish-looking man with a rake in his hands appeared in the doorway.

The little man's eyes went wide, and he bowed as low as he could. "I'm Hanillingsly Elvenroot, at your service, O Great Being from the Heavens!"

"I'm not from the Heavens." Dean chuckled.

"You fell from the sky into my home. Why have you come?"

Dean tried to raise himself up. "Sorry. I'm just here to find a guy. Volsur."

The man's eyes became even bigger. "Are you here to stop Volsur?"

"Stop him? Yeah. I'm here to stop him."

"I knew you were from the Heavens. You're here to stop Volsur!" The man leaped into the air. "What may I do to help you, O Great Being from the Heavens?" He bowed low again.

"Stop that. Don't call me 'O Great Being from the Heavens.' My name's Dean." He finally managed to raise himself off what he guessed had been a bed—although his landing had quite thoroughly crushed it. "Well, Hanillingsly Elvenroot, was it? Do you mind if I call you something a little shorter than that?"

"Oh, yes, O Great—I mean, Dean." The man blushed. "My friends call me Han. Not implying that you are my friend. I don't mean that you're not my friend either. What I mean is—"

"Whoa. Slow down. I know what you mean. Are you a Leprechaun? No. No, you're too big. An Elf? No. You're too small. You're an Elvana, right?" Panadur had spoken at length of the various races of this world, and Dean had listened carefully.

"Yes, I'm an Elvana."

"Good. I knew it. Where am I, anyway?" Dean looked around the little cottage. At the center of the single room was a small plain wooden table and chairs, and off to the side stood a little wooden bureau. Two colorful paintings of summer fields hung on the walls.

"You're in the Lallamine Valley." Han looked puzzled, then the look suddenly vanished. "Oh, of course you don't know where you are. You're from the Heavens!" he exclaimed.

"Listen, I'm not from the Heavens, okay? I'm from another . . . planet? I guess. That sounds weird. I'm just from another place, and I'm here to stop Volsur."

"You're going to stop Volsur? Please let me accompany you on your quest," Han begged.

"I don't know. Panadur didn't say anything about getting help," Dean said, almost to himself.

"Panadur the Wizard? You know Panadur?" Han's face filled with awe.

"I knew him. He's dead."

Han sat down right on the dirt floor. "That's very sad news. I'm sorry." He drew a circle in the dirt. "But you'll need help to get to Volsur. More help than I can offer, too. The road is very long and very dangerous. Evil creatures roam freely, even in the daylight." Han closed his eyes. After only a moment, they snapped back open. "If you want to go, I'm not going to let you go alone." He stood up and squared his shoulders.

"Panadur never said anything about getting help. And I don't want you to get hurt."

"I can get hurt staying here! In fact, I will probably starve to death."

Dean shook his head. "I don't know."

"Do you know how to get there?"

"I don't even know where 'there' is," Dean muttered. "I don't even know where here is." He exhaled and brushed back his hair. "So, okay, I do need your help. But it could be really dangerous."

"I can help. I'm not afraid." Han stuck out his chin.

Dean paced back and forth in the little cabin. Finally, he looked back at Han, who seemed ready to burst with anticipation. "All right, you can come with me."

"Great. When do we leave?" Han ran to the little bureau.

"I don't know. What time is it?"

"It's morning. If I pack now, I can be ready in no time." Han threw clothes into a large burlap sack, then looked up at Dean. "Do you have anything to pack as well?"

"Oh, man. I didn't bring anything." Dean's hands dug into the pockets of his leather jacket and pulled out thirty-four cents and the roll of hundred-dollar bills Panadur had given him over his weeks with the old man. From his inside pocket he pulled out a lighter and a couple of scraps of paper. "I don't believe this."

"They didn't prepare you well in the Heavens—no offense. Hmm. My cousin Falivan, who works here but has gone to the seller, is rather large. His clothes might serve as short pants for you for the time being." He stared at the objects in Dean's hands. "What are those?" he asked.

"Thirty-four cents, a roll of bills, and a lighter." Dean smiled sarcastically as he lit the lighter, but Han gasped, nearly falling over.

"You're a wizard," Han whispered. His eyes grew wide.

Dean laughed. "No, it's just a lighter. Everyone has one where I come from."

"That's because you're from the Heavens," Han exclaimed, and Dean laughed harder.

"You said your cousin is in the basement?" Dean looked for the way down.

"No, he's at the seller's." Han's face scrunched up. "As in the opposite of buyer. The seller is one of Volsur's men. There's one in every part of the realm now. He's the only one with any goods. He's the only one who's selling anything. Many Elvana have had to trade their land to him when their crops stopped growing. After he gets the land, the soil becomes good once more, and the previous owner is forced to work his own land and live off Volsur's scraps." Han's voice was full of hate, and the look in his eyes almost scared Dean.

"Well, if your cousin won't mind, it'd be great if I can borrow his clothes. What about food?" Dean asked.

"I have some food and enough supplies, but I'm afraid we'll have to walk. I don't have any horses." Han looked embarrassed.

"It'll be good exercise," Dean said brightly. "Do you have any money?" He put the change and money roll back in his pocket. They would obviously do him no good here.

"They really didn't prepare you, did they? I have very little money, but I'll bring it. Oh—and I have to leave a note for my family. I don't want to tell them I'm leaving in person; they'd try to talk me out of it." Han grabbed a scrap of parchment and a quill and sat down at the table.

"Family? Wait a minute . . . I don't know if I should let you go," Dean said.

"I have five brothers and four sisters who can take care of my parents." Han talked even as he wrote. "My family can hold on, but not for much longer. The best way for me to help them is by going with you. Besides, I don't have any place to sleep. I don't have a bed anymore—you crushed it." Han grinned from pointed ear to pointed ear.

When Han had finished his note, he went off to get clothes from his cousin, leaving Dean to wait—and kick himself for being so poorly prepared. Fortunately, the clothes did prove to fit him, although Dean decided to stick with his own jeans. The cousin's pants would fit around his waist, but they'd come down to right below his knees.

After Han made a quick lunch, they set off down the dirt road to the north—the road that would lead them to Volsur.

Then Dean remembered Panadur's instructions. "I need to find Carimus," he blurted out.

Han didn't stop walking. "I don't know where to look for a famous wizard."

"Who would?"

"Who would know where a wizard is?" Han closed his eyes and tapped his foot.

"Would the Kilacouqua?"

"You know the Elves?"

"Not personally. Panadur said he and Carimus helped them."

Han stroked his chin. "That's a great idea. We'll go right through their lands. If anyone knows where Carimus is, they do."

***

Han explained that his farm was near the edge of the valley, and that they were heading in the direction of the Haraden Mountains. As they walked, they passed farms that looked just as bad as Han's. Nothing grew in the dry, dark soil. They saw half-starved animals and Elvanas who looked only slightly better off. But soon enough, to Dean's relief, they left the farms behind and pine trees loomed over them.

As they walked, Han talked like they were old friends catching up after a long time apart. He spoke of how more and more Elvanas were being forced to sell their farms. He told of the evil night creatures, like the Krulgs and Varlugs, who now walked by day. He recounted the battles of the different peoples of his world: the Dwarves, Elves, and Humans fighting the Krulgs and other foul folk—and among themselves. None of the creatures except the wicked ones worked together, he said; all the good folk seemed to be concerned only with protecting themselves.

As night approached, the darkness grew deeper, and the two decided to camp just off the road. They put two Elvana sleeping mats together for Dean and placed them beneath a large elm tree for shelter, as a light rain was beginning to fall. They had a small supper without a fire, for Han claimed evil creatures could be lurking anywhere, and neither wanted to chance attracting the attention of one.

"This darn rain." Han pulled his sleeping mat over himself.

Lightning streaked across the sky far away, and thunder rumbled into the valley. Dean rolled onto his back and put his hands behind his head.

"The lightning crackles like a witch cackling as she stirs her billowing cauldron, which bubbles and boils over. The foul fluid falls like black rain, hissing as it touches the burning city with a fire no water can quench. The liquid seeps into every crack and crevice, in search of all the grime, and sweeps it to the surface. Her laughter causes the wind to stir the filth from the swirling puddles until it rises like a black fog, embracing in its evil grasp all that it touches."

"That's creepy." Han made a face as if he'd eaten a bug.

"I wrote it," Dean said. "Before I met Panadur."

"You write?"

"Sometimes. Just poems and stuff."

"It's good. But eerie." Han shuddered and rolled over.

"Thanks, I guess. Goodnight, Han," Dean whispered.

"Goodnight, Dean."

Dean fell asleep to the sounds of the storm spreading across the land.

***

The night passed without incident, and the two awoke to continue on their way. This new day was even grayer than the one before, and the ashen clouds seemed to hold back the wind, for not a leaf rustled in the still air.

"What route are we taking, Han?" Dean asked a couple of hours into their hike. "I should get to know the geography."

"Well, the quickest way to Volsur's city, Naviak—that's what he named it; it used to be called Arieot—is to head north by the Horns of the Warriors. The Horns are peaks that sound like many horns when the wind blows through them. Some say it's not the wind that makes the horns blow, but the last dying breaths of all the dead warriors." Han looked ominously at Dean.

"Now you're creeping me out. Enough with the ghost stories." Dean chuckled, but he still looked nervously around.

"Our first stop along the way will be in Vinrell—that's after we pass through the Haraden Mountains. The Dwarves there might be able to aid our quest; they're very mighty warriors."

"Then we go to the Elves to find out about Carimus?"

"Yes. But we have to go through the Dwarven land first."

"Aren't the Dwarves in a battle?" Dean asked.

"Yes, so we'll either have to skirt around the battle area or avoid them altogether. I for one don't want to run up against any mean Krulgs."

"Um, how about some really ugly ones?" Dean shouted as he pointed behind them.

Nine or ten creatures with greenish skin and tusks, just like Panadur had described, rushed out of the woods. They wore dirty leather armor and carried either curved swords or long, barbed spears. Their black eyes flashed with hate.

"What shall we do, Dean?" Han's voice was surprisingly calm.

"RUN!" Dean grabbed the Elvana and bolted down the path.

The Krulgs raised their weapons in the air and screamed in what sounded like delight at the prospect of a chase.

Dean and Han scrambled over the rocks with the creatures at their heels. Dean silently thanked Panadur for his training and hoped he could outrun the creatures he'd imagined racing and beating so many times before. They ran as fast as their legs would carry them, gradually putting some distance between themselves and the Krulgs.

Soon the path wound its way up a steep hill. Dean ran behind Han, almost pushing the Elvana up the rocky trail. When they reached the top, Han collapsed on the ground.

"I can't run any farther," he panted.

"You have to run, or they'll catch you and eat you," Dean snapped.

But apparently, Han could do nothing but gasp for breath. The sound of the approaching Krulgs grew closer, and then the first Krulg came into sight on the path behind them.

"C'mon, Han! They're almost here!"

A horn call split the air.

"What's that?" Dean looked around for a new threat.

"The Horns of the Warriors," Han gasped.

Another horn blast ripped through the air, seeming closer than before.

"Attack, men! Attack!" Dean cried at the top of his lungs. He waved his arms over his head.

The Krulgs stopped in their tracks and looked nervously around.

"What're you doing?" Han asked. "There aren't any men. It's just the wind." He rose unsteadily to his feet.

"I know that, and you know that, but they don't know that. At least I hope they don't know about it."

A third call split the air, then a fourth. Each call sounded like a battle horn coming closer.

"Kill them all!" Dean screamed. "Take no prisoners! Kill the big ugly one first! Kill them as slowly and as painfully as you can!" He drew his sword and charged the group of Krulgs, waving his blade above his head.

The creatures turned and fled, scampering and sliding down the hill. The largest one shoved the others out of his way before disappearing into the woods.

Dean spun around and sprinted back to Han. "Let's get out of here. They won't fall for that forever." He pulled the Elvana along.

They ran for a few more minutes before Han needed to slow to a walk again—and even then they moved at a brisk pace. After many miles, only when they were sure they had lost their pursuers, they stopped to rest.

"Pretty nice bluff, don't you think?" Dean panted with a grin.

"What bluff? That rock over there isn't a bluff. It's barely a hill." Han flopped to the ground and stared up at Dean, puzzled.

"No, what I did. I tricked them. Attack! Attack! I can't believe they fell for that." A broad smile spread across Dean's face.

"I can't believe they believed that either. Krulgs only speak Krulg."

Dean's smile dropped, and then they both burst out laughing so hard they were soon panting for breath again.

**

They continued to travel for the remainder of the day. Han imitated Dean's charade over and over, each time making it more comical. When the sun set behind the mountains, they camped in a small clearing, ate a light supper, and, as they got ready to sleep, talked about Han's world.

"Does this world have a name?" Dean asked.

"It's known as Kisch, the shining planet," Han said.

Dean lay back and looked up at the stars. "This is so bizarre. I can't believe I'm on a whole different planet. I've never even been to a different state and now . . ." His voice trailed off as the moon poked out from behind a cloud. "You have a moon here?"

"Of course. You don't?" Han rolled up on his elbow.

"No, we have a moon. We landed on it."

Han jumped up. "You've been on the moon?" His hands went to the sides of his face.

"Yeah." Dean shrugged. "Not me personally, but guys walked up there."

"What? They walked to the moon! How? Is it because the Heavens are so close you can just walk to the moon?"

Dean laughed. "No. They took a spaceship."

Han's mouth dropped open. "They have ships that can sail in space?"

Dean waved his hands. "You know what? Maybe I shouldn't talk about this stuff. Maybe it will screw up the progress of your planet or something."

Han shook his head. "No, please tell me more. It's unbelievable."

"But you're getting freaked out."

"I'll be good. It's just so . . . awesome." Han sat back down on his sleeping mat, but he was still shaking with excitement.

"Well, it's kind of weird for me too." Dean folded his hands behind his head.

"I'll stick to easy questions," Han whispered. "Are the stars much different here than on your world?"

Dean shrugged. "I . . . I don't know. I never really looked." He watched them for a few moments.

"I guess you can start now." Han grinned. "Then when you go home, you can see the difference."

"Yeah. Hey—you're an Elvana, so you're related to Elves, right?"

"Very far back. That's what Elvana means: little Elves."

"Is it true that Elves live to be a thousand years old or something like that?"

"Did Panadur tell you that?"

"No. I heard it someplace."

Han's lips pressed together. "Oh, no. Elves live at least twice that long. And Elvana live, on average that is, for four or five thousand years."

Dean's eyes widened and he looked at Han in amazement.

Then Han burst out laughing. "And if you believe that, have I got a castle to sell you!"

Dean groaned. "I know that saying."

"I'm sorry, Dean, but I just couldn't let that opportunity slip by."

"I don't know these things, so cut me some slack. Okay?"

"Cut you what?" Han asked.

"Never mind. But stop laughing at me, or those Krulgs will come back. And this time I'll trip you."

"All right. I'm sorry. Good night, Dean." Han rolled over on his sleeping mat.

"Good night." Dean lay back on his mats. "Buy a castle. Oh, man."

"Dean, can I ask you a favor?" Han asked.

"Sure. What?"

"Would you please stop referring to me as a man? I'm an Elvana." He giggled.

"Go to sleep, will you?" Dean threw an acorn Han's way.

The two of them fell asleep beneath the stars, with Han quietly laughing to himself.

6

THE HUNT

They traveled through the mountains for days. Han hunted small game with his tiny bow. The little archer proved to be deadly accurate. Dean watched or tried to flush out the game. In daylight they made a fire, but at night they feared to because the creatures could be about. Each morning the sky was a brilliant red, but the days were overcast and gray. The nights were mostly starless, and the moon could rarely be seen through the clouds.

As they neared the second week in the mountains, the pass through which they were traveling descended into a large valley below. And it was while they were camped in that valley one night that Dean's eyes flew open.

He'd heard the crack of dead wood somewhere near the camp.

His heart raced. He stayed still for many minutes as he listened to hear the sound again, but there was nothing. Finally, he closed his eyes.

And heard the sound again.

While the hairs on the back of his neck rose, he slowly reached his arm out and clamped his hand over Han's mouth. Han's eyes fluttered open, and Dean motioned for him to be silent. The two lay unmoving as they listened for any foreign noise amid the sounds of the woods.

Han struggled to open his mouth. When he stuck out his

tongue, Dean yanked his hand away.

"Shh," Dean whispered.

"It's the wind. I heard it too," Han whispered back.

"There is no wind. And you didn't have to slime my hand." Dean made a face as he wiped his hand on his jeans.

"I couldn't breathe. You're just being paranoid." Han rolled over. "I grew up in the outdoors. I know these things."

"I'm paranoid? Oh yeah, I'm in a valley on the side of a mountain with a leprechaun in The Twilight Zone with a bunch of monsters around every corner, and I'm paranoid," Dean muttered under his breath.

There was a loud crack in the tree above, and Dean quickly leapt to his feet, dragging Han up behind him. A large net fell where they had been, and a cry of rage came from above.

"You were right," Han yelped.

"Great," muttered Dean. "Now let's run!"

Pausing only for Han to grab their packs and Dean to grab and unsheathe his sword, they took off—and ran almost directly into a Krulg. It stepped out from the shadows cast by a thick tree, dressed in dirty chain armor, a curved sword clasped in its gnarled hands. Its face twisted into an evil smile as it swung the dark blade at Dean's chest.

But Dean didn't even slow. His sword cut upward and sliced through the Krulg's armor, into its ribs. The Krulg's cry of pain echoed through the woods, and was answered by screams of fury.

Another Krulg now raced straight for Dean. It held a spiked mace over its head. Dean lunged forward and ducked low. He caught the beast in the stomach with his shoulder. With a heave, he flung it over his back. As he spun around to strike the Krulg down, he saw Han thrusting a long dagger into the prone Krulg's chest.

The two companions resumed their sprint down the trail, the

Krulgs crashing through the forest after them. Dean and Han raced ahead, but when the little path widened, they slid to a stop. Blocking the trail was a man in black plate armor sitting atop a massive horse. The man's ebony helmet had a crossed visor that was down, and in his hands was a huge lance with a silver tip.

"Don't run like rabbits." The man raised his lance in the air. "Feel proud to meet your end with the bravest hunter in all the lands. You're now Taviak's. You belong to me. Stay where you are."

"Yeah, right. Run, Han!" Dean sprang into the woods, and Han chased after him.

"You will not live to see the end of this valley!" Taviak bellowed.

Through the dark woods they ran. The noise of barked orders and Krulgs rushed after them. Remembering his lessons, Dean zipped up his leather jacket to hide his white shirt. He heard the rushing water of a stream ahead and strange barking from behind.

"Dogs?" he asked. "This guy is hunting us with dogs?"

"No." Han gulped and went pale. "Durhunds. They're like really mean boars with four tusks."

"Even worse. Crud. Follow me." Dean headed for the sounds of the stream. When they reached it, Han stopped on the bank, but Dean grabbed him and dove into the water. The two of them lay in the stream, the water rushing over them, their mouths just barely exposed.

And not a moment too soon. Just seconds later, Taviak, along with several Krulgs and Durhunds, appeared on the bank. "The fools tried to lose their scent in the water," cried Taviak. "Tragrik ubrunik alke varnik vuergrak!"

That must have been some kind of order, because the Krulgs and Durhunds took off along the stream in both directions. Dean held Han still, and they both waited several minutes.

Just when Dean was about to raise himself up from the stream, he heard footsteps. They both held their breath and sank beneath the surface of the water.

A figure appeared on the bank next to them. Dean felt Han shake as something jabbed the water near them. Again and again something stabbed the water, coming closer and closer. Dean's lungs burned, and his mind raced.

A spearhead flashed as it passed next to Dean's face. He sat bolt upright and thrust his sword at the figure. His blade sank deep into the Krulg's chest. He yanked his sword back, and the Krulg fell onto the bank, dead.

"Look out!" Han screamed as a second Krulg ran up and thrust at Dean with his barbed spear.

Dean spun to the side and grabbed the shaft of the spear. In one motion, he pulled both it and the Krulg forward, and he drove his sword into the Krulg's belly. Screaming, the beast fell into the water, which swallowed its cries but not the echo that rang through the woods.

Han looked at him, wide-eyed. "You're the bravest warrior I've ever seen. Actually, I haven't seen too many in battle, but if I had, I bet you'd be the best. I've never really seen a battle—"

Han was cut off as Dean dragged him to the opposite bank. "I'm running on luck right now, and I'm pushing it. That Krulg's screaming is going to bring them all back, and I don't want to be here to meet the black tin can again. Let's go."

The two ran once more. The pale moon peeked out from the clouds overhead.

"Great. Like they really needed more light to hunt us," Dean grumbled.

"Dean," Han panted, "I hear the Durhunds."

Dean stopped. "We'll never lose those stupid things. I thought the water would cover our scent. I have to think. The Durhunds will be running in front of those guys. If they are, we can try to kill the Durhunds and then run. That's what they'd do in the movies."

"Movies?" Han asked, puzzled.

"Motion pictures? Oh, skip it. How many do you think there are?"

"Three or four. It's hard to tell with them all barking, but that's what I would guess."

"Do you think you can kill them with your bow?"

"Four? I don't know if I can if they're all trying to get at me at once."

"Get up in this tree. I think I can get one or two on the ground while you get the others."

Han scurried up the tree, and Dean assumed a defensive stance as the barking of the Durhunds drew closer.

Suddenly, a growling Krulg charged from behind the tree. It swung its mace in a huge arc. Dean blocked and pivoted around the mace, and the mace fell to the ground. But the Krulg grabbed Dean's sword arm and punched him in the face. As Dean staggered to the side, the Krulg grabbed Dean from behind, its large arms wrapping around his chest. His sword arm was pinned and his weapon fell to the ground.

Dean did the only thing he could do: he planted his feet and pushed backward, slamming the Krulg into the trunk of the tree.

But the Krulg only tightened its grip. It grasped Dean's throat with a clawed hand, and Dean could smell the creature's foul odor. Its rancid breath was hot on his face. With a growl, it whipped Dean around and smashed him into the tree.

As Dean fell to his knees, the Krulg stepped back and drew a rusted, curved dagger. The beast looked down at Dean with hate in its eyes and it raised the weapon.

Han bounded from the tree and landed hard on the creature's head. With a loud groan, the Krulg fell backward, and Han tumbled onto the ground.

"I did it!" Han looked at Dean with a wide grin.

"He's not out. Help me tie him up."

While Han rummaged inside his pack and drew out a short length of cord, Dean unzipped his jacket and pulled his shirt off, then pulled the shirt over the Krulg's head.

"Just tie his arms," he instructed Han.

Soon, Dean and Han had tied the Krulg's arms behind its back and lashed a gag in its mouth.

"What're we doing?" Han asked.

"It's a white shirt. They'll see him from a mile off. It also has my scent. I'm hoping the Durhunds will follow him, and we won't have to fight them."

He heaved the Krulg to its feet. It snarled and stared menacingly at him.

"Run." Dean pushed the Krulg, but the beast just stood and glared. "Run, you stupid jerk," Dean ordered again, with another shove. Still, the Krulg just stood and stared blankly.

"Wait a minute." Han rushed to the base of the tree. He bent down and turned over rocks and branches.

"What are you doing? The Durhunds are almost here." Dean leveled his sword at the Krulg.

"Here." Han picked something up and cupped it in his hands. "A Wahelli bug." He grinned as he held out his hands to reveal a large brown bug with big pincers in the front. "I don't know if that's their real name, but that's what I call them."

"What are you going to do with it?"

"This." Han dropped the bug down the Krulg's pants. "It will make him run."

The Krulg yelped and ran.

Han climbed the tree again, and Dean climbed up after him.

The Durhunds appeared seconds later—and as Dean had hoped, they followed the scent of the fleeing Krulg. Dean and Han waited, and soon after, Taviak and six or seven Krulgs crashed through the woods and raced after the barking Durhunds.

Only then did Dean and Han toss down their packs and scramble from the tree. They ran in the opposite direction. After a mile or so, they came to a large field and slowed their pace.

"It worked." Han gave a large grin as he patted Dean on the shoulder.

"It wouldn't have if it wasn't for your Wahelli bug."

"The Durhunds followed the scent of your shirt. That was smart."

"I'm just glad it worked."

"Actually . . ." Han's voice rose. "It didn't work for long."

Taviak, on top of his horse, crashed through the brush behind them. "We meet again, my little fleeing rabbits." He laughed.

"Split up!" Dean shouted. He dashed to the right, and Han sprinted for the woods on the left. "After me, Tin-can Man!" Dean taunted as he fled.

As Han ran, he unslung his bow and tried to nock an arrow. Turning around, he slipped and fell. Taviak immediately changed direction targets and headed for Han. Dean turned and raced toward his friend as well.

The horse's hooves churned up the ground as it bore down on Han. The lance's silver tip flashed. Han scrambled to his feet.

Dean knew he couldn't reach Han in time. He grabbed a rock and threw it as hard as he could.

The rock struck the side of Taviak's helmet with a clang. The lance flew over Han's head.

Taviak reined the horse to a stop and turned to face Dean.

"Hey, tin-can man. Are you wearing pink under all that armor or what?" Dean sneered.

With a yank on the reins, the horse changed direction and charged straight at Dean.

"I can do this," Dean muttered. "It's like the pole at the stream. Except for the four-hundred-pound horse at the end of it . . ."

As the horse thundered toward Dean, everything seemed to slow: the grass flying up behind the hooves, the weaving of the silver lance tip, and the pounding of Dean's heart in his chest. He spun sideways, but the lance ripped into his leather jacket, pulling Dean off his feet and dragging him along in the dirt.

"The rabbit is snagged," Taviak laughed as he pushed the head of the lance into the ground.

The horse suddenly whinnied and shied. Dean saw Han grab Taviak's leg and scramble up behind him. The Elvana grabbed Taviak's black helmet and, with a grunt, turned it sideways.

Dean took advantage of the distraction. He grabbed the lance, which Taviak still grasped firmly, and pushed it to the side, sending Taviak tumbling from his mount and onto the ground below. His helmet came off and rolled along the dirt.

The horse reared, and Han, still mounted, held onto its neck for dear life. The horse turned, bucked, bolted across the field, and disappeared into the woods with Han.

Dean pulled the lance free and jumped to his feet at the same time that Taviak rose, swearing.

"You're dead, boy," he growled.

"Try to catch me, tin-can man," Dean jeered, walking backward.

"I don't need a horse to kill you." Taviak bent over, grabbed his helmet, and put it back on. His hand flashed, and a knife whizzed by Dean's ear.

"You want to throw things? Well, I hope you want to catch them, too." Dean heaved a rock that rang off Taviak's shoulder.

"Stand and die," Taviak challenged as he ran toward Dean.

"I think I'll go with run and live." Backpedaling, Dean bounced another rock off Taviak's armor. Then he turned and sprinted away, with Taviak on his heels.

He dashed into the shelter of the woods, with Taviak's thunderous footsteps behind him. But when he turned around, Taviak was nowhere to be seen. The forest was hushed. Dean stayed low and tried to calm his breathing. The woods were completely silent.

Then a sword swept around a tree, straight at Dean's neck. Dean ducked just in time, and the blade cut deeply into the tree. Taviak yanked the sword from the wood and slashed again, but this time Dean parried with his own blade. The sound of metal on metal filled the forest.

"Decided to fight, boy?" Taviak jeered.

"Yeah, because I think you're wearing a dress under all that fancy armor."

Taviak screamed, and as his sword crashed and locked with Dean's, he punched Dean in the face with his gauntleted fist.

Dean spun around and fell onto his stomach. His head rang, and blood ran from his lip.

"You hit like my nanny," Dean growled as he rolled, jumped to his feet, and lunged.

Taviak turned the blade to the side. "Insolence!" His weapon crashed into Dean's, and the force knocked Dean back to the ground.

Dean landed hard on his back. His hand pressed into the dirt.

"Now die, boy." Taviak raised his sword over his head.

Dean flung a handful of dirt into Taviak's open visor. Taviak's hand went to his face, and Dean thrust upward with his sword. The blade struck Taviak's armor and bounced aside.

"Fool." Taviak laughed. "No blade can pierce my armor."

"Crud."

Dean rolled to his feet and ran. The forest opened onto a small clearing with a high mound of large rocks and a single tree in the center.

"Stop, rabbit!" Taviak taunted from behind.

Dean ran for the stone mound, for the advantage of higher ground. He grabbed the rocks and hurriedly pulled himself up.

"Don't hide, rabbit," Taviak sneered as he stopped at the base of the mound.

Dean stood above him, out of the reach of Taviak's sword. "I'm not technically hiding, since you know where I am." He tossed another rock.

"You've found my weakness, rabbit. I cannot climb. Now I must wait to kill you. Don't be happy, though. Now you must wait to die." Taviak walked to the base of the tree and sat down.

Dean scanned the open field. He knew there was no way he could outrun Taviak before getting to the safety of the forest. He was trapped.

"Can I ask you a question?" Dean bent down and picked up a large, round stone.

"You may speak, rabbit."

"Stop calling me rabbit, tin-can man."

"Fine. What's your question?"

"Why are you so set on killing me?"

"It's what I like best. Hunting people down and killing them," he said plainly.

"I think you need another hobby."

"Don't think of running again. I will catch you. Why not just come down and let me kill you?"

"Thank you for the pleasant offer, but I sort of want to stay alive a little longer. If you want to see someone die so badly, why don't you just fall on your sword?"

"You have a sharp tongue. But you fought well, boy. Who taught you how to fight?"

Dean thought of Panadur. "My father taught me how to fight."

"Who is he? Maybe I killed him too."

"You couldn't shake a stick at Panadur."

"Panadur! You're Panadur's son?" Taviak jumped up. "Oh, it will be a joy to kill you."

"Don't get all excited. I'm not dead yet."

"You don't think I could best Panadur? Then you don't know anything about me, boy. I've killed just about every type of creature alive. I used to kill Wardevar, before they died out. Some say I'm the reason that the Leomane are so rare."

"You should take up fishing. No"—Dean shook his head— "I like fish. Why don't you plant flowers or something?"

"I'm not just a hunter, boy. I enjoy seeing things suffer. Sometimes I torture them before I kill them. Sometimes I watch them die slowly."

"That's really creepy. You've got issues." Dean walked to the other side of the mound.

Taviak followed him on the ground. "There was only one thing I hunted down and let live."

"That was nice of you. How about you make it two?"

Taviak laughed. "I let it live because I was paid to."

"I have money." Dean reached into his pocket and pulled out the roll of bills.

Taviak laughed harder. "Paper? You would offer paper for your life?"

Dean pressed his tongue against his cheek. "Great. The only time I have money, and it's worthless," he muttered.

"Do you know what it was I caught, Dean? It was your uncle, Carimus."

Before Dean could respond, Taviak suddenly turned and dashed over to the edge of the field. There was a muffled yell, and then Taviak returned, dragging Han. One hand held a knife to the Elvana's throat.

"It's time for your friend to die," Taviak said. "I'll let you watch."

"Stop. Let him go, and I'll come down."

Han opened his mouth to speak, but Taviak's hand clamped down on his throat.

Dean climbed down from the rocks and walked to Taviak. He stopped only six feet away. He held his sword in his left hand and hid a rock in his right hand. "Let him go," he said. "Just you and me."

"Wonderful!" Taviak flung Han away like a rag doll. The night sky was just starting to lighten. "Dawn," Taviak said. "That's a good time for you to die, boy."

Dean's muscles tightened. With all his power, he threw the rock at Taviak's head. The rock slammed into Taviak's helmet. As Taviak's head snapped back, his neck was exposed. Dean's sword flashed as the first rays of morning came into the clearing.

Taviak fell to the ground with a thud. Dean stood, panting, and his hand trembled.

"Is he dead?" Han scurried away from the body.

"Dead as a doornail."

"Are you sure?"

"The guy doesn't have a head. Usually when you don't have a head, you're dead."

"Are you okay?"

Dean shook his head. "I've never killed anyone before."

"You killed the Krulgs."

"They were monsters." Dean cleaned his sword on the grass.

Han looked down at Taviak's corpse. "He was a monster, too."

Dean swallowed and closed his eyes. He took a deep breath and nodded. "Let's get out of here."

"The horse got away, but I got our packs. They're in the woods."

"Nice work."

"Thank you." Han walked beside Dean. "I mean . . . thank

you for saving my life. If you hadn't thrown that rock . . ."

"Don't worry about it. You've been saving my neck too," Dean said. "And hey, was that a throw or was that a throw? I was just like Babe Ruth."

"You weren't like a little girl. You were great!"

"What? A little girl?" Dean wrinkled his nose.

"Baby Ruth," Han said.

"No. Babe Ruth. He's a guy. He's a baseball player."

"Baseball?" Han asked.

"It's a game. Baseball. You throw the ball and eat hot dogs."

"Dogs? They eat dogs in the Heavens?" Han shrieked.

"They don't eat dogs in the Heavens."

"That's what you said."

"I didn't . . . Oh, skip it."

"Oh, skip it. That's what you always say. Oh, skip it. I just want you to know if I go to the Heavens, I'm not going to eat a dog."

Dean burst out laughing. "Don't worry, you won't go to the Heavens."

Han's mouth fell open. "I won't go to the Heavens?"

"No. I mean, you will someday. Not my Heavens but the Heaven. You know what I mean?"

Han shook his head and looked dejectedly at the ground.

"Don't get all bummed out. When I go back, you'll come to the Heavens with me, I promise." Dean held up a hand.

"I knew you were from the Heavens." Han laughed and then took off running, and Dean chased him into the woods.

7

THE TINY VIKING

The Dwarves all stood in a battle line, their massive two-headed battle-axes in their hands and their metal shields slung over their broad backs. A new wave of Krulgs approached them, led by Varlugs, the creatures' larger brethren, who stood nearly eight feet tall. Both sides had taken heavy losses in the earlier attacks; the field before them was littered with the dead, the ground turned a sickly red. The wicked beasts had lost far more, but they had the advantage of numbers on their side; they still outnumbered the Dwarves nearly four to one. The sky was in shadow, and the lack of wind stirred the smell of death now hanging in the air as thick as the darkest fog.

"Bravic, my brother, if I fail to make it through this next attack, I leave to you my belongings." A tall Dwarf, nearly five feet, laid his hand on a smaller Dwarf's armored shoulder.

"We'll both survive, Braga. We'll make it through all of this. Besides, you haven't got anything except me." The smaller Dwarf chuckled.

The two braced themselves for the awaited battle horn. Bravic stood with his short, stocky legs set. He had brown eyes and his dark hair, tied back, was nearly as long as the braided beard that rested on his chest plate. His leather boots, fringed with fur, were over his leather breeches, his gray metal shield was strapped to his back, and his battle-axe was in his thick hands.

The Dwarven horn echoed rich and deep through the

mountains, and both sides swarmed forward like waves smashing against rocks. The Dwarves sounded their booming battle cry, and the creatures answered with their wicked, guttural screams.

At the front of the ranks of the Krulgs, flanked by Varlugs, rode a Tearog, a demon warrior. The creature's features might have made it appear almost Human if not for its deathly pale skin, slanted black eyes, and seven-foot height. It wore midnight-black armor, and a black moon decorated its huge shield. It rode on a Ravinulk, a beast with the body of a huge wolf and the head of a dragon.

As the two fronts clashed, their weapons crackled like lightning, their screams of death echoed like thunder, and their blood poured down like rain. The Dwarves' line swept around both sides of the approaching force, but the Varlugs, led by the Tearog, ripped into the middle of the Dwarf formation, splitting it in two. As Dwarf, Krulg, and Varlug fell, the cloud of dust from the dry earth grew thicker and the sun grew fainter.

The two Dwarven brothers stood back to back. All around them lay a ring of fallen enemies. Braga blew his horn to rally the Dwarves to attack with renewed fury. The Dwarves came together, and again the creatures started to retreat.

But the Tearog cut a path through the Dwarves, until only the Dwarven brothers stood in its way. They both turned to attack the Tearog, but only Braga saw the spear flying from a Varlug's dark hand—straight for Bravic's side. Braga didn't hesitate: he jumped in front of it. The barbed spear sank deep into his breast, and he crashed to the ground. His dying words were lost, as though they were cried in the midst of a storm.

Unaware that his brother had fallen, Bravic rushed at the Tearog. He swung his axe in a massive arc, only for it to crash into the Tearog's huge shield. The Tearog's bloody mace struck out, but only clipped the Dwarf's helmet. Had it struck him full on, the blow would have caved in his head. As it was, the glancing blow was still hard enough to knock the Dwarf unconscious.

As the other Dwarven warriors rallied around their fallen comrades, the Tearog threw back its head and laughed a wicked laugh. Its evil mouth twisted into a vicious smile and revealed its pointed teeth. Then the Ravinulk turned and raced back to rejoin the rest of the foul creatures.

***

When Bravic came to, he was lying on the side of the battlefield, next to the woods. The bodies of fallen Dwarf warriors lay all around him. Rolling over, he saw his brother's still form, his battle-axe clutched in his cold hands. He wept as he pried the axe free. His tears fell onto the bloodstained grass.

"We can't win," Bravic sighed. "Volsur's army is all around, and all we're doing is dying—for nothing. Braga, I'm sorry. I have to leave. I want no part of this anymore. Volsur has won. This is just needless death."

He rose and walked into the woods, away from the two forces that were even now preparing to face each other yet again. He walked away from the bloodstained battlefield. He walked away from his fallen brother.

***

As the first rays of morning fought vainly to drive away the shadows, Dean and Han were already on the road. They both agreed that the few berries they'd had for breakfast were not the best way to start their day, but they were better than nothing at all.

As they traveled, Dean spotted familiar animals, birds, and trees: squirrels, rabbits, and foxes; blue jays, sparrows, and hawks; elms, pines, and maples. The animals were unremarkable, but the trees did not look healthy. Barren branches clutched at the gray sky. Some were already mere skeletons whose dead leaves broke off in the infrequent breezes.

Toward the middle of the day, the sun beat down upon them, making the walk a little too warm. They trekked on, heading down the straightening path.

"Hey, Han. When does a Krulg look good?" Dean asked as they stopped to rest.

"What?"

"It's a joke. You're supposed to say, 'I don't know. When does a Krulg look good?'"

"I know what a joke is. You don't think we have jokes?"

"I didn't really think about it, but I figure you must have jokes. Let's start over. When does a Krulg look good?"

"I don't know." Han smirked. "When does a Krulg look good?"

"When it's on the end of a spear!" Dean laughed.

"Hey, that's good. Do you have any more?"

"Yeah. How many Krulgs does it take to screw in—that won't work. How do you save a Krulg from drowning?"

"How?"

"Take your foot off its head."

They both laughed, and Dean stretched out on the grass.

"Can I ask you a question about the Heavens—I mean, where you're from?" Han asked.

"Yeah. What do you want to know?"

"Well, how did you get the name Dean? I never heard of a Dean before."

"I'm named after the movie star James Dean."

"Movie star? If you're named after a star, then you must be from the Heavens!" Han stared wide-eyed at Dean again.

"I'm not from the Heavens. I was born in America, but my

parents went on a trip to France—"

"France? What's France?"

"Shut up and listen, and I'll tell you," Dean blurted out in frustration.

The Elvana's smile vanished, and he looked at the ground. "All I did was ask a question. That's no reason to yell," he said dejectedly. "I'm not from the Heavens, so how am I supposed to know what a France is?"

"I'm sorry I yelled," Dean said softly, now upset at himself, seeing how sad Han looked. "It's just part of my life that I never talk about. It hurts."

"Please tell me, and I promise not to interrupt."

Dean shrugged. "Well, I got my name in France, like I said. It's a country in my world. Anyway, so I was told, my parents went to France when I was a baby. They were robbed and killed." As Dean continued, the Elvana's frown deepened. "Some French people found me. They knew I was an American—America is another country in my world. Wow, that still sounds bizarre. Anyway, they had to give me a name so I could get a visa or something, and they must have liked James Dean, so they named me after him."

Han was the first person Dean had ever told the story to, and it made him feel good to share it with someone.

"That's so sad," Han said. "I thought Panadur was your father."

"No. My real last name is Walker." Dean exhaled. "Or at least, that's the name the French people gave me. And Panadur . . . well, I didn't know him long, but he was more of a father to me than anyone. I grew up in foster homes mostly, but they didn't work out. I don't know if the problem was I didn't want pity or they didn't offer any. When Panadur took me in, I . . . Do you mind if we stop talking about this right now?" Dean quickly turned away.

"Sure. We can stop talking about it." The Elvana changed the subject. "We're making good time. If we hurry, I think we can reach Vinrell—that's the Dwarven stronghold—by nightfall."

Dean's legs ached at the thought of hurrying. He couldn't understand how Han moved so fast over such a long distance with such small legs. And now Han was up again, ready to set off, looking as if he could walk forever. With a groan, Dean got to his feet and followed the Elvana, who skipped down the road before him.

Before long, they topped a little hill. Down below, a small stream wound its way beside the path and curved into a little pool that sparkled invitingly.

"I think I'd better drink from that pool before you," Han said. "You're such a glutton there might not be any left by the time I get there." Han laughed as he ran down to the water.

"You can walk faster, but there's no way you can outrun me."

Dean chased after Han. Han had a good lead, but Dean quickly caught up, and before they reached halfway, Dean overtook him. As he put a little distance between the Elvana and himself, Dean turned partway around and started to run backward, infuriating Han, who pushed himself harder. Han caught up and started to pull ahead, but Dean turned back around and, with a leap, reached the side of the pool just before the Elvana.

They both lay on the bank, trying to catch their breath, as they splashed the cool water on their faces.

"Nice try." Dean raised himself up on his knees to drink from the small pool. "Better luck next time."

"We Elvanas have a saying." Han was panting, still quite winded from his run. "People who say 'Better luck next time' are all wet," he yelled—and he shoved Dean into the water.

Dean came up sputtering and flailing his arms. "Help me,

you stupid Elvana. I don't know how to swim!" he screamed.

Han's eyes went wide, and he sprang through the air to dive into the pool headfirst. His little hand reached down for Dean, but instead he found himself hoisted out of the water by his arms.

"We humans have a saying, too: 'You fell for it!'" Dean laughed.

Dean set Han down in the water. The scowl on Han's face deepened when he realized the water only came up to his chin. Dean tried to contain the smirk on his face, but it quickly spread to a broad grin.

"Try to play me for the fool, will you?" Han said. "Well then, prepare to meet your match!" With that, Han reached underwater, grabbed Dean's legs, and pulled them out from under him.

Dean pitched backward, but as he fell, he blindly grabbed Han by the front of his shirt and pulled him underwater too. "Now who's the victor?" he said as he stood.

"What the heck are you talking about?" Han asked from behind him.

Dean's head turned. Han stood five feet behind him with a puzzled look on his wet face. Dean looked down at his hands. He held on to a shirt, but it wasn't Han's. It belonged to the corpse of a man whose face was just beneath the water. Still eyes stared blankly upward, and the man's mouth was frozen in a twisted scream.

Dean let go of the corpse and raced for the side of the pool.

Han looked perplexed. "What's going on?"

"It's a dead guy. A real dead guy," Dean said.

They both scrambled from the pool.

"Shouldn't we get him out?" Han asked.

Dean looked at Han and then back at the pool. He couldn't see where the corpse was now. The water was cloudy from the dirt stirred up from the bottom.

"You get him out. I'm not touching a dead guy." Dean backed away. "He has his eyes open. It's the creepiest thing I've ever seen." He suddenly went white. "Gross!" He spit and ran up the stream.

Han chased after him. "What's the matter now?"

Dean stuck his whole head in the water. He came up spitting, sputtering, and wiping his mouth. "We drank out of that pool." He made a face and stuck his head back under the water.

"GROSS!" Han dropped down and washed his mouth out too.

When they finally felt that they were clean, they walked back to the pool.

"It just doesn't feel right," Han muttered.

"What doesn't?"

"Leaving him in there. If it were me, I'd want someone to take my body out." Han looked at Dean, but Dean didn't move. So Han slipped back into the water.

Dean paced back and forth on the bank, scanning the pool for some sign of the body. He sighed, then stepped into the pool. "I can't believe I'm going to look for a dead guy," he mumbled.

The two of them felt around for the corpse, sticking their arms down while trying to keep their heads above the surface. Their faces were contorted with looks of disgust. The water swirled around their necks, and their feet stirred up the mud at the bottom. Soon a smell of decay rose to hang above the pool.

"This is gross. We don't even know how the guy died," Dean said.

"Or what killed him," Han added.

At that moment, the hair on the back of Dean's neck stood on end. He looked up—and froze.

"Um, Han? I think I know what killed him." He pointed at the huge creature now standing on the bank of the pool. The

Varlug stood nearly eight feet tall, with broad shoulders and bowed legs. Its hideous face featured a flattened nose, large ears, and two tusk-like teeth that rose from its lower jaw to cover its upper lip. "He did!"

Dean and Han both ran for the other edge of the pool just as the Varlug's whip snapped through the air with a crack, barely missing Dean's head. Its gray, hairy face twisted in glee as it snapped the whip again, and this time the leather wrapped around Dean's neck. The Varlug laughed as it pulled in its struggling prey.

Dean's breath caught in his throat as the whip cut into his skin. With one hand he pulled on the whip to relieve the tension, while with his other he fumbled for the sword at his side.

The creature yanked him closer and raised a barbed spear.

Dean's feet were dragged across the slippery floor of the pool. He dug in his heels, and managed to turn and face the creature.

The Varlug lifted his spear. And at that moment, Dean yanked as hard as he could on the whip. The Varlug stumbled forward and fell into the pool.

With a wicked growl, the Varlug burst out of the water and jumped at Dean. Both of them disappeared beneath the surface.

Only the Varlug emerged. Its spear struck again and again into the water as it searched for its victim. Then the hideous creature felt its spear strike flesh and bone, and the Varlug roared triumphantly.

Han was pulling his dagger from his pack when he heard the Varlug's roar. He spun around in time to see the creature throwing a limp body to the deeper side of the pool.

"Dean!" he screamed.

Han raised the dagger and threw it with all his might. As the blade spun through the air, Han saw everything in slow motion—the dagger spinning, the creature raising its spear . . .

and the top of a head appearing from under the water. Dean's head. He wasn't dead! The body the Varlug had thrown must have belonged to the dead guy.

Han's dagger struck the Varlug in its arm. It roared in pain and dropped its spear.

Dean took the opportunity to pull himself onto the shore and scramble to his feet. But with another crack, the whip once again circled Dean's neck. The Varlug yanked Dean off his feet. Dean's hands fumbled for his sword as the Varlug dragged him back toward the water.

Han ran forward. The Varlug picked his spear up and swung it like a staff to ward off the little figure. He struck Han in the side and sent him flying.

Dean finally managed to draw his sword from its sheath. With a cry of rage, he cut the whip around his neck and spun to strike the creature. But before he could, the butt of the spear crashed down on Dean's head. It felt as though an explosion went off in his brain, and he fell backward. He landed flat on his back, the air forced from his lungs.

The Varlug stomped triumphantly forward. Dean stared up at the creature that towered over him. The Varlug raised its spear over its head, prepared to drive it through Dean's body.

But instead, the Varlug froze. The front of its leather shirt pushed forward and split open, revealing the bloody, razor-sharp head of an axe. Two trails of black fluid ran from the corners of the Varlug's mouth, and the creature tumbled to the side.

A Dwarf stood on the opposite bank.

"A tiny Viking?" Dean said. "I got saved by a tiny Viking."

Then he closed his eyes and fell into blackness.

8

A FISH, A CHICKEN, AND A SQUIRREL

Dean opened his eyes and saw Han's familiar face filled with worry.

"Bravic, he's awake," Han said cheerfully.

"Where are we?" Dean mumbled and licked his lips. "I feel like I ate sand, my mouth is so dry."

"We're about a mile from the pool. You've been unconscious for a whole day now. Bravic and I carried you here. Actually, he did most of the carrying. Oh, you haven't really met him." He gestured to the Dwarf. "This is Bravic Volesunga. If it weren't for him, we'd both be dead. I think—"

"Hold on, Elvana." Bravic's thick hand landed on Han's shoulder. His voice was deep and rich. "He's just woken up. Give him some time to get his legs."

"Thank you, Bravic." Dean tried to raise himself up on his elbows, but slumped back down.

"Here," Han said. "Drink this tea." He passed Dean a dented metal cup. "It's an herb tea to help you sleep. Rest now, my friend. I'll see you in the morning."

Dean drank thirstily, then lay back down. He was asleep again almost immediately.

***

Dean awoke to a gray morning and the sounds of swords

clashing. He sprang to his feet. His head spun, and he swayed in a large circle, but he managed to remain standing. He rubbed his eyes and saw that Bravic was instructing Han on how to use a dagger against a battle-axe in combat. Dean stretched and approached the two figures.

"Dean, you're awake." Han beamed. "Bravic is showing me how to be a warrior. Something you've neglected to do, I might add. I didn't think of it until this morning, when Bravic asked me if I knew how to fight and I realized I didn't. I know how to fight a little, but I've never been formally trained. I've never been trained at all, actually. Though I do know how to shoot a bow." Han did his best imitation of the Dwarf as he said, "If you ever met a Daehtar, he'd cut you in half before you could draw that little bow."

"That's right, he would," Bravic growled, but a smile crept across his face. "That's why I'm going with the two of you. Without me, you two wouldn't last a day on this quest."

"Han! Have you told him everything?" Dean asked.

"Yes." Han gulped. "After all, he did save our lives . . . and he's a mighty warrior."

"I don't know," Dean said. "I appreciate you wanting to help, but I don't know if it's right to drag you into this."

Bravic pressed his lips together and squared his wide shoulders. "The way I see it, you need my help. Right now I don't have any place to go, so I'm going to come along."

Dean looked at the imposing Dwarf for a moment, then nodded. "Okay. My name's Dean Theradine, at your service." Dean bowed, trying to remember how Panadur had taught him. "If I was out a whole day, then Han must have told you all about me already."

"He's told me a great deal about you, indeed. What I believe and what I don't, is yet to be determined. I mainly question the part about you being from the Heavens."

"I'm not from the Heavens." Dean glared at Han.

"Whoops." Han smiled impishly.

Dean's stomach rumbled. "Is there anything to eat?"

"This little woodsman is a fair shot with that little bow. On small game," Bravic added when he noticed Han's grin. "He managed to down quite a few rabbits. They're all skinned, cleaned, and cooked. We thought we should wait for you before eating, much to my own dismay."

After the three sat down and ate a hot breakfast, they continued on their way. And for the next several days, whenever they stopped to rest, Bravic taught them both how to fight against an opponent with an axe. Soon Dean and Han were covered with bruises, but they learned quickly. Han ducked and dodged, then tried to spring in and jab quickly. Dean attacked aggressively, trying to turn the blows aside with his sword and sweep in, using the speed of his weapon.

The days were gray and dark; storm clouds turned thicker and seemed to sink closer, hiding the sun and smothering their spirits as well. To pass the hours as they walked, they talked and told tales. At one point Bravic burst into a boisterous and spirited song of the Dwarves:

> Since the days of Caltic we dig deep
> Into the mountain for gold to reap
> We dig all day, we dig all night
> We dig till we see that golden light
> We are Dwarves! We are Dwarves!
>
> We dig under mountain
> We dig under light
> We dig all day and we dig all night
> We dig till we see that golden light
> We are Dwarves! We are Dwarves!

Our backs are stone
Our arms are steel
Deep under mountain
Our hammers we wield
We dig all day, we dig all night
We dig till we see that golden light
We are Dwarves! We are Dwarves!

Eventually, the land became less rocky and more level. Small shrubs became trees and the gravelly path turned to moss. Soon they were out of the mountains and passing over grassy hills that spread in front of them like a green sea in a storm. Travel was much easier, though Bravic seemed to miss the mountains.

After five days on the plains, as dusk fell, they came to the edge of a great forest and decided to set up camp for the night before venturing forward. As Dean gazed upon the sky that evening, the clouds parted for a moment, and a shadow passed between him and the almost-full moon.

"Did you see that?" he whispered to Bravic. "It was some big flying thing."

Bravic leaped to his feet. "Did it look like a bird?"

"No. It wasn't a bird. It looked like a—" Dean was cut off as Han tackled him from behind. A four-taloned paw swept just over his unprotected head.

"They're Tarlugs!" Han said. "Flying Krulgs. Should we stand and fight?" He drew his little dagger and got to his feet.

"No, we run and hide!" Dean yelled. He flung his pack over his shoulder and ran to the forest.

"Good idea, Human." Bravic grabbed his own pack and raced after him.

As the three ran, Han nocked an arrow, and all three looked to the black sky. Dean saw what looked like a Krulg with huge, dark-green wings flying toward them.

"Twelve o'clock high!" Dean screamed, turning and setting his feet in preparation for the creature's attack. As the Tarlug descended on him, Dean's sword struck it in the chest and sent it skidding along the ground. "I got it!" he cheered. "I got it!"

Dean felt talons rip into his jacket and pull him off his feet. "Help! It's got me!"

An arrow flew from Han's bow and sank into the back of the Tarlug that now held Dean. The Tarlug went limp, and both Tarlug and Dean crashed to the ground.

Bravic raised his ax and screamed at the sky. "Come and stand your ground where I can hit you, you cowardly flying dogs!"

"Run for the woods!" Dean shouted. "They can't fly in there."

The Tarlugs descended after their fleeing prey. Dean and Han reached the treeline first. Bravic was still racing toward them when a Tarlug dove at his unprotected back. Two more arrows flew from Han's bow. The first struck the Tarlug in the wing, but the second hit its chest. The beast hit the ground in a bone-cracking heap.

The Dwarf sprang for the safety of the trees. A pursuing Tarlug tried to pull out of its downward plummet but smashed into the upper branches of a tree and fell to the ground. With a single swing of his ax, Bravic made sure it was dead.

"I think we should keep going," Dean panted. "I don't want those things chasing us all night."

"I wouldn't advise it. The Palutaried Swamp is in this forest, and I wouldn't want to journey into it in the day, let alone at night," Bravic said grimly.

"Yeah, and we're safe right here." Han crossed his arms and leaned against a tree. "Tarlugs can't fly in a forest, so we have nothing to worry about."

"Unless they walk, too." Dean pointed to the Tarlugs. They had landed at the edge of the woods and were walking into the forest. "Let's get out of here. Palutaried Swamp, here we come."

Again they ran. Dean and Han had to slow down for the Dwarf, but they still easily outdistanced the creatures. The Tarlugs were not very fast runners.

Soon the ground became spongy, and pools of dark, muddy water appeared around them. After a while, the pools grew into one, and they had to wade through ever-deepening muck. Dean looked nervously at Han. The water was now up to the Elvana's chest.

"I think we lost them," Bravic whispered.

"I think you're right. Should we go on?" Dean asked.

"I think we have to keep going straight. I have no idea where we are," Bravic grumbled.

"Then we don't have any choice." Dean shrugged. "Han, I think you'd better get up on my shoulders. The ground seems like it's leveling off, but I don't want you to fall into a hole or something."

"Sounds like an excellent idea to me," Han said.

They picked their way through the swamp, heading north, as far as they could tell, as they twisted and turned around vine-covered trees and mounds of earth. Their feet sank in thick ooze, and with each step it became harder to pull their feet free. Their footsteps also churned up the murky waters, making them even blacker and releasing a foul, rotten odor that lingered in the stagnant air. But as they walked, the swamp swallowed any trace of their passage. Behind them, the water seemed to transform into smooth muck once again.

"Dean, something bumped my leg!" Bravic yelped nervously.

"Imagine it's a fish," Dean called back.

"Yeah, imagine it's a fish," Han repeated from atop Dean's shoulders.

The Dwarf glared up at him.

After traveling a little farther, something bumped Bravic's leg again.

"There it is again!"

"Imagine it's a fish," Dean snapped.

"Yeah, imagine it's a fish," Han teased.

Dean stopped to rest—Han, as light as he was, had started to tire him—and Bravic let out a muffled call from behind.

Han turned. "Imagine it's a—" he started, then screamed, "It's not a fish!"

Bravic's feet were sticking out of the mouth of an enormous snake. With its prey in its jaws, the creature dove back under the water and sped off.

Dean lunged after the fleeing snake. Han tumbled from his back and landed with a splash. But the snake moved so fast it was soon lost from sight in the dark water.

"Han, come on, we have to go after Bravic!" Dean cried. "It's going to eat him!"

"I don't think so." Han shook the water from his hair. "At least not right away. It's an Aliandor. They like to save their prey and eat them later, after they do all their hunting. There are some in the Weeping Meadow Marsh, but I never heard of one that big."

"So Bravic could still be alive? It didn't bite him in half or squeeze him to death or—"

"I hope not." Han made a horrified face. "A fisherman from my village was taken one time, so my dad and some men went to rescue him. And he was fine—mostly. The Aliandor probably has a nest or home around here somewhere. We just have to find it."

"Bravic! Bravic!" Dean called and then listened. There was

no response but the sound of buzzing insects. "BRAVIC!" Dean screamed as loudly as he could, but again, he heard only the sounds of the swamp in reply. "How are we going to find him, Han? Do you think we could see its lair?"

Han's voice cracked with frustration. "I don't know. It could be anywhere."

"You said it does all its hunting before eating?" Dean asked.

Han nodded. "My dad said the snake came out and caught a member of the rescue party. They followed the snake back and saved both men," he said proudly.

"We'll do the same thing," Dean said excitedly. "If we can get that snake to come back after one of us, we'll follow it back to its lair." He splashed around in the water, trying to get the snake's attention.

Nothing.

"Why did it take Bravic?" he asked Han.

Han shrugged. "You're probably too big."

"That's it! I'm too big to attract its attention. But you're not."

"Not me," Han cried. He nervously climbed one of the vine-covered trees. "You're not going to use me as snake bait!"

"Come on, Han. It's Bravic's only chance. We'll never find its lair if we don't," Dean pleaded.

"I might be little, but I'm not a mouse for some oversized snake," Han yelled down.

"Yeah . . . you're not a mouse, you're a chicken," Dean yelled back.

"Well, I'm an alive chicken," Han snapped. "And that's the way I'm going to stay: alive."

"Fine, be a chicken and stay up in the tree. I'm going to get Bravic," Dean growled.

He knelt in the muck so the filthy water came to his chest, then walked on his knees. "Come on, snake. I'm a nice, fat, juicy Dwarf," Dean bellowed, trying to imitate Bravic. He started to sing, in his best Dwarven voice, "I dig all night, I dig all day, for the gold, for the gold, because I'm a Dwarf, I'm a Dwarf."

"What're you doing?" Han called down to him. "That's not how the song goes. And even if it did, snakes can't hear."

"Well, they feel vibrations or something," Dean muttered. "And if I—"

Dean was cut off as his whole upper body was swallowed into the giant mouth of the snake. It lifted him high in the air and dove back under the water. As Dean felt himself being dragged along, he hoped he'd made the right decision, and this creature was not going to drown him.

Just as he felt his lungs were about to burst, the snake came above water again in some enclosed den. Dean was dropped unceremoniously into a deep pit, and the snake disappeared once again under the water.

Dean wiped the slime off his face and looked around the pit. The sides rose over twelve feet. Above that was a domed ceiling made from sticks woven together.

Bravic stretched out a hand to help Dean up. "Imagine it's a fish," he said. "It got you too, huh?"

"Yeah. How do we get out of here?" Dean looked around.

"It's a giant beaver lodge. The snake must have taken it over. The walls are too slimy for climbing and too hard for using spikes, but if I get on your shoulders I may be able to jump out," Bravic said hopefully.

They tried that strategy repeatedly, but Bravic fell back each time, reaching far short of the edge. Then they tried switching it around, with Dean climbing onto Bravic's shoulders, but Dean, too, fell short of grabbing the edge of the pit.

"Do you know what we need?" Bravic grumbled.

"A rope?"

"No—Han."

"Well, don't hold your breath," Dean muttered.

Outside the pit, they heard a splash of water. The shadow of the creature appeared over them, and a body and a large pack dropped from the creature's mouth to land at their feet. As the body rolled over, Dean saw Han's familiar face.

"Han!" Dean cried and he helped the Elvana to his feet.

"Were you expecting a chicken?" Han snapped, trying to clean the slime from his face.

"You brought my pack?" Dean said, picking it up. "Thanks!"

"I was hoping to choke the stupid snake with it," Han grumbled as he shook the water out of his ears. "So. What're we going to do now that all three of us are in this predicament?"

"Let's get out of here before that snake comes back." Dean stood against the wall. "Quick, Bravic, climb back on my shoulders, then Han, you climb on his."

Between the three of them, they had enough height for Han to almost reach the edge of the pit. He jumped up and snagged a hanging root—but his feet still dangled.

"Pull yourself up," Bravic growled.

"I'm trying." Han's feet slid on the side of the pit. "The side of the pit is slimy too. See how my feet are slipping? Why is that snake so slimy? It's not a worm, but it has a coat of slime that—"

"Stop talking," Dean snapped. "Pull yourself up."

"I'm trying!" Han finally climbed out and disappeared from sight.

"I wonder what was harder for him," Bravic huffed, "pulling himself up or not talking?"

"Now what do I do?" Han called down, peering over the edge.

"Look for a rope or a vine or something," Dean said.

Han looked around. "It looks like an abandoned beaver lodge," he said.

"I already told him that," Bravic complained.

"I'll try to pull one of these sticks down." Han jumped at a limb that hung from the ceiling.

"No!" Bravic yelled as Han jumped up and snagged the branch. "Look at the structure. It uses tensional force to dissipate the weight. You'll need to find a branch that doesn't bear any load."

Han hung from the stick, and his body twisted around in a slow circle. "What?" One eyebrow arched. The branch suddenly pulled free. "I did it!" Han cheered.

The ceiling groaned, and the sound of branches snapping made them all duck. A second branch fell from the ceiling and a third quickly followed.

"Yep, I think you really did it . . ." Dean grabbed Bravic and moved against the wall of the pit.

The whole ceiling caved in around them. Han dove into the water as Bravic and Dean hid against the wall.

"Sorry!" Han yelled.

"It's okay—we can use the branches to get out now." Dean helped Bravic climb. "But if snakes feel vibrations, it surely felt that."

Han waited at the edge of the pit as Bravic pulled himself up on the branches. "It worked, didn't it?" Han snapped in response to Bravic's scowl.

"It could have easily gotten us killed as well," Bravic said. "I told you not to pull that one out."

"No, you didn't." Han planted his foot.

"I clearly did."

"What you said was about as clear as mud." Han's hands went out. "Grab a cross-tensional blah-blah-blah."

"A Dwarf would have understood."

"I'm not a Dwarf."

"That's obvious."

Dean climbed out. "Can you kids stop fighting until we get

out so the giant snake doesn't eat us?"

"Fine." Han rolled his eyes. "You could at least say thank you." He cast a sideways scowl at Bravic.

"For what?" Bravic roared. "Almost getting me killed?"

"How about thank you for letting a huge snake eat me, getting half drowned and totally slimy, and almost getting you killed—I mean, getting you out of the pit." Han glared.

"For the first two things that you said, I thank you." Bravic glared back.

"Kiss and make up," Dean said, "and let's go."

Both Han and Bravic made a face before they followed Dean to the edge of the collapsed structure.

"We can get out there." Dean pointed to an opening in the side.

The creature's lair was very near the edge of the swamp. The forest was only a short distance away.

"Let's get to land before that thing comes back," Han said, hurrying out. "I don't feel like being a piece of bait again."

Dean let Han climb onto his back again, then waded from the little wooded island toward firmer ground. Bravic swore as he sank up to his chin in the water, but they made it to dry ground without incident.

Still, they hurried onward. They didn't know for sure whether the snake could come onto land.

Soon, Dean noticed a cave opening in the side of a hill, and gestured for the others to follow. The opening was tall enough for Dean to easily walk into, and the floor was dry earth.

"Do you want to camp here?" Dean motioned the others forward.

As Bravic leaned into the darkness, a deep, guttural growl came from far back in the cave. A foul smell rose with it.

"If you tell me to imagine it's a squirrel, I'll beat you both senseless," Bravic yelled as all three sprinted away from the cave.

It was late in the day when they finally stopped to camp in a small, dry clearing, well clear of both the swamp and the cave. Tired and grimy, the three sat around a small fire, drying their clothes. They were covered with dirt and grime, and twigs and leaves hung in their hair. As the night swallowed the faint light, they fell asleep beneath the starless sky in the now strangely silent forest.

9

COWBOYS AND INDIANS

Their food had been ruined in the swamp, and Han's bow had been lost when he was taken by the snake, so for breakfast they had to settle for a few berries. They needed supplies, and when Bravic realized they were only a few days' walk from the Elven forest of Kilacouqua, they decided to pass through it. Despite their hungry stomachs, their spirits were high from surviving the snake, and with the sun glowing like fire, they set off. As they walked, Han sang a song of the Elvana:

With a hi and a hey! We start along our way.
Traveling down to somewhere.

With a hey and a hi! We make the time fly.
Traveling down to somewhere.

With a yip and a yeah! We journey where we may.
Traveling down to somewhere.

With a yeah and a yip! We enjoy the trip.
Traveling down to somewhere.

With a hee and a ho! We sing as we go.
Traveling down to somewhere.

If the road gets too long.
Then we'll just sing this song.
Bringing us down to somewhere.

After two days, the trees gave way to a sea of emerald-green grass. It was the spongy type of grass that felt good underfoot, and with heightening spirits they headed for the shadow that marked the beginning of Kilacouqua, the Elven woods.

But although the woods looked near, the distance was misleading. For three days they traveled across the grassy plain, scavenging what few berries they could find. But at last the trees grew larger before them, and as they made camp they knew they would reach Kilacouqua the following day.

That night, clouds galloped across the sky and thunder rolled like the sound of hooves across the plains. And the next morning, although the storm had passed, Dean, with his ear pressed to the ground, still heard rumbling.

"Bravic," he whispered. "The ground is rumbling."

"That's my stomach. Let me sleep," Bravic mumbled as he rolled over.

"No, really. The ground is—" Dean could clearly feel the ground vibrating now. "We've got trouble," he cried.

He looked up and saw a line of silhouetted figures standing between them and the trees. There were hundreds of them. As he spun around to tell Bravic, he saw another line of figures on the other side of them. They, too, were just barely illuminated by the rising sun.

"Han, Bravic, we've got big, big problems!"

Han rubbed his eyes and looked back and forth between the two rows of figures.

Bravic jumped up. "We're in the middle of a battlefield! Run to the forest."

"Why to the forest?" Dean asked, gathering up his pack. "We

don't know if that side is the good side."

"They're Elves," Han said. "Just run!"

While the three of them ran, Dean risked a glance over his shoulder. He saw the figures behind them surge forward, and as the first dim rays of the red morning drove back the shadows, he saw what they were: Krulgs.

"I think this thing is about to kick off," Dean warned, and all three burst into a sprint.

Suddenly, a loud, long horn blast split the air, and the Elves spurred their horses forward. The ground shook, and Dean felt his heart beat faster as excitement and fear caused a newfound energy to surge through him.

As the Elves charged toward him, Dean looked upon the first Elf he'd ever seen. The warrior was dressed in rich, brown leather armor. Secured to one arm was a small leather shield, and a long spear was strapped to his back. He was slightly smaller than Dean, with long brown hair that flowed behind him and revealed his thin, angular features. Across his cheeks were two black and red stripes of paint, and on his biceps he wore a circle of leather with feathers that waved as he sped to clash with the enemy. His mount was a dappled gray horse, which he rode bareback.

When the three came into the midst of the riders, they had to almost stop to avoid being trampled. Dean looked behind him and saw that, only a short distance away, the first of the Elven riders had engaged the Krulgs. Screams and the crash of metal echoed.

Han sprang out of the way of a horse, lost his footing, and fell. He rolled over a few times before he came to a stop on his back. Another horse galloped straight for him. Just as the horse was about to trample him, a Krulg's black arrow struck the rider. The Elf tumbled from the horse's back. The horse neighed and shied around Han.

Bravic grabbed Han and ran over to the horse. He picked Han up and slung him over the back of the mount. "I don't want you to get trampled."

"But I can fight," Han protested.

Bravic turned the horse around and gave it a stinging slap, which sent it galloping toward the forest with the Elvana clutching its mane with all his might.

More horses galloped past, sending Dean farther away from Bravic. Soon he couldn't see the Dwarf anywhere. He grabbed the mane of a riderless light-brown horse and swung onto its back.

The battle now raged all around him, and a group of Krulgs was heading his way. He drew his silver sword and raised it above his head. The red rays of the sun streaked across the plains and wrapped around the blade, causing it to flash bright red. At the sight, the Elven warriors cried in triumph and pressed harder into the fray.

The Elven cries were too much for the Krulgs; they fell back. And like a wave collapsing on itself, the Krulgs that tried to turn around smashed into the others that pushed forward. Soon they fought one another as they struggled to retreat.

Dean saw one Elven warrior on foot trying to fend off three Krulgs on foot. Dean spurred his mount forward, slashed his sword down and took out one of the Krulgs, while the Elf slew another one. But the third Krulg's gnarled hands pulled Dean halfway off his horse. Dean hung on to his horse's mane with one hand while trying to fend off the Krulg with his sword.

Suddenly, Bravic's axe smashed into the creature's back, sending it crashing to the ground. Bravic grinned fiercely up at Dean.

"Thanks. Ten o'clock!" Dean warned as a group of maybe twenty Krulgs rushed them.

"O'what?" Bravic cocked an eyebrow.

"Never mind. Stand back to back!" Dean leaped from the horse.

Bravic's face went white. He remembered Braga saying the same thing. "Get back on the horse!" he hollered. "I will hold them this time."

Bravic planted his feet and swung his axe in a huge arc, cutting down anything in his way. Krulgs fell before him, and he roared in unbridled rage. The Krulgs parted around the Dwarf, who attacked them with a fury none had seen before.

Seven Krulgs broke away from him and came for Dean. Dean desperately blocked blow after blow as he backed up. A number of Elven warriors came to shield him from being swallowed by the undertow of the tide of the battle, and as a group they managed to drive the Krulgs back.

Bravic's axe swept down again and again. Each time, a Krulg fell to the side. As he stood unmoving against the sea of Krulgs, a Varlug grabbed him from behind. Its burly arms wrapped around his chest and pinned his arms to his sides. Bravic struggled to break its hold, but could not—and a Krulg rushed forward to impale him on its barbed spear.

But just before the Krulg drove him through, a horse raced up, and a small, snarling form vaulted onto the Krulg's back.

Han.

One of the Elvana's arms wrapped around the Krulg's neck while he punched the creature in the face with the other. The Krulg struck Han with the side of its spear and, with a heave, flung Han from its back. Han rolled across the ground. Beside him lay the broken shaft of a spear. He grabbed it, and as the Krulg lunged at him, Han closed his eyes and pushed forward with the spear. The Krulg landed on the spear and screamed.

Han looked at Bravic, who was still being held by the Varlug. "Bravic, duck!" he shouted as he pulled out one of his little knives.

Bravic put his head on his chest. He heard the blade fly by and strike the Varlug in the throat. The beast gasped and staggered back. It ripped the knife out, then fell dead.

By this time, the Krulgs were in full retreat across the plain. The Elves did not pursue them.

"I told you it was a good weapon." Han grinned.

"Thank you. I owe you my life." Bravic picked up his axe.

"Well, maybe this will teach you not to go throwing me on a horse and sending me off just when things are starting to get interesting." Han stood toe to toe with the Dwarf and glared up at him.

"Well, the next time you want to jump in front of a charging horse, I think I'll leave you there." Bravic thumped his finger against Han's chest.

"You didn't get me out of the way. I moved myself!" Han jammed his finger against Bravic's chest, and it bent against his armor. "Ow!"

"Hail!" A loud voice cut them off. They turned as a mounted Elven warrior approached with his hand held in the air. "Stop your talk. Now you ride." He gestured to two horses whose reins he held in his hand.

"I'm Hanil—" Han began to say.

"No talk. Ride." The warrior's jaw clenched as he leaned down and pushed the reins into their hands.

"How very rude," Han whispered rather loudly to Bravic.

"Quiet. They're Kilacouquen," Bravic whispered with a glare.

They got up on their horses and saw Dean approach on horseback, flanked by Elven riders. Dean greeted his two friends with a smile, but upon seeing Bravic's stern look, he said nothing. Dean and Han rode in silence, surrounded by Elven warriors, across the grassy plain toward the forest.

Dean whispered to Han, "Is this like Cowboys and Indians, or what?"

"Cow Boy? Is that like a Minotaur? Part cow and part boy?" Han asked.

The lead Elf turned to them and glared.

"Sorry," Han mumbled.

As they entered the forest, the three rode in the front of the procession of warriors and just behind the Elf who had greeted them. They traveled until almost noon, resting only twice, before they saw wooden buildings before them. Elves came out of the buildings to watch the return of the warriors. They were all dressed in forest shades—deep brown and rich green. Most were slender, with angular facial features and light-brown skin.

Dean saw individual faces light up when they saw a warrior they recognized. They didn't move or speak, but he could see relief ripple through their bodies.

Then they passed one home where a teenage girl stood in the doorway. Tears ran down her face as a warrior held out the spear of a fallen comrade. Her hand trembled as she received the weapon. She turned her head, and her green eyes locked on Dean's. He could see pain there. He knew that pain well. Dean bowed his head, and she did too.

He gripped the horse's mane tighter and stared straight ahead. He remembered Panadur's words. Unless he stopped Volsur, there would be more death. More tears.

They came to a stop before a very large building. The outer walls were flat and covered in bark that seemed to be part of the building itself. From a large archway in the center came an older Elf, dressed in a dull green robe with long gray hair tied back in a braid. As he walked forward, a hush descended over the forest.

His smooth voice split the silence. "How fared the Lords of the Woods?"

"The Lords of the Woods were victorious, as we have always been." The lead Elf raised his spear and let loose a battle cry. The cry was answered by all in the village, their voices becoming one.

"Then tonight we feast," the older Elf proclaimed. He looked at Dean and the others. "You will prepare to be received at the feast tonight, carrier of the sword of Panadur." He turned and addressed a warrior who stood at attention at his side. "Before the feast, bring them to me."

The Elf who had led them to the village took Dean, Han, and Bravic to another wooden building, much smaller than the first. As they dismounted, a young boy took their horses, and the Elf led them through an open archway. Inside, large canvas flaps on the roof were thrown back to let in light. Painted leather tapestries, depicting scenes from Elven life, hung on the walls. There was no furniture in the room, only a few padded mats.

The Elf bowed his head and crossed his right arm over his chest. "For now, rest. The feast will begin shortly. If you need anything, send for me. My name is Manitu."

"Manitu, thank you for your kindness." Bravic bowed low. "My name is Bravic Volesunga. This is Hanillingsly Elvenroot." He held his hand toward Han, who bowed too. "And this is Dean Theradine."

Before Dean could bow, Manitu stepped forward. "Dean Theradine? You not only bear the sword of Panadur but his name as well? Your father was a friend of the Kilacouquen; it is with honor I meet you. Ahulata will wish to know this." Manitu turned and rushed out the door.

"I didn't expect that." Han grinned and held his hands out toward the doorway.

As Dean gazed at the opening, three Elven women entered with flasks of water and clothes, and one carried Dean's pack. They set the water down between the mats in the center of the room.

"We have been sent to see that you are ready for the feast," the youngest of the women said in a high-pitched voice. She held Dean's pack out to him. "Manitu said this belongs to you as well."

"Great." Han pouted. "You still have your pack, but we've lost ours."

Dean shrugged. "Sorry."

The girl grinned. "We have brought new clothes for all of you. We will lay them out in the baths." She pointed to an opening in the far wall, and the other two girls bowed and walked through. "Is there anything else you need?"

Han stepped forward. "Can I get something to eat? You see, we ran out of supplies days ago, and there wasn't a lot of foraging available out in the plains, and I lost my bow so I couldn't hunt. Then there was that battle and a long ride, and if this feast isn't going to happen for a while, I'd like to get something to tide me over." Han grinned up at the girl.

"We'll come back with something, Hanillingsly." She smiled sweetly before walking out the door. Han stared after her, the smile seemingly stuck on his face.

"She's a cutie," Dean said.

"A little tall for him, though," Bravic added.

"I'm just grateful for the bath," Han stammered, turning bright red.

"A bath? I hope it's a shower."

The three of them walked into the other room, where the women had laid out long cloths and set out folded piles of new clothes. Three intricately carved tubs were filled with steaming hot water.

Han held up a cloth and raised his eyebrow. "Is this like a huge towel?" he asked before Dean and Bravic could shush him.

"Just get in the tub," Bravic grumbled.

The women left, giving them privacy, and Dean, Han, and Bravic peeled off their clothes and slid into the warm water. The women then returned to retrieve the companions' gear and clothes.

"We will clean your things," one explained as Dean looked

worriedly at his jeans.

"You don't have to do that." Dean shook his head and sank a little deeper into the bath.

"We'll have them back before the feast." She smiled and hurried out.

While they were bathing, a young man came in with three plates of fresh fruits and more water, which he set beside them. They all dug in immediately.

After the bath, Bravic polished his chain armor while Han dressed in his new clothes. Dean pulled on his new white shirt and light wool pants and cringed. The pants clung to him awkwardly. Pulling at the fabric, he asked Bravic, "Is it against some custom if I wear my own clothes?"

Bravic shrugged.

"There would be no disrespect," said one of the girls as she carried in more drinks. "We want you to be comfortable."

"Thanks. I don't want to sound ungrateful, but I'd be happier in my own things."

"It is understandable." The girl handed him a drink. "You are Human. Your body is different from an Elf's." She lowered her eyes and blushed.

"Thanks."

The girl bowed her head and departed, and soon returned with Dean's old clothes. The cuts and holes in his leather jacket were mended, and the dirt from weeks of travel on his worn sneakers was gone.

Dean quickly dressed. As he finished lacing his shoes, he looked over at Bravic. "Do I look okay? I just feel more comfortable in my own stuff."

Bravic scratched his chin. "The pants and jacket are odd. I've never seen anything like them. And your sandals . . . I'm thinking Han may have been telling the truth, and you are from the Heavens."

"Don't start that Heavens thing again. Anyway, these clothes will have to do," Dean snapped as he tried to brush his hair with an Elven comb.

A young warrior appeared at the door. "The feast will soon begin. Ahulata is ready to see you. Follow me."

He went out the door; Bravic and Dean followed. Han took a large bite of an apple before hurrying after them.

Beautiful flowers covered the wooden buildings. Trees grew everywhere, making it hard to tell where the forest ended and the city began. And as they walked down the wide streets, they saw Elves moving here and there. The Elves were dressed in deep-brown leather and brightly dyed greens, and most were adorned with jewelry. Many of them smiled and pointed at Dean, making him feel awkward. It probably didn't help that at five foot ten, Dean was taller than the tallest Elf. Han would have stopped and talked to everyone if Bravic had not had a firm hold on his shirt collar. As it was, the Dwarf had to practically drag him down the street.

When at last they arrived at the largest building, two Elven guards raised their crossed spears to let them pass. Inside was a huge chamber with row upon row of tables, and flowers had been hung in a rainbow of bright, vibrant colors. Elves were all about, making preparations, and one hurried over to escort the three to a door at the other end of the hall where two more Elven guards stood. The Elf who escorted them went back to his duties as the three passed through the door into another room.

Seated on a large chair, almost a throne, was Ahulata, the older Elf they had met before. Manitu stood beside him.

"Welcome," Ahulata said, a smile spreading across his face. "I know all of your names. I am Ahulata, Lord of the Kilacouquen. Dean, what news do you bring of Panadur?"

Dean walked forward and stopped directly before the chair. He looked at his feet for a moment before he spoke. "Panadur has passed away."

Ahulata's hand gripped the arm of the chair tighter. "This is grave news. And we had hoped that he and his brother Carimus could defeat Volsur. Yet Carimus has been captured. Volsur keeps him prisoner as a warning to all."

"Where?" Dean asked.

"In Mount Hope. Volsur keeps him there as a symbol of defeat. Now that Carimus is a prisoner and Panadur is no longer, I do not know where hope may lie."

Dean straightened. "I've taken on the quest to stop Volsur."

Ahulata pressed his lips together and sat forward in his chair. "That quest is not something you can choose. The one who stops Volsur will be the one who has been chosen."

Dean stood taller. "Panadur chose me."

"You are very young, but Panadur was a friend, and I believe in his judgment." He gave Dean an appraising look. "As you know, the people of the lands are trying to stay alive. You have seen that the Dark One's legions have come now even to our own forest. Because of this, the aid the Kilacouquen can offer you is limited." After a long pause, he continued. "But I will send a hundred of my mightiest warriors with you."

Han wiggled his eyebrows at Dean, but Dean shook his head.

"Thank you, sir, but I've thought about this. We can't do that. If we bring that many men, Volsur will crush us. We need to slip in. Covertly. We need to act like a SEAL team."

Ahulata's eyes narrowed. "There is no ocean along the road to Naviak."

Dean was confused. "An ocean?"

Han cleared his throat and took a step closer to Dean. "You said you wanted a team of seals," he whispered. "That's really weird."

"No. I mean . . ." Dean shook his head. "A Navy SEAL team."

Ahulata's brows rose higher.

Dean's mind raced and his thoughts piled together. "Never mind. What I mean is, we have to be like ninjas. They're Japanese warriors. Japan is—"

Bravic groaned.

"Let me start again. We need a small group," Dean said. "A large force would draw too much attention."

Manitu leaned over and whispered something to Ahulata. Ahulata nodded, then considered the three companions for a moment. "I will let you choose the mightiest of my warriors to accompany you. The way to Volsur is long, and time is growing short. His evil spreads through the land like fire through the woods. If you don't reach him soon, the evil will spread so deep into everyone's heart that no good will be left. Even here, even now, my warriors feel his pull. The woods themselves are affected. The trees at the edge of the forest are sick and dying. So tonight at the feast, make your selection, whoever it may be."

"Thank you, Ahulata." Dean bowed.

"When is this feast?" Han poked his head around Dean.

"Come. It will now commence." A broad grin crossed Ahulata's face.

As they walked back into the large hall, Bravic elbowed Han. "Between the two of you, I think I'll die of embarrassment," he muttered.

Once again, an Elf at work in the hall hurried over to escort them, this time to their seats. Dean sat on the left of Ahulata, with Bravic and Han next to him, and Manitu sat on Ahulata's right. They sat quietly as the final preparations were made and the rest of the hall filled with Elves. The warriors sat close to Ahulata's table, and the back of the room appeared to be for some sort of general seating. As far as Dean could tell, every Elf from the village had been invited.

Ahulata rose, and the hubbub in the room subsided. "Lords

of the Woods," he began. "Today, as in the past, we were victorious." Cheers erupted throughout the room. "And from the middle of the battlefield came one carrying the sword of Panadur. Tonight the son of Panadur will choose the bravest warrior here to accompany him on a quest. Right now, though, we hail—To the fallen! To the battle! To Panadur! To the three! To the chosen!" With each toast, everyone raised their wooden cups and drank.

Dean examined his own cup as he drank. Made of a smooth wood with no grain, it was intricately carved into the shape of a head—part lion and part man.

Ahulata explained, "That is the Leomane cup. It is very old. In the days of my father, the Leomane passed frequently through these woods."

Elven servants brought out huge trays of food: fruits, meats, and all kinds of bread. The three companions ate heartily, as the food was incredibly good and they were all still very hungry. But they had barely started when Ahulata stood, and silence once again descended upon the room.

"I now present to you Dean Theradine," he announced.

Dean's heart raced. He hadn't expected this.

"Stand up," Bravic whispered.

Dean stayed frozen in his seat. He swallowed hard and stared straight ahead.

Bravic poked Dean with his fork.

Dean leapt to his feet and looked out over the vast hall. All eyes were on him. "Lords of the Woods," he said. His booming voice sounded foreign to him. "I come here . . . seeking your aid. I'm looking for someone among you who'll accompany my companions and me on a quest." He held out a hand toward Bravic and Han. "It's dangerous, and you're likely to die."

Dean shifted his weight. He could feel sweat forming on his back.

"The chance is small that we will make it to Volsur. It's more of a suicide mission." Dean wiped his hands on his jeans. "I understand if no one wants to go, since . . . we're probably going to die, but . . . someone has to try."

The room was perfectly quiet now. Not even the servers moved.

Han jumped to his feet and raised his glass. "To the Kilacouquen, the bravest warriors in all the lands!" he screamed.

The whole crowd surged to its feet and cheered wildly. Warriors pounded both the tables and their chests as they bellowed their battle cry.

Dean breathed a sigh of relief and sat down.

Han beamed from ear to ear. "You just had to work on the ending," he said, and Bravic burst out laughing.

10

"DOCTOR DOLITTLE"

After Dean's speech, the warriors vied for the chance to be selected for Dean's journey. Each in turn stood and described the many deeds he'd done in battle, how brave he was, and why he should be the one chosen.

Han tapped Dean's arm. "What about that one? He's like a giant Elf." He pointed at an Elf who had just stood to stretch. Not only was he taller than any other Elf in the room, but he was even taller than Dean.

Bravic nodded. "He's strong, too."

"He hasn't spoken yet, right?" Dean stifled a yawn. "They're all starting to blend together. Let's hear what he has to say."

The night stretched on. Most of the women and children had long since gone to bed, and the warriors who had already told their tales had perhaps now had a bit too much to drink. One especially rowdy table kept summoning their server girl, rather rudely, to bring them more food and ale. As Dan looked on disapprovingly, he realized with surprise that he recognized the server: it was the girl who had been handed the spear of the warrior who died. She had green eyes and long brown hair, and looked to be about his age, but it was hard to tell from the hardened expression on her face. Her hair was pulled back into a high ponytail, and her simple tan and green dress was tied around her waist with a light leather belt. She moved with a crispness that gave away her underlying annoyance, but Dean saw her grace as she hurried around. And despite the scowl, she was breathtaking.

Dean eyed a rather heavy Elf who yelled for ale, and he thought of one of his foster homes—the one that was most horrid. He remembered the fat man who wanted not a son but a servant. He recalled the time he didn't bring the slob a beer quickly enough to satisfy him, and he was beaten. The beating was so savage that when the police came Dean couldn't tell them what had happened because his mouth was too swollen to speak.

The fat Elf pounded the table and held his goblet high but the girl didn't seem to be paying attention. She was moving through the crowd but was heading for the side door and not toward the tables. When she reached the door, her eyes darted around the room before she slipped outside.

The heavy Elf rose and snorted. "I'll show that girl how to serve warriors." The other men laughed, and he stormed toward the door.

Dean felt his stomach churn. He got to his feet and pursued the rapidly departing Elf, who swayed drunkenly through the hall. Dean darted between warriors to catch up. When the Elf got outside and went around the back of the building, Dean followed him to a stable.

Keeping to the shadows, Dean hurried to the entrance of the stable. Inside, the girl knelt beside a horse that was lying on a straw mat, covered with a blood-soaked blanket.

The fat Elf cursed at the girl. "So this is what you do instead of serving warriors," he boomed. "Tending to lame creatures?"

"I'm sorry," she replied in a quiet voice, but Dean saw her jaw tighten. "It will die unless I help."

"That lame thing should die," the stout Elf bellowed, and he unsheathed his sword, raised it, and swung.

The blade stopped just before the horse's neck with a loud clang. The portly Elf stared in disbelief. The girl had grabbed an old pitchfork and blocked his sword with it.

Her eyes blazed. She swung the wooden end of the pitchfork at the fat Elf's head. He blocked her swing with his sword just inches from his face.

"You'll pay for that," he growled. The rotund Elf lifted his blade—but stopped when Dean's sword pressed against his neck.

"Go." Dean's voice was cold.

"Do you think you can order me?" the Elf snarled.

"He is a guest of Ahulata," the girl said. "You cannot touch him." She pointed the prongs of the pitchfork at the fat Elf's belly.

The Elf glared at both of them but raised his hands and walked backward. "I don't have to touch him. Volsur will do the job for me."

Dean never took his eyes from the Elf as he stumbled out of the stables.

"You should have let me hit him," the girl snapped as she turned back to the horse and stroked its neck. In the light from the lanterns, Dean could see she had been crying.

"I probably should have, but then I'd have to help you hide the body."

She chuckled, but her smile quickly faded.

Dean sheathed his sword. "I'm sorry for your loss."

"How do you know?" she asked without looking at him.

"I saw you. When we rode into the village. A warrior gave you a spear."

Her hand stopped moving. She pulled the blanket up over the horse and whispered, "My father fell in the battle today."

"I'm sorry."

She stood and glared at Dean. "I'm sorry he's not here. If he lived, you would have chosen him. If I had hietas, I would be picked, or I would have been on the battlefield with him."

"Hietas?"

The girl shook her head. "If I were male, I would be allowed to go to battle. Because I am female, you look down on me." Her ponytail swayed back and forth as she set the pitchfork against the wall.

"What?" Dean's hands went out. "I'm not looking down on anyone."

"You would never pick me."

"You?" Dean's eyes widened. "No. It honestly never occurred to me to pick you."

"Because I am female." She stepped forward so she was nose to nose with Dean. She was only five foot three but stood with her feet shoulder-width apart and her hands balled into fists.

Dean could feel her breath hot on his face as she glared up at him. He swallowed and bit his lower lip before taking a step back. "No. Because you don't know how to fight, and—"

In a flash, she snagged the pitchfork from the wall, spun it around, and placed it an inch from Dean's throat. "Only one in the village is better than me with a spear."

"Take a chill pill." Dean held his hands up.

"You take . . . this pill," the girl stammered. "I can fight. You said you would take me if I could fight, and then you stopped talking."

"Because you stuck a pitchfork in my face." Dean paused. "I'll give it to you that you can fight. Okay?"

"Agreed." She spun the pitchfork around and thrust it into the ground. "But you still won't take me. I can ride, hunt, fish, and track. I also know the way. I journeyed to Naviak when I was young, with my father."

"But—"

"I am female." She thrust her chin forward.

"That's not it," Dean snapped.

"Then what is it?"

"We're going to die." Dean hoped his words would impact on her. They did, just not the way he expected.

"Is that all?" She laughed.

"All? Look. I don't want to burst anyone's bubble, but the chances of me and two guys stopping a wizard aren't good. I don't care who the fourth guy is. It could be a guy, a girl, Dwarf, Elvana, Elf, or a monkey for all I care. I didn't want Han to come. I still don't. I don't want to get Bravic killed, but he won't leave. I certainly don't want you to throw your life away."

"I understand," she sneered. "It's not because I have no hietas that you will not pick me. It's because you don't have any."

Dean held up a hand. "I'm pretty sure I know what hietas are now, and yes, I have them. It's not about me being scared. Don't you get it? You come with me, you die."

"Do you not get it?" She stepped forward so she was now toe to toe with him again. "The Kilacouquen will fight. They will lose. My father told me this. The enemy are many. Our men will die, and then the Krulgs will come. I will fight then because there will be no more men left to tell me I can't. I will die with a spear in my hands. One way or another, I will die like a warrior. Your way, I die here, with the women and children. But I am still dead. It is you who doesn't get it." Her green eyes searched his face for a moment, then she turned and stomped out of the stable.

Dean looked out into the darkness while her words echoed in his head. He pulled the pitchfork out of the ground and leaned it against the wall.

He took his time walking back. When he re-entered the hall, Manitu waved him over to the head table.

Ahulata motioned for Dean to take his place next to him. "It is time for your decision."

Manitu walked over to the wall, took down a polished silver horn, and raised it to his lips. He blew three long, loud blasts. The latter two were not necessary, for after the first, all conversation had ceased.

"Lords of the Woods," Manitu boomed, "Dean Theradine has decided."

Dean swallowed and stood. He looked over the hall filled with mighty warriors. There were men here tonight whose acts of bravery and strength were legendary. He looked from the warrior who claimed the title of the best swordsman, to the fastest, to another who had killed over a dozen Krulgs that morning alone.

But before he could say anything, the tall Elf whom Han had noted earlier jumped to his feet. "I have not spoken." His voice boomed across the room. "Everyone knows I am the best warrior in the village. The right is mine to claim. I choose me. Does anyone challenge?"

His eyes swept the room. When no one said anything, the Elf looked Dean up and down and frowned. "It is decided. I will lead you to Naviak." He grinned smugly as he walked around the table to stand with Dean and the others.

Dean raised his hand. "Hold up. Sorry to burst your bubble, but you don't make the decisions. I pick the guy."

The Elf scoffed. "Look. There is no one else." His hand gestured around the hall.

Dean looked out at the warriors, who shifted uncomfortably. No one challenged the huge Elf.

"It's still my pick. Thanks for your offer, but I pick . . . her." Dean pointed to the green-eyed Elf, who was still serving ale.

Everyone looked at the girl, and her mouth fell open.

"I didn't see that coming," Bravic mumbled.

"She's not a warrior!" screamed one Elf.

"She's a servant!" another cried.

"She's nothing but a girl!" a third scoffed.

"She is a Kilacouquen," Ahulata growled as he rose to his feet. The room fell into silence. "And she is the one the bearer of the sword of Panadur has chosen. Come here."

The girl hurried forward.

"Dean has chosen Oieda Halotic to be one of his company. It is decided."

An awkward silence fell over the room. Then the fat, drunken Elf stood up and swayed against the archway. "She's not the best warrior. She's a nursemaid to crippled animals," he sneered.

"I am the best warrior." The huge Elf grabbed Dean's shoulder, and Bravic put his hand on his axe.

"Kecheta, hold your tongue," Ahulata commanded.

"I challenge this so-called warrior," Kecheta continued. "I challenge her for the right to be the chosen. I challenge her to a duel with swords."

The room was silent. The warriors murmured among themselves.

Dean looked to Bravic and Han, but they turned up their hands, unsure what to do.

"I've made my choice, and I'll not change it," Dean snarled.

"It is his right to challenge," Ahulata said.

Dean drew his sword. "Then he duels with me."

Ahulata shook his head. "That is not our way. You cannot interfere, son of Panadur. But the form of the contest is not yours to pick, Kecheta. It is the challenged's right to pick what form the challenge will take."

"Wait a minute. Oieda can pick the contest?" Dean asked.

Ahulata nodded.

Dean leaned closer to Oieda, despite the fact that she looked as though she wanted to bite his face off. "You said you were the best with the spear, right?"

Her hands balled into fists. "I said there was only one person better."

"Don't tell me it's him."

Oieda nodded and pressed her lips together.

Dean exhaled. "You can hunt?"

"Yes. So?" She rolled her eyes.

"Can you? Are you good?"

"Very."

Dean leaned closer and whispered something in Oieda's ear. The Elf tilted her head, and a smile spread across her lips.

Then she looked at Kecheta and spoke. "I accept the challenge. It will be in the form of a hunt. The first person to bring back a fox will be the winner."

"A fox?" spat Kecheta. "A warrior hunting a fox?" The whole room erupted into howls of laughter. "No. If you will not fight me . . ." The corner of his mouth curled up. "We hunt wolves."

"Fine. A wolf," Oieda growled, her anger rising.

"The competition is decided," Ahulata proclaimed. "The first warrior to bring back a wolf will be the victor. Let the competition begin now."

Dean grabbed Oieda by her arm, but she yanked it free.

"Hold up," he whispered. "Did you see the smug grin on his face? He has an ace up his sleeve."

"What?" She looked at Dean like he had two heads.

"He's got an angle." Dean stepped so close he was cheek to cheek with her. "He picked the wolf for a reason; I could see it in his face. Be ready for some trick."

"I don't need your worry." She spun on her heel and ran from the hall.

Kecheta laughed as he strutted haughtily after her. Dean and the others raced outside to wait and see which warrior would be the first to return. Oieda dashed down the road and disappeared into the dark forest.

"That fool girl hunting a wolf." Kecheta laughed. "Now I won't have to kill her. The wolves will do it for me."

"Big talk from a big oaf," Han scoffed.

"You little—" Kecheta began, but seeing Bravic and Dean put their hands on their weapons, he stopped.

"Your fight is with the wolf, Kecheta." Ahulata motioned down the road.

"I will fight it with my own hands." Kecheta glared at Han.

"Oh? I was hoping you'd fight it with your face," Han sneered.

Dean smirked but his grip tightened around the hilt of his sword as he watched Kecheta's face turn a dark crimson. Cursing and mumbling, Kecheta turned and jogged down the road.

***

Oieda moved as silently as the shadows that clung to the trees. Her keen eyes searched the ground for any trace of passage. The underbrush was thin, and the rocks on either side made this the perfect trail for wolves to travel. There were many tracks, but after a few moments she found fresh ones. Her fingers traced the outline of an enormous wolf's paw print.

Noiselessly, she followed the tracks. The blood raced in her veins, and her heart pounded in her ears. She was led to a small cave between two hills. Looking in the opening, she saw that the wolf had gone in but had not yet come back out. She moved behind a tall boulder and unslung her father's spear from her back. Then she crouched down and waited.

***

Kecheta walked down the paths that twisted through the forest. He moved deliberately, because he knew exactly where he was going. He climbed to the top of a mound and looked down to its hollow center. At the bottom, he could see the cage trap that he'd set days before.

For the Kilacouquen, trapping was illegal. The Elves respected the animals and hunted them accordingly. But Kecheta didn't care whether a creature suffered; he always picked the path of least resistance. And now the trap he'd forgotten to check on might bring him fame and money.

He slid down into the wide depression and saw something in the cage.

"A pup," he spat. The little brown wolf was huddled in the back of the cage, whimpering. "Pup or not, it's a wolf." Kecheta smiled and drew his spear.

***

Oieda froze as she heard the wolf approach. Without a sound, she raised her spear and held it above her head, poised to strike. She could hear her heartbeat, but she concentrated on the soft sound of the wolf as it trotted out of its den.

When the giant wolf's brown head appeared, Oieda gritted her teeth, but the spear remained at its zenith. She was a hunter and killed for food, never for sport. Her hand shook. She could not strike.

The wolf scampered sideways and turned to look at her. Cold coal-black eyes searched her face.

With a sigh, Oieda lowered her spear and dropped it to the ground. The wolf tilted its head. Oieda reached out her hand. The wolf growled, and its teeth flashed. Oieda whispered softly to it, and the growling stopped. After another moment, it sat back on its haunches.

Oieda walked slowly forward until her hand touched the brown fur of the wolf's neck. She gently scratched its head. Sighing, she looked into the beast's big brown eyes. "I cannot kill you," she said softly. "Now Kecheta will win."

She walked back to the city with her head hanging down.

***

Kecheta eyed the frightened little wolf with a wicked gleam in his eye. He thrust the tip of his spear in the cage and watched the pup knock it aside with its paw. Repeatedly, he poked at the wolf, toying with it. Then, with a laugh, he stood and slammed the spear against the cage. The wolf huddled in the back and howled a pitiful little howl, like a baby calling for its mother.

"What's the matter, wolf? Should I just kill you right now and not make you suffer?" Kecheta smashed the top of the cage with his fist. "You were dumb enough to fall into my trap, so you should pay. I have played too long already. That stupid girl might get lucky—"

A howl split the night, and Kecheta spun. A gigantic wolf stood at the top of the ridge, its eyes glowing.

The enormous wolf raced down the slope toward Kecheta. Grinning, Kecheta threw his spear, but the wolf nimbly leapt aside, and the weapon fell harmlessly to the ground. With a curse, Kecheta reached for his sword.

Then, from all around the hollow, howls filled the night. Many more wolves appeared on the ridge around him—and all raced for the Elven warrior.

In fear, Kecheta ran to a tree and pulled himself onto a low branch. The branch creaked and groaned beneath his weight. The jaws of the wolves snapped below him. He reached up for a higher branch, but the one he was on cracked loudly, and he moved closer to the ground. Closer to the wolves.

The largest wolf sprang up. Its teeth flashed, and its jaws just missed his thigh.

"Help!" he cried out. "Help!"

Suddenly, the wolves stopped jumping, though they still

snarled, and their jaws clacked as they bit the air.

"So the pig has been treed?" Oieda laughed as she walked down the slope.

Kecheta looked in disbelief from the wolves to the thin girl. "Oieda, help me," he pleaded.

"Help you?" Oieda saw the cage, and her eyes narrowed. "No. It's your turn to feel what it's like to be trapped. I don't want to aid you at all."

"Oieda, I'll do anything that you want. Name it. Please." Kecheta shrieked as the branch moved even closer to the ground.

"Why? Why shouldn't I let these wolves rip your body into pieces?"

"Please, Oieda. I'm sorry. Please." Kecheta wept.

"Give me your word you'll never harm another animal out of hate as long as you live. Give me your word as a Kilacouquen."

Kecheta stared at her cold green eyes. "I give you my word," he said quietly.

"Go," Oieda growled.

***

Dean paced back and forth in the square. He'd lost track of the time but was sure it had been many hours since they'd left. Still, not one of the Elven warriors had gone home; all were anxious to see the outcome of the competition. Bravic and Han were there as well, seated on a bench. The Elvana frequently jumped up to look down the empty street.

Finally, a call echoed from down the road, and everyone stood. In the torchlight, they could see a figure walking down the center of the street. Kecheta. He walked up to Ahulata with his head hung low and stood, unmoving.

Ahulata's eyes narrowed and his lips pressed together. "Why

do you return without a wolf?" he demanded.

"I failed in my hunt. I have lost. The girl has won." Kecheta looked up to meet Ahulata's gaze.

"Hurray," Han cheered.

Ahulata raised his hand. "The competition is not over. Oieda has not returned." He turned back to Kecheta. "Again, I ask you why you return with nothing." There was now anger in his voice.

"I threw my spear in haste and missed my wolf. As I went to take my sword, I found myself in the middle of a hunting pack. I had to climb a tree or be killed," Kecheta said bitterly.

"So the big brave warrior hides up in a tree like a chicken," Han said cheerfully.

"How did you get away?" Ahulata interjected.

"The . . . the girl saved me," Kecheta mumbled.

"Oieda? How did she—" Ahulata was cut off by a shout from up the street.

As Oieda came down the road, there was a collective gasp from the crowd. She was surrounded by a pack of wolves.

"That . . . is . . . awesome!" Han cried out.

Dean took a step back. "Wolves in this world are way bigger than in mine. They're as tall as a ponies."

"What I would give to ride one." Han clapped his hands together.

Ahulata stepped forward, and silence descended upon the square. "I declare Oieda the winner of the challenge. She has earned the right to accompany the son of Panadur on his quest to defeat Volsur."

Oieda turned to the huge brown wolf. She scratched it behind its ear, and it affectionately licked her face. She touched her forehead to the wolf's, then the pack turned and ran back toward the woods. Before they disappeared into the night, the grand wolf stopped and looked back at Oieda. It howled a heart-stirring call and then vanished into the blackness.

"Is she Doctor Dolittle or what?" Dean smiled. "Ask her to bring back a wolf, and she brings back the whole pack."

"That was a lot," Han said.

"What?"

"You should call her Doctor Do-lots, not Doctor Do-little. What's a doctor anyway?"

"No. I meant . . . there's this guy who talks to the animals . . . oh, skip it," Dean said.

"He always says that," Han whispered loudly to Bravic.

"Glad you can join us, Oieda." Dean held out his hand.

Oieda opened her mouth and quickly closed it. She stared at Dean for a moment and crossed her right arm over her chest. "I will not fail you." She dropped to one knee and bowed her head. "My life is yours to use."

"Okay . . ." Dean looked awkwardly around. "Seriously, you're helping me out, so stop kneeling like that."

Oieda rose. Bravic and Han came over and shook her hand.

"I have lots of questions—" Han said, but Ahulata cut him off.

"I'm sure you do, little Elvana, but it is now very late. You all must get an early start tomorrow. All that you need will be supplied for you, but for now, go to bed."

As the crowd dispersed, the companions went to their room. After Dean washed up, he came out and saw Han and Oieda sitting and talking.

"Dean," Han called. "We just finished telling Oieda about our journey. When Bravic comes back, he wants to sing a song." He rolled his eyes. "But I told him that you had to sing your song first, because we've never heard one of your songs and we've heard lots of Bravic's."

"Me? No way. It's the new guy's turn." Dean jerked his thumb at Oieda.

"I am not singing." She frowned. "Han said you."

"I don't do everything Han says." Dean lay down on a padded mat. "Besides, isn't there some Elven custom where you have to be a good host and sing?"

"No," she snapped.

Bravic walked back into the room. "I'm ready to sing."

Han looked desperately at Oieda, but she shook her head. Han sighed. "It's okay, Oieda." He crossed his legs on the mat. "Some people are afraid of singing." He almost fell over when she glared at him.

"I am not afraid." She closed her eyes. Then she sang:

In the forest of Kilacouqua, we are at home.
In the forest of Kilacouqua, we will always roam.

Our spears are lightning,
Our horses thunder,
Our cries the wind,
Splitting all foes asunder.

Under the boughs of Kilacouqua, with a harp in our hands.
Under the boughs of Kilacouqua, with our bows we rule the land.

Our arrows are swift,
Our aim is true,
Our bows are cut,
From the mightiest yew.

In the woods of Kilacouqua, we are its swords.
In the woods of Kilacouqua, we are its lords.

Her eyes snapped open as everyone clapped. Dean smiled awkwardly when he realized he'd been clapping a little too enthusiastically. He noticed her cheeks flush, too.

"That was beautiful," Han said.

"Agreed." Bravic stood. "Is it my turn?"

"Nope. It's Dean's," Han said.

"I don't know a song."

"You don't? Come on. You have to know at least one song. Just pick one," Han pleaded.

"You really want me to sing?"

"It's either you or Bravic." Han groaned.

"Are you afraid?" Oieda tucked her legs underneath her.

"No. Okay. I'll sing." Dean shook his head and held up his hands. "I feel like I'm at summer camp. You guys have to help me out here. Now when I point to you, you're going to sing the chorus part."

"Okay," Han said.

"The chorus goes something like:

"Beat, beat, beat, beat, a beat, beat.
Beat, beat, beat, beat, a beat, beat.
My little heart just skipped a beat."

"Hey, that's neat," Han said.

"It's a strange song." Bravic raised an eyebrow.

"You just sang one about Dwarves playing at the beach. I'm still trying to get the picture out of my head." Dean smirked. "Just sing it when I point to you. It wasn't my idea, anyway."

As Dean pointed to them, they all began to sing:

Beat, beat, beat, beat, a beat, beat.
Beat, beat, beat, beat, a beat, beat.
My little heart just skipped a beat.

I met a girl who's oh so neat
And my heart just skipped a beat.

Oh, oh, I can't wait to see her.
Whoa, whoa, I really miss her.
Oh how I want to kiss her.

Beat, beat, beat, beat, a beat, beat.
Beat, beat, beat, beat, a beat, beat.
My little heart just skipped a beat.

I can see my baby walking down the street,
And that girl is oh so sweet.
Oh no, she's coming nearer.
Whoa, whoa, my heart's starting to quiver.
Oh how I'm starting to shiver.

Beat, beat, beat, beat, a beat, beat.
Beat, beat, beat, beat, a beat, beat.
My little heart just skipped a beat.

I can see her smile ever so sweet
And my little heart just skipped a beat.
Oh, now I'm gonna hug her.
Whoa, whoa, just gonna hold her.
Oh how I'm gonna love her.

Beat, beat, beat, beat, a beat, beat.
Beat, beat, beat, beat, a beat, beat.
My little heart just skipped a beat.

"A beat, beat," Han cheered, and they all laughed.
"Do you have a child?" Oieda asked.
"What?" Dean looked around. "Me? No."
Oieda look confused. "But, you sang about your baby."
Dean laughed. "No. Not that kind of baby. It means your

girl. You know? Like a girlfriend."

All three stared at Dean.

"Do you mean your betrothed?" Bravic rubbed his beard.

"Betrothed? That's like the girl you're going to marry, right?" Dean asked, and Bravic nodded. "No. It doesn't have to be that serious. Baby. It's like calling a girl sweetie or angel or something."

"Angel?" Han sat up. "I knew—"

"Don't say it," Dean snapped. "It's just a term of endearment. Look, I didn't even want to sing. Let's talk about something else."

The four sat up for hours and talked. Oieda fit into the group as if she'd been a part of it all along. The four were now bonded by friendship—and the realization that tomorrow they would leave on the road to Naviak. The road that would take them to Volsur.

***

When Dean awoke, the sun was still down and Oieda was gone. One of the girls who'd brought him a plate of fruit must have noticed him looking around, because she said, "Oieda went to prepare the horses." She smiled at Dean, and he saw the color rise in her cheeks.

"Thank you." He brushed back his hair and stretched.

Dean, Han, and Bravic had a large breakfast laid out for them. After they ate, they stepped outside and found Oieda next to five horses. One was loaded with supplies. Oieda was dressed in leather armor and had a spear strapped across her back. Her long brown hair was in a braided ponytail.

"Are you sure you won't take the Elven armor?" Bravic asked Dean for the third time that morning.

"I'm good. Listen, I plan on doing way more running than

fighting. Our goal is Volsur. If it's up to me, we fight only one time—against him. Besides"—Dean climbed onto his horse—"I like my look."

Han laughed, Bravic scowled, and Oieda rolled her eyes.

Manitu and Ahulata walked out of the main hall. "Fare well wherever the road to Volsur takes you, warriors," said Ahulata. "Time grows short for your quest to be done. You four are the chosen. You four are the only ones who can save the world from Volsur's evil. You will have no fears under the bows of Kilacouqua. Once you leave the safety of the forest, do not stray, but fly like the rays of the sun through the darkness." Both he and Manitu bowed low.

"Thank you, Lord of the Woods," Dean replied, and all four bowed their heads.

"And thanks for my bow," Han added with a smile as he held up the new short bow he had been given.

The four turned and rode down the street. Han moved up next to Oieda. "What's that?" He pointed to a leather band around her arm with a feather dangling from it.

"It's a Taristaku," Oieda said. "You wear it on your right arm into battle. You look at it to remember something you are fighting for."

"What are you fighting for?" Han asked.

"Many things. But I will look at it and remember my father. This Taristaku was his."

"What does Oieda mean?"

She blushed and let out a little laugh. "It means 'Sent from the Heavens.'"

"Hey, that's neat." Han turned around in his saddle and wiggled his eyebrows at Dean. "Her name means 'Sent from the Heavens'—and you are sent from the Heavens."

"I told you not to say that anymore," Dean grumbled as he chased Han's fleeing horse down the road.

11

THE GOLDEN CITY

The four journeyed through the forest of Kilacouqua for nearly a week, but then the woods ended and they traveled over rolling hills with the sun occasionally breaking through the gray clouds. The days wore on, and they made good time, for the weather was fine and the travel was easy. They'd often catch glimpses of wolves running alongside them, and at night, the wolves stayed close and watched over their camp.

On one particularly fine day, as they came to the top of a gentle rise, they could see a large city that shone like gold in the sun.

"What city is that?" Dean gasped.

"That is Modos. The Golden City," Oieda said.

"Is the city safe?" Dean asked. "We need to restock supplies."

"I think some of us have eaten in excess," Bravic grumbled, frowning at Han.

"It's safe enough," Oieda said with a frown. "They have been allies."

"Is there something you don't like about them?" Dean asked.

She sat up a little straighter on her horse. "The people are ... pampered."

"Oieda, why do they call it the Golden City?" Han asked. "Is it really made of gold or does it just look like gold? Or maybe it's just a very rich city so people say, 'Gold flows like water there.'

Or, 'That city is full of gold.' Or—"

"Han, I'll race you to the far end of the road." Dean spurred his mount forward to try to get the Elvana to stop talking.

The four rode the rest of the way to the city. It was surrounded by huge walls, but above those walls they could see the tops of buildings covered with real gold. The gates into the city were swung wide open, and the guards posted there barely lifted their heads as the four rode past.

"If they were Dwarves, they'd be hung for neglecting their posts," Bravic spat.

"If they were Elves, they would be hung at the posts," Oieda said.

"Yeah? Well, if they were Elvana, they'd be beaten, hung, all cut up, and then fed to wild pigs," Han growled.

Everyone turned to him in horror. When he saw their faces, Han burst out laughing. "Got ya."

They rode down the beautiful cobblestoned streets. The buildings sparkled. Some were painted in bright colors, while marble and stone gleamed on others. The people who were out and about wore outlandish, gaudy clothes, which hung loosely over their bodies to hide their fat. Jewels adorned their outfits. Some wore wide necklaces or large rings. Others had gems in their pierced noses, ears, and even their cheeks.

As they passed one store, Bravic reined in his horse to gaze upon a jewel-encrusted battle-ax plated in pure gold. The blade gleamed brightly, and Bravic almost had to shield his eyes. He looked up from the weapon into the dark eyes of a thin, old shopkeeper, who smiled at him. Bravic's eyes locked on the shopkeeper's. He seemed unable to look away. The shopkeeper leaned forward, and Bravic's eyelids became so heavy he closed his eyes. When he opened them again, the shopkeeper was gone. Bravic shook his head before turning and hurrying to join the others.

As they neared the center of town, an ornamented carriage drawn by a team of ten horses came down the road, followed by a dozen soldiers on horseback. The carriage pulled across the street and blocked their path. A servant hopped to the ground, opened a gilded door, and lowered an attached step.

Out stepped an obese man in his later years. His hair, what little was left of it, was gray; his eyes were deeply set, seeming to hide behind his bloated cheeks. He was dressed in a long, wide bright-red robe. Thick gold chains extended down below his fat chin.

"Welcome to Modos," he said to Dean. "I'm Anganese Falvidor, mayor of the Golden City." He bowed as low as he could, but his great stomach meant that wasn't far. "We've been expecting you. You are the son of Panadur?"

Oieda's hand reached back for her spear, and Bravic moved his horse slightly in front of Han's.

"Let me spare you the awkwardness of deciding whether to trust me or not." Anganese smiled and twirled his hand. "I received word from Ahulata. He requested we extend the same pleasantries as if you were his personal dignitaries. The Kilacouqua have been allies of Modos for years. I intend to honor that alliance. As proof, I say to you: Ashota delnita kiatee."

Oieda's eyes widened, and she looked at Dean. Dean searched her face. She nodded.

"My name's Dean," he said to the mayor. "Nice to meet you."

"The pleasure is mine. I have had my humble home prepared for your stay. Will you be here long?"

"We're just passing through," Dean said.

"We're on a quest," Han added.

Dean shot Han a sideways look.

"Oh, a quest." The fat man rubbed his plump hands together. "I can't wait to hear all about it. Modos is a city for travelers, and I love to hear their tales, especially if they're on a quest. Follow my wagon, and I'll show you the way to my home. I have prepared a banquet for you tonight." He bowed again and waved. The many rings on his chubby hand flashed in the light.

The servant shut the door and climbed onto a narrow seat. The soldiers turned their horses and trotted around so they were behind the companions.

"Another feast." Han beamed.

"Just don't say anything else, okay?" Dean whispered to Han.

"Why?" Han asked.

"I don't trust him yet." Dean's jaw clenched. "I learned growing up that nothing is free. Everyone has an angle."

"I don't think we have much of a choice right now but to go along with him," Bravic grumbled. He tilted his head back toward the soldiers, who were moving up behind them.

They trotted along after the carriage, the soldiers following behind. After many twists and turns through the crowded city streets, they came to a large, lavish house atop a steep hill. The wagon passed through a gate where two more guards dozed at their posts.

The mayor's house was white, but its edges and domed roof were gilded. The wagon stopped in front of two massive front doors, and servants rushed to take the companions' horses. Anganese stepped from the carriage and motioned them to him.

"This is my home." He waved his hand. "I insist you stay with me while you visit the city. I hope you'll find your quarters comfortable."

The inside of the house was filled with expensive objects from all over the land. Everything seemed to shine or sparkle. As they walked through wide corridors Anganese pointed out one object or another and explained where it was from and how expensive it was. Then he led them to their rooms.

"This is where you'll be staying, friends of the city. The

banquet will begin shortly. If you need anything at all, please tell the servants." Again, he tried to bow low before he turned and waddled down the hallway.

The four opened the doors to their new rooms. They were furnished in the same rich manner as the rest of the house. After each cleaned up, they gathered in Dean's room to await supper.

Dean grabbed Oieda and pulled her close. Her green eyes flashed. She pulled her arm away and stepped back. Dean rolled his eyes, leaned in close, and whispered, "What did Anganese say to you when we arrived? Those strange words? Why did you trust him?"

"He repeated the current kitarama."

"The what?"

"It's a pass phrase," Oieda explained. "We change them frequently, but it was the last one set right before we left. If Ahulata sent a rider, he would have used that phrase so I would know it was safe."

"That's good news, but …" Dean sighed. "Something still doesn't feel right. Why is every other place we've gone through hurting, and these guys aren't?"

Oieda squared her shoulders. "Ahulata said they are allies."

"No offense, but alliances change."

"Don't look a gift horse in the mouth." Han yawned. "Especially if it's made of gold and there's a banquet attached."

Just as Han got up to pace the floor for the fifth time, a knock at the door preceded the entrance of a well-dressed servant. "Dinner is now ready," he announced. "Please follow me."

They set off down the hallway. Bravic had to grab hold of Han's shirt to prevent him from dashing ahead of the servant when the smell of food filled the air.

The dining hall was large, but held only one small table with five places set for supper. "Please, sit and be merry," said

Anganese, already seated at the head of the table. "Any food you wish, I have." He waved to the large assortment of foods the servants held.

The four ate everything from roast duck to sea fish to exotic fruits from over the sea. Han ate more than everyone except, of course, Anganese. When they finished, servants came with bottles of wine from around their world and any ale the Dwarf could name.

Finally, Anganese pushed his thrice-cleaned enormous plate away. "Well, journeyers, tell me something of your quest."

Dean cleared his throat. "We are heading north."

Anganese held up a hand while he raised his goblet to his mouth again and drained it. "As I mentioned, we are allies of the Kilacouquen. Ahulata requested my assistance, and I assure you I intend to aid you in any way I can. Do you really plan to go all the way to Naviak?" Anganese asked. "Just you four?"

Oieda nodded.

Anganese sighed. "Volsur's? That's a very dangerous journey. And why would you head to the Dark Lord's realm?"

"We plan to stop him," Han answered plainly, taking another bite of chicken.

"You four are braver than I thought." Anganese gave a smile. "Everyone else is going the other way, but you four head straight to him. But to stop Volsur, surely you'll need more than just yourselves? You'll need men and money. I can provide you with both. The Golden City has no love for Volsur." Anganese pushed backward in his chair.

"Will the men be the same type as your guards?" Bravic scoffed.

"The lazy loafs I have outside are not what I meant for warriors, my friend. No, I mean real warriors from all the lands."

"We have no need of men," Dean said. "We just need supplies, and we'll be on our way."

"Supplies we have in abundance. Make a list, and all that is on it will be provided. All you have to do is ask."

"Thank you for your help, Anganese." Dean rose to shake the man's outstretched hand. "If it would be okay with you, we'd like to rest here for a few days."

"By all means, my boy," he said. "Stay as long as you want. I'll start gathering what you desire. In the morning, you'll be able to rest far easier. For tonight, I thank you for joining me."

"No, thank you." Han groaned as he sat up, wishing he'd stopped eating long before.

As a servant took them back to their rooms, they all wished they had eaten less. Except Bravic, who had only picked at his food. He had been thinking of something else.

Han yawned. "I have to sleep. It's past midnight, and with my belly so full, bed will feel so good."

"We're getting up early and leaving," Dean said.

Han tossed up his hands. "You just said we would stay a few days and rest. I for one would like another banquet."

"No," said Dean. "I want to get moving."

"He is helping us," Oieda said. "We should rest while we can."

"I agree," Bravic grumbled. "The horses could use it too."

"And me," Han added.

Dean looked at his three friends and shook his head. "No. We go first thing. Agreed?"

They all nodded, but Oieda spun on her heel, Han pouted, and Bravic walked away muttering.

Dean sank into the mattress of his extra-soft bed. Between the comfort of not sleeping on the hard ground and his full stomach, the last thing he wanted to do was leave right away, but his nagging feeling won. He planned to leave as soon as they could.

***

A short time later, Bravic's door opened and he slipped quietly down the hallway. He crept by the sleeping guards and went out the gate into the darkened streets. He didn't notice the silent form following him down the deserted road like a shadow.

He walked to the store window they'd passed earlier that day—the window in which the golden ax lay. He stared at the gleam of tainted yellow light that seeped up the blade. In one motion, he thrust his gauntleted fist through one of the window panels and grasped the handle. He looked around, turned, and started to walk back down the street.

When Bravic neared an alleyway, a cloaked figure stepped in his path. He swung his golden ax upward. The blade gleamed in the moonlight. As he prepared to strike the figure down, it pulled back its hood.

"Do you not believe in the quest?" Han asked with hurt in his eyes.

"I believe in it. But this ax is mine," Bravic spat, his weapon still raised.

"How can you believe, yet steal? I thought you were a nobler warrior than that." Han's pain turned to anger.

"Warrior?" Bravic snarled. Shame welled up inside him. "I'm not a warrior—I'm a coward. I deserted a battle. That's the 'warrior' you look upon."

Han scoffed. "You're no coward. You've been saving Dean and me since we met you. We both would have died if we hadn't met you. The Varlug would have killed us in the pool. What about the horse that would have trampled me? You're the bravest—"

"I'm not brave."

"Do you think that ax will make you brave?"

"The axe is mine. Whether it makes me brave or not. I want

the best axe in the lands," Bravic growled, gripping the ax harder.

"The best ax in the lands? Then I guess your brother's ax wasn't good enough for you."

Bravic froze. His eyes burned. He looked down at the golden blade and hung his head.

Han stormed away, unsure what to do. Should he go back and tell Dean or try to talk to Bravic again?

He paused as he heard footsteps running back toward the store. He waited, and after a minute the Dwarf ran back to him.

"Forgive me," Bravic whispered. "I've added to my shame."

"No, you haven't." Han shook his head.

"I'm a coward and a thief. I saw that ax and . . . I couldn't stop thinking about it. I just wanted it."

"But you put it back. So you're not a thief. We all have temptations. Look at me. I ate nine donuts. And that was after dessert."

"It's not the same thing." Bravic shook his head.

"It is. I didn't need nine donuts. I was full. I knew I shouldn't, but I did it because they tasted so good."

Bravic chuckled. He looked at the Elvana and then up at the black sky. "I'm still a coward."

"You? No. You're one of the bravest warriors I've ever seen. Besides, you came back to this battle, right?"

Bravic's brows pressed together and he nodded curtly. "Thank you."

Han gave him a quick hug, and they returned together to Anganese's house.

***

The next morning, a knock came on all four of the companions' doors. When they rose, a servant was waiting outside.

"Anganese has urgent news for you all," announced the servant when they were all gathered in the hall.

"Give us a second to get ready," Dean said.

"The mayor has requested your presence immediately," the servant pressed.

"I have to use the bathroom," Dean said.

The servant frowned as Dean pulled everyone into his room and shut the door.

Dean motioned everyone to him. "This doesn't feel right. Take what you can carry—and your weapons."

"We requested his aid," Oieda said, her expression hard. "We will bring shame on Kilacouqua if we just sneak out now."

"We need the supplies," Han said.

"And the horses," Bravic added.

"Fine." Dean strapped his sword on. "We'll meet with him. But I want everyone to be on guard. And I do the talking."

The others returned to their rooms to grab their weapons, then they all followed the servant down the hallway. When they reached the dining hall, the servant held the door open for them.

"Bravic, watch our backs," Dean whispered.

As they stepped into the room, Anganese was seated at the far end of the table, as he had been last night, but this time he rose to greet them. "My friends, I am truly sorry for waking you, but I have urgent news." He motioned them into the room. "You'll be able to see Volsur with greater ease than you'd hoped."

As he said this, twenty armed guards poured into the room from all sides. Kecheta was among them.

"Traitor!" Oieda shouted. She reached back for her spear, but Dean grabbed her arm. "I should have let the wolves eat you," she spat at the tall Elf. "You lose your challenge to me so you betray your people?"

Kecheta sneered. "You are your father's daughter. You

refuse to see the truth. We ally with Volsur, or we will be wiped out."

Anganese's eyes were ice-cold. "I'm sorry I have to do this, but you see, Volsur and I are having a disagreement as of late. He wants me to turn over most of the money from my city, and I ... well, I do not want to. Now, if I give him four little rebels who wish to kill him, then maybe that'll count for a great deal of gold. I'm not an evil man; I hate Volsur as much as all of you. But I'll not part with any of my gold, so I must part with you. I'm sorry." As he said these last words, he graced them with a wicked little smile.

"You fat jerk," Han yelled.

"Listen, Elvana," Anganese spat menacingly, "I have not decided if I'll give you to Volsur dead or alive. So watch your tongue, or I'll have it cut out."

Oieda and Bravic put their hands on their weapons, but Dean held out his hand. "Not now."

"I'd listen to him," Anganese said. "If you draw your weapons, you will die."

A scream came from behind the closed door to the hallway they had come through. Soon more screams split the air. The doors burst open, and a bloodied guard rushed in.

"Volsur's attacked," he panted. "Krulgs have overrun the house gates."

"Looks like you've got problems of your own," Dean said to Anganese with a grin.

"Cut his tongue—" Anganese started to order, but just then Krulgs came streaming into the room, and the guards turned to face these new enemies.

All except Kecheta. He pulled back his spear and aimed it not at the Krulgs, but at Oieda.

But just before he flung it, Han sent a dagger to his head. Kecheta stepped to the side, but it caused his spear to fly wide of his target.

"Wait," Anganese was pleading with a Krulg. "They're the traitors to Volsur." He pointed at Dean. "They want to kill him. He is Dean—"

The Krulg's ax ran him through.

"Out the back!" Dean cried as his sword cut into a Krulg's chest.

The companions moved to the back of the room. The Dwarf and Elf fought side by side and dropped many Krulgs, while Han shot any that managed to get by the two. Dean pulled open the rear door and ushered everyone out.

"Wait!" Kecheta yelled. He sprang over the table and raced toward the back, but three Krulgs grabbed him and pulled him screaming to the floor.

Dean slammed the door and shut its deadbolt after all the companions were through. "That isn't going to hold those guys for long," he said.

"This corridor leads to the back of the house." Bravic pointed with his ax. The corridor was dark, but they saw light coming from around a corner.

"Bravic," Dean said, "you guard the caboose, and I'll take point."

"Huh? What do you want me to guard?"

"I have the lead. My eyes are best." Oieda slipped past Dean and started down the corridor.

"Actually, my eyes are best," Han said.

"Just GO!" Dean shouted as the blade of an ax cut through the door.

They raced down the corridor. As they turned the corner, they saw a servant with a torch darting through a doorway into a room halfway down the hall.

Dean pointed. "We should follow him."

"Let him flee. We need to leave here," Oieda yelled. The

sounds of fighting now came from all directions.

"Why's he running into a room?" Dean asked. "He must know another way out."

The four ran through the door just in time to see the servant disappearing through a hole in the floor and trying to slide the floor panel back in place over his head.

"Grab him!"

Han dove toward the floor panel before it was fully back in place. The panel flipped, and Han and the servant disappeared.

"Why doesn't he ever wait?" Bravic grumbled.

Dean pulled aside the panel. Below it was a short vertical shaft leading to a tunnel below.

Han stood at the bottom. "Well, I kept him from shutting it," he yelled up to them, rubbing his head.

They all jumped down. They could see the servant's torchlight bobbing away down the tunnel.

"Let's hope this tunnel runs out of the city," Dean said as Oieda put the panel back in place.

The tunnel was relatively dry and ran straight. They traveled along it as quickly as they could, but the torchlight kept the same distance from them. Suddenly, the torchlight came to a stop.

"He might be at a door, warning someone about us," Oieda said.

"Or locking it." Dean sprinted forward.

"Oh, I hope he dies," Han cursed.

A scream filled the corridor, and the light up ahead fell to the ground.

"I think he just did," Dean muttered.

They ran to the end of the tunnel. The body of the servant lay before a closed door. As they neared him, they could see the gleam of a needle sticking out of the handle on the door.

"That greedy pig Anganese didn't want anyone to get out of here except himself," Oieda said. "He set a trap on the door."

She pushed the door open with her spear.

Behind the door was a ladder with a trapdoor at the top. Dean went up first and pushed the heavy trapdoor open. He climbed out onto the top of a hill. The city was only a short distance away, and it was engulfed in flames.

"Let's keep moving," Dean said as the others climbed out behind him.

As they ran through the night, monstrous catapults rained burning spheres down upon the city. Screams drifted on the wind.

Traveling north, they soon came to a wide trail that dipped between two hills covered in brush. The sounds of the siege had faded, but Dean could still see the glow of the fires in the distance.

Oieda froze. "Something is near," she whispered.

The companions drew their weapons.

Suddenly, a Krulg battle cry filled the air, and the evil beasts sprang from behind the brush, where they'd lain in wait for anyone fleeing the city. Two made it no farther than a few steps before Han's arrows struck them down, and then the four companions formed a circle, back to back, as they prepared to face their attackers.

Bravic swung his mighty ax and felled one Krulg in a single blow. Dean blocked an attacker's ax and cut up under its weapon; his sword struck bone and the Krulg screamed in pain as it flew back. Oieda's spear thrust out in quick jabs at the Krulg in front of her until it, too, fell.

The Krulgs backed away, snarling and stamping the ground. They numbered close to twenty, and their wicked eyes gleamed in the fiery moonlight.

"There are too many of them, my friends," Bravic said. "We'll die the deaths of warriors."

"How about 'We'll live the lives of heroes'?" Dean suggested.

One Krulg tilted his head back and let loose a battle cry. To the Krulgs' evident surprise, it was answered—by howls.

A dozen huge wolves sprang from the forest. In the glow from the moon, the wolves' eyes gleamed as they ripped into the Krulgs' ranks.

"The wolves!" Han cried. He let two arrows fly into a Krulg.

"We must save them!" Oieda cried. She leaped into the battle. Her spear darted at the Krulgs' unprotected backs.

"Save them?" Dean drove his sword through a Krulg whose throat was in the maw of a massive wolf. "I don't think they need—Han!" Dean screamed as he saw three Krulgs rushing the Elvana.

Han's arrow pierced one Krulg's chest. Dean's sword cut the second one down. But the third swung at Han's head with its ax.

Han ducked, avoiding the blade, but the beast crashed into him hard. They tumbled together, and the Krulg was first to its feet. As Han fumbled for his little dagger, the beast raised its ax again. Han held up his dagger, knowing he would never be able to block the blow.

Spear, ax, and sword hit the Krulg from three separate directions. The creature fell to the ground. There was silence in the clearing, save for the breathing of the warriors and the wolves.

Oieda stepped up to the leader of the wolves and scratched behind its ear. She said something that was too faint—or perhaps in a tongue too strange—for anyone but the beast to understand.

Then she rose. "We will follow them," she said. "They will take us to safety."

"Anything you say, Doctor Dolittle." Dean smiled.

They started to run, but immediately Han fell forward, howling in pain. "That stupid, clumsy Krulg stepped on my ankle," he muttered.

Bravic looked at the Elvana's swelling ankle. "He can't walk, let alone run. It's not badly hurt, though."

Han winced at Bravic's touch. "It feels badly hurt."

"We'll have to carry him," Dean said.

Oieda whispered something to the giant wolf, then turned back to Dean. "She will carry him."

Han's eyes widened. "You want me to ride a wolf?"

"Don't look a gift wolf in the mouth," Dean said, and he set Han on the wolf's broad back.

And they set off with the pack. The wolves slowed somewhat so the others could keep up, but soon Dean, Bravic, and Oieda were soaked with sweat. Meanwhile Han hung on anxiously, trying not to pull too hard on the wolf's fur.

Oieda ran up alongside him. "Do not worry. You can hold on as tightly as you need."

"Okay," Han said, but he was still very pale. "I'm not worried."

Dean saw Oieda look away to hide her smile.

They ran for many hours. When they finally stopped, now many miles from the city, Dean, Bravic, and Oieda fell to the ground, panting, and Han slid off the wolf's back as it moved over to nuzzle Oieda. She stroked the wolf's fur and whispered things only the two could understand. The wolf licked Oieda's face. Then it raised its head and howled, and the pack disappeared into the woods.

12

THE LAST OF THE WARDEVAR

They traveled only a little distance over the next two days, for they were now without horses, and they had to take turns carrying Han. Their spirits were low due to the loss of equipment, the lack of food, and the gloomy weather. The days were especially gray with a constant mist.

On the third day, Han was able to walk again, much to the delight of everyone except Bravic. Before, Han had been able to talk constantly in the ear of whoever carried him. Now he solely leaned on Bravic for support, since he was the closest in height, and that made the Dwarf the main audience for Han's constant questions and tales.

By the fifth day, Han could walk on his own, and it raised everyone's spirits, because he hunted and brought back plenty of fresh food. After they ate, Bravic set a very fast pace, and they stopped much less often to rest.

As the sun began to set on the fifth day, Han wanted to stop and camp early—his ankle was still sore. But Bravic disagreed.

"The Hall of Fallen Warriors is supposed to be somewhere in this vale," he said, "and I'd rather be tired than spend more time here."

"The Hall of Fallen Warriors!" Han and Oieda shouted together. They looked around nervously.

"What's this hall?" Dean asked.

"The place where the spirits of great, good warriors go to rest before they leave this world," Oieda explained. "It is said if a living being enters the hall, he will not come out. We should not have come this way."

"It was the fastest," Bravic grumbled.

"I—I think I can travel a little farther," Han stuttered.

They got moving again and soon came to a fork in the path. Bravic stopped. "I don't know which way to go."

Dean tossed his hands up. "Please don't say one path takes us out and one takes us to the hall."

"I don't know," Bravic muttered.

Oieda scanned the ground. "The path to the left is more traveled. I think we should take that one."

"How do you figure?" Dean asked.

"The dead leave no trace of passage."

"Well, thanks for giving me the creeps," Dean said.

"Me too," Han added.

They went down the path to the left as the shadows lengthened. It took them to a clearing where four statues stretched skyward, standing almost twenty feet tall. They were carved in the form of armed warriors: an Elvana, an Elf, a Dwarf, and a Human. Behind the statues was an enormous arched entryway.

"Oh, major creeps," Han groaned as he stared up at the figures. "There are four of them and four of us."

"Maybe that's a good thing," Dean said. "There's writing on the bases. Should we read it?"

"I wonder if it'll do something. I say we read it." Han rushed up to the base of the Elvana statue. "Everybody read in turn, okay?"

"Something bad could come of this," Bravic said nervously, but he walked to the base of the Dwarf statue.

"What's the worst that could happen?" Han asked.

"In my world," Dean said, walking over to the statue of the

Human, "when someone says that, it's usually right before something really bad happens."

"Should we not read it then?" Oieda moved into place. "No offense intended, Han, but following your decision is not my first instinct."

Dean and Bravic chuckled while Han frowned. "Thanks."

"Now I'm curious too." Dean grinned roguishly. "Let's do it."

One by one, they read the words inscribed on the stones.

"In this Hall of Fallen Warriors,
There lie those who cared.
They cared for others and not themselves,
they were the few who dared."

"In this Hall of Fallen Warriors,
are those who gave their lives.
They died for what they believed;
their sacrifice saved lives."

"In this Hall of Fallen Warriors,
those courageous souls do stay.
They had the courage to seek peace,
but they fought when there was no other way."

"In this Hall of Fallen Warriors,
are heroes of the past.
They want only one thing now ...
that what they died for will last."

As the echo of Dean's voice faded, a silence fell. The four stood as motionless as the statues above them.

"Nothing happened? I can't believe nothing happened." Han

looked around. "That stinks."

"I thought something might happen, too," Bravic said. "We need to—"

"Something did happen. Look!" Dean pointed back to the mouth of the valley. Dozens of black forms were flying straight toward them.

"Tarlugs!" Oieda spat.

"Those stupid flying Krulgs," Han said.

"We can't fight so many. Into the entryway," Dean ordered.

"Do what you want. I'm not going in there," Oieda said, raising her spear.

Dean stepped into the archway with Han and Bravic. A recessed alcove surrounded a large metal door. "It's a better vantage point than out in the open!" he shouted.

The approaching Tarlugs numbered at least thirty. They screamed in glee at the sight of the four figures.

"Maybe you're right," Oieda said as she turned and ran to the others.

As the first of the beasts flew at them, Dean skewered it on the end of his sword. Han leaped backward, bumping against the massive iron door. It swung open, and the Elvana tumbled through.

"Han!" Dean yelled. He ran into the darkness after the Elvana.

The other Tarlugs approached more cautiously, landing at the edge of the alcove and drawing their weapons. Bravic grabbed Oieda by the arm and pulled her through the door.

"Let go," she growled.

"There are too many out there," Bravic said.

"We can take them one at a time," Dean said. "Bravic, get on that side—"

But Han was already pushing at the door.

"Don't!" Dean yelled.

But it was too late. The massive door swung shut, and the companions were plunged into darkness.

"Crud," Dean said. "Did you forget about the part where if we go in, we won't leave alive?"

"Oops. Sorry," Han said.

"I heard a lock click in place," Bravic said.

"You're kidding me." Dean set his back against the door. "Does it only open from the other side?"

Oieda pounded on the door with her spear. "Open the door!" she screamed.

"What are you doing?" Dean said. "We don't want them to get in."

"I want out." Oieda's voice was strained.

"Hold on. There's a torch on the wall." Bravic took flint from his pocket and lit it.

A glow arose, and they could see they were in a long stonework hall. Bravic studied the door and frowned.

"Can you open it?" Oieda squeezed his shoulder.

The Dwarf shook his head. "There is a lock here, and here ... and here." He pointed to three places on the door. "I can't tell how to unlock it."

"You're a Dwarf," Oieda snapped, "and you don't know how to open a lock?"

Bravic scowled. "Locks aren't designed to be opened. That door's not opening for me or anyone else."

Dean stepped between the two of them. "Shall we go forward then?" he asked.

"Do we have a choice?" Oieda snapped.

Dean looked from Bravic to Oieda to Han and back to Oieda. "Oieda, you're really pale. Are you okay?"

"I'm fine," she said, but her eyes darted all around.

"Seriously, did you get hit or—"

"I am unhurt." In the torchlight, her green eyes flashed. "I do not like enclosed places."

"Neither do I." Han moved closer to her. "Especially when it feels like the walls are right in your face. It makes it hard to breathe when you think we're in a tomb and—"

"Stop talking, Han," Dean said as Oieda turned even paler. "Let's get moving."

Bravic held the torch up and led the way across the tiled floor. Han walked next to Oieda, while Dean guarded their backs. Their footsteps echoed from far away, but Dean could only guess how big the hall was.

"Do you think that's right?" Han asked. "That no humans leave alive?"

"No," Dean scoffed. "Shh."

"I'm not scared," Han whispered. "I'm an Elvana."

"Why does being an Elvana make you not scared?" Dean asked.

"Because they say that no human being comes out alive."

"They said no living being comes out alive."

Han frowned and gulped loudly. "Thanks."

"Sorry."

Light gleamed on something on the wall to the left, revealing it to be a suit of gray plate armor, standing as if worn. It was in front of a small raised iron door with carving on it.

"Don't touch anything," Dean said to Han.

"I won't."

"Don't read anything either," Bravic added.

"I said I won't. But I don't think that us reading the text on the statues brought the Tarlugs. I think they followed us from Modos or they—"

Dean held up his hand. "Don't say anything either."

"Now I can't even talk?" Han asked loudly.

Suddenly, torches on the walls burst to life. The flames seemed to jump from torch to torch until the whole massive hall was filled with light. All down the hall, suits of armor seemingly hung in the air, each in front of small metal doors.

Han threw his hands up. "My talking did not do that. That was a coinciden—"

"Quiet," Bravic whispered.

A voice echoed through the chamber: "Any who enter the Hall of Fallen Warriors must die."

"Oh, great . . . I knew it," Dean grumbled as everyone drew their weapons. "I just knew it."

At the far reaches of the light, an armored figure walked toward them. "You have defiled the dead of this hall, and now you must pay with your lives," it said ominously.

"I didn't read anything. I didn't touch anything. All I did was ask a question," Han whined as he nocked an arrow.

"We didn't defile anything," Dean called to the figure.

"Thieves," the man spat. "You'll steal nothing from this tomb."

"I'm not a thief," Bravic retorted, now truly offended.

"All who come into this tomb are thieves." The figure was now only fifteen feet in front of them. "Choose who'll die first."

"We didn't come here to steal." Dean stepped forward.

"Choose who will die first," he repeated.

"If someone has to die, can we pick you?" Dean asked.

Oieda groaned.

"Your choice is made. You will all die," the man announced.

The man took four long strides and lunged forward. His sword swept down, aiming to cut Dean in half. Dean jumped to the side, and the man's sword rang like a bell as it struck the floor.

"I don't want to fight you," Dean yelled as he backed away.

"But you must." The man's sword cut at Dean's chest and barely missed.

"We were seeking shelter," Dean explained, parrying another blow.

Growling, Bravic rushed at the man. The man sprang forward, grabbed Bravic, and flung him sideways. The Dwarf crashed into the wall and slumped to the ground.

The man struck at Dean once more.

While Han backed up with Dean, Oieda circled the man.

"Listen! We don't want to fight you," Dean growled again.

"Die!" the man yelled. He thrust at Dean, who parried once more.

"Don't move!" Oieda ordered. She pressed the tip of her spear against the man's back.

Dean exhaled. "Nice move."

Oieda smiled.

With one sudden motion, the man twisted, grabbed the spear, and pulled it forward. His elbow hit Oieda squarely in the chest and sent her sprawling to the floor.

Han drew back his bow, but the man leaped at him and, using his leg, swept Han's feet out from underneath him. Han crashed onto his back with a groan.

Then it was Dean's turn. He lunged with his sword; the armored man turned and parried. They stood toe to toe, their swords pressed together.

Then Dean slipped to the side and smashed the handle of the sword into the side of the man's head.

The man fell to his knees. He put his hands on the floor like he was going to jump up, but he did not stand.

Han drew back his bow, Bravic grabbed his ax, and Oieda lowered her spear at the man's chest. They were all panting for breath, but the man seemed more winded than any of the four. He took off his helmet and let it fall to the floor with a loud clang. His hair was gray but so light it was almost white. He raised his head, and his steel-blue eyes glanced first at Dean's lowered sword then his own sword, lying well out of his reach.

"Why don't you run me through now that you have the

chance, thief?" the old man asked.

"You're alive," Dean said in disbelief.

"You think a nick like that would kill me?" the man grumbled as he stood.

"You're not a ghost?" Han yelped, wide-eyed.

"And how do you know I'm not?" the man asked ominously. He leaned toward the Elvana, who quickly moved back to stand behind Bravic and Oieda.

"We do not want to steal anything, ghost or man. Or should I call you a Wardevar?" Oieda kept her spear pointed at him.

"The Wardevar have been dead for fifty years," Bravic said. "They were all defeated and killed."

"They were not defeated," the man said. "They were murdered. And there is still one who lives. And one is all that's needed to kill you, spawn of Volsur." The man's hands balled into fists.

"You have it all wrong. We're going to stop Volsur!" Han jabbed his finger at the man.

"Stop Volsur?" The man stared questioningly at Dean. "Maybe you're not thieves. Who are you?"

"My name is Dean Theradine. My friends are Bravic Volesunga, Oieda Halotic, and Hanillingsly Elvenroot," Dean said. The companions bowed low as they were each introduced.

"Dean Theradine? Let me see the sword you bear," the man demanded with an outstretched hand.

Dean didn't hesitate in handing it over.

The man eyed the blade appraisingly. "This is the sword of Panadur. You are not thieves."

"How do you know we didn't steal it from Panadur?" Han asked.

"Han!" the other three snapped.

"I know you are not thieves," the man repeated.

"Did you know Panadur?" Dean asked.

"No. I never knew him." The man handed the sword back to Dean.

"Then how do you know we're not thieves?" Han asked again.

"No thief would give his sword to an enemy, unless he was a fool." The man gave Dean a half-grin. "Follow me. And don't speak any more before the shadows of the warriors." He picked up his helmet and walked, now with a noticeable limp, down the immense hall.

The companions marched in silence for a long time; the hall seemed to go on forever. They passed many suits of armor, all of the finest craftsmanship. As they walked, their feet sounded like the drums of battle ringing off the stones. No matter how they tried to break up this rhythm, they'd all fall right back into the slow, steady beat.

Finally, the hall came to an end, and the man stopped before two massive iron doors. Carved in the walls on either side were long, rounded stone benches.

"Sit," the man ordered, though he continued to stand. "Let me hear your tale."

Dean spoke. He started his story with meeting Panadur, but he didn't mention the Middle Stone or his world, and he continued through everything that had happened leading up to their arrival at this hall. Han interrupted here and there to add details or tell how much he liked or didn't like certain parts of their journey.

When Dean was finished, the old man turned and moved away from them. He gazed down into the darkness of the hall for a long time. They sat in solemn silence as they waited. Then, suddenly, without saying a word, the man strode away and vanished in the darkness.

"Where do you think—" Han began, but Bravic's elbow in his side cut him off.

Soon they heard the man's footsteps returning. As he came into the light, they saw he carried a large, flat bundle under one arm. "I believe what you've told me," he said. "Now you must believe what I'm going to tell you."

Han leaned forward with burning curiosity in his bright eyes.

"Many years ago, before Volsur was banished, there lived a young lord named Coren. He ruled a land called Wardevar. It was a dry, barren land where it was a struggle just to survive from day to day. But Wardevar bred the strongest and bravest warriors in all the lands; their fierceness in battle was unparalleled. This strength enabled them to live in peace, for none would, or could, challenge them. Lord Coren sought peace, and not just in his own land; the warriors of Wardevar would often go to the aid of any in need.

"Of course, Volsur wanted their aid, but not for peace. Volsur wanted it for war. With the Wardevar behind him, he knew he could not fail. So he tried to sway young Lord Coren to his side. He offered Coren money and power, anything and everything. But Coren refused.

"So Volsur laid a trap. First, he won over a Wardevar warrior named Norouk—may the traitor forever burn—with promises of riches and power. Next, he used Norouk to lead the others to the valley of Grenadil. The valley lies between steep cliffs; it was the perfect place for Norouk's betrayal. When the traitor led his comrades and Lord Coren into the valley, the Vereortu fell upon them. The Vereortu are evil creatures who thrive on fear. The warriors fought with all their might, but the sheer numbers of Vereortu cut through them.

"As they died, Norouk watched from atop a tall rock. He stood up there so he could get the best view as his comrades were butchered. The screams of the dying mixed with the sound of his laughter. He even murdered some with his own hands. The coward didn't have enough honor to go down to the battlefield, though; instead, he had the Vereortu drag the fallen warriors up to him. Then he'd kill them slowly as they lay dying at his feet.

"That's where Lord Coren died. He did not go easily, however; as the Vereortu threw him before Norouk, the young Lord Coren slashed at Norouk, his sword cutting deeply into Norouk's face. As Norouk howled, dozens of Vereortu attacked and killed Coren—but he took many evil creatures with him.

"The rest of the Wardevar did not die easily either, but in the end, their valor was not enough. Soon only Graylen stood— Graylen, who was said to have been a descendant of the people from the Isle of Mist: the people of magic. His body was battered and torn, his wounds fatal, his life flowing away.

"Norouk called the Vereortu off, and Graylen asked to speak his last words. I don't know why, but Norouk agreed to listen to Graylen. Maybe he just wanted to see him suffer longer. Graylen had something else in mind, though. In the middle of all his fallen comrades, as he himself stood dying, he picked up his shield. The Vereortu came and dragged Graylen up to the rock where Norouk stood. They drove Graylen to his knees. When Graylen spoke, his voice was so faint, it was like a whisper in the wind:

> As their screams of vengeance go unspoken
> Let their spirits fly to the shield unbroken
> On this spot, there again you will see
> On that day their spirits will be free
> Their souls will fly
> Yours will surely die.

"After Graylen said this, Norouk ran his sword through him, and Graylen fell upon his shield. Then the creatures and the traitor left. One thousand warriors went into the valley that day.

Only two came out."

"If the first was Norouk, who was the other who came out?" Han asked.

"One was Norouk. The other was the flag carrier, a man named Ranadin. Ranadin was among the first to fall in the battle. A spear ripped through his leg, but the wound was not fatal. A young warrior dragged him beside a fallen horse, where Ranadin hid for the remainder of the battle. And when all was over, Ranadin crawled to Graylen's body. He saw that his once plain shield was now covered with many runes. Ranadin brought that shield here, knowing one day it could be used to avenge the Wardevar' deaths."

"But all this happened before Volsur was banished. Is Norouk still alive? Is he with Volsur now?" Han asked.

"Norouk, curse his name, went into the Barren Lands with Volsur. Now he's master of the Vereortu and dresses in armor made from the gold Volsur paid him to betray his fellow warriors. Volsur's power keeps Norouk from aging. If you plan to stop Volsur, you'll have to face Norouk."

Han groaned. "But if he killed all the Wardevar, how can we stop him?"

Dean shook his head. "Listen. There are only four of us. If we do run into this Norouk guy and the Vereortu, we can't fight them. We have no chance."

"We will try." Oieda jumped to her feet and held out her spear.

Dean sighed, but the old man smiled. "I admire her courage. It would indeed be madness for you to face Norouk, but if you head to Volsur, you will meet him. Or he will come after you."

The old man unwrapped the bundle underneath his arm. It was a silver shield on which were inscribed hundreds of dark runes. "It is to you, Dean Theradine, that I give this shield of Graylen." As he handed the shield to Dean, he added, "I know not how to use it. But you'll know when the time is right."

"I thank you," Dean said.

"Give me no thanks. It was my duty," the old man snapped. He moved to the massive doors and opened them. They led back outside. "The time has come," he said. "You must now leave the hall."

Dean opened his mouth to speak, but the old man held up his hands. The companions bowed low, then walked past the old man into the darkness.

As the huge doors closed behind them, Han turned and called, "But you never gave us your name."

"My name is Ranadin," the man answered as the great doors swung shut.

13

THE FALLEN WARRIORS

The companions walked away from the hall and followed the only path—a narrow, rocky trail along the side of a cliff. On one side, the sheer cliff towered above them, and on the other side, the ground dropped off, the bottom of the valley nearly one hundred feet below. Han constantly looked behind him as they walked, and a look of fascination appeared on his face whenever he glanced at the cloth bundle underneath Dean's arm.

Then screams split the air. Dean cursed and pointed to the sky, where thirty shadowy shapes swept toward them. "Not again. Tarlugs."

Two Tarlugs dove straight at them. The first fell shrieking, impaled by one of Han's arrows. The second flew at Oieda, who stabbed it in its chest with her spear. The wounded Tarlug grasped Oieda as it fell. With a cry, she tumbled toward the edge of the cliff.

Dean lunged forward. Landing hard on his stomach, he grabbed Oieda's arm just as she fell over the edge. Dean started to slide over too. His sneakers dug into the stone, but Oieda's weight kept dragging him forward. He grabbed her arm with both hands. Bravic grasped Dean's legs.

"Pull me up!" she screamed, dangling over the valley below.

"I'm trying!" Dean yelled back. "You weigh two hundred pounds."

Oieda's eyes went wide. "I do not!"

"Stop yelling at each other and pull!" Han cried. While Bravic held Dean's legs, Han helped Oieda back onto the path.

"You can't pull up a girl?" Oieda huffed as she pressed her back against the wall.

"Now you're a girl?" Dean rolled his eyes.

"What does that mean?" Oieda snapped.

"You gave me a ration of crud back in the stable about how a girl can do anything a guy can and how you want to be treated like a guy. But now you throw I'm just a girl in my face—"

"I did not mean it that way. I didn't think you were so weak that you weren't able to lift a girl."

"You're wearing forty pounds of armor and ten pounds of weapons. You alone have to weigh at least one hundred and—"

"I know how much I weigh."

"Can we fight the Tarlugs and not each other?" Han said.

All four looked up. "I don't see them. Did they flee?" Bravic asked.

The sound of rolling stone came from somewhere above them, and a large rock crashed onto the path just behind them.

"They're bombing us with stones!" Dean pointed at the ridge above them where Tarlugs held large rocks in their arms.

Another boulder slammed into the ground and showered them with splintered pieces, flying like little daggers through the air.

"Ah-ooh-ga! Ah-ooh-ga! Dive! Dive!" Dean ordered as he sprinted down the path.

The companions raced along the trail. Boulders fell all around, blowing apart as they landed. One shattered right before Dean, and a fragment hit him just above his eye. The cut was thin, but blood flowed down his cheek.

He held his hand to his face. "I'm going to get those stupid flying Krulgs."

"There's a cave up ahead!" Bravic shouted.

They darted inside the opening. Crack! A boulder landed just outside the opening. Several more rocks tumbled down in the same spot, and the whole cave shook. Bits of the ceiling cracked and fell.

"The cave is collapsing," Bravic gasped. "We must do something, or we'll be crushed."

"We can't go out there. One of those rocks would crush us like bugs. How far back does the cave go?" Dean looked back into the darkness.

Crack! The mouth of the cave crumbled inward and shards of rock flew all around.

"I think we're about to find out," Han muttered, and they dashed into the blackness.

***

A deep rumble behind them told them the cave had been sealed.

"Why are we stopping?" Bravic asked.

"Because I can't see a thing," Han said.

"Bravic, can you make a torch?"

Dean could hear Bravic huffing and puffing for a minute. "No," Bravic muttered. "I can't find my flint."

"What?" Oieda gasped.

"Han, take Oieda's hand," Dean said quickly.

"Sure," Han answered nervously.

"Bravic, grab Han's hand. You can see a little?"

"Not exactly," Bravic mumbled. "But I can sense where the rock is."

"Well, lead on then. Just move slowly. Oieda, I'll take your other hand."

"Hey! That is not my hand," Oieda snapped.

"Sorry." Dean coughed. "Got it."

"Bravic?" Han's voice trembled. "We don't know what's down ... I mean, never mind. I'm not saying anything."

"If you keep not saying anything so loudly, anything down here will know we're here. Light or no light," Bravic grumbled.

"Ouch! Stop squeezing my hand so hard," Dean said to Oieda.

"Sorry," Oieda said.

Dean heard the angst in her voice and remembered her fear of enclosed spaces. "I'm sure we'll be just fine, Han. You don't have anything to worry about." He tried to sound as confident as possible.

"I'm not afraid of enclosed spaces," Han said. "You don't have to try to make me feel better. Ow! You're hurting my hand, Bravic."

"Then be quiet," Bravic snapped.

They traveled in silence for a long time. Although Bravic led the way, they moved very slowly. They tripped over unseen rocks and bumped into one another in the dark. The invisible path they traveled was relatively flat but rocky, so they kept next to the cave's rough wall.

"Bravic, no offense, but do you have any idea where we are?" Han asked finally.

Bravic sighed. "This path has doubled back. We're now beneath the Hall of the Fallen Warriors."

"How can you be sure?"

Bravic sounded annoyed. "I'm a Dwarf—a miner. I don't get lost underground. Ever. That's like asking a Dwarven seaman if he knows the way back to his port of call."

"Dwarves sail? I didn't think that Dwarves even—" Dean began, but Oieda's grip tightened painfully.

"We are beneath the hall?" she asked. The dread in her voice was plain.

"Oieda, what's the matter with this place?" Dean asked.

"There is another part of the legend about the Hall of the Fallen Warriors. You know the great warriors above us were good in spirit and heart. But it's said the great evil warriors lurk beneath the hall. Their hate for the warriors above keeps them prisoners here. The legend says they walk in the dark shadows with a hate for the living, never able to leave this hall, never able to rest."

Dean groaned. "Let me get this straight: you're saying this is where all the best dead bad guys hang out?"

Suddenly, an eerie light filled the space around them, and they could see that they were in a huge underground chamber. The ceiling was too far above to see, and the walls were two hundred or more feet apart. At the far end of the chamber, a long way off, was an opening.

"I didn't touch anything," Han muttered.

The companions let go of one another's hands and drew their weapons.

"Run for the opening," Dean ordered.

As they sprinted across the space, the sound of galloping hooves rang on the stone behind them. They dashed across the smooth floor as fast as they could.

But Oieda stopped. She turned and raised her spear in the air. The other three continued to run, unaware that Oieda was no longer running behind them.

A mounted horseman appeared and galloped straight toward Oieda. Oieda tightened her grip on her spear. Light flashed white on the horse's flanks. When the rider came into full view, Oieda's heart stopped. The beast was bare bone. The rider was a skeleton.

The tip of the skeleton's lance lowered, and Oieda put one foot back and readied her spear. The rider raised a large shield on its other arm.

"Oieda?" Dean looked around and stopped. "Oieda!"

The Elf spoke in a tongue no man could understand.

"Run, Oieda!" Dean screamed.

"That crazy Elf!" Bravic cursed as they all ran back.

The horse's hooves rang like rolling thunder across the stone floor. Oieda lowered her spear. Han fumbled to nock an arrow. Bravic and Dean ran forward. The tip of the skeleton's lance flashed dully, and the skeleton's eyes glowed with a pale-green light. Then Oieda held out her hand, and the horse stopped so sharply that the skeleton was launched from its mount. It sailed through the air and crashed to the floor.

Sword and axe swung as one to cleave its body in two. Even then the skeleton's arms continued to strike, until Dean and Bravic broke all its bones.

Dean glared at Oieda. "What did you think you were doing?"

The skeletal horse stood before Oieda with its head lowered. She stood silently, then turned and walked to Dean and Bravic.

"Bravic, I need your ax."

"My axe? But—"

"Please."

Bravic handed her the ax. Oieda strode back to the horse and bowed her head for a moment. Then the ax slashed down and the horse fell.

When Oieda turned back to the others, her eyes glistened. "It was not evil," she said. "Now it is free."

"We'd better go," Dean said softly.

"Wait." Bravic kicked the bones of the skeleton. "I know this shield." He picked up the circular shield. It was so small it only covered his forearm. "It's called the Buckler."

"It's tiny." Han giggled. "Even for me."

Bravic twisted his wrist, and the metal plates on the shield snapped open with a swift click. The shield was now taller than Han.

Dean whistled. "That's cool."

"Do you want it?" Bravic twisted his wrist again, and the shield returned to its small size.

"Wow. But no, thank you. I don't know how to fight with a shield."

"I'll teach you." Bravic held out the shield.

"Until you do, you should keep it."

Bravic nodded.

"What about the skeleton's spear?" Han asked. "Do you want that, Oieda?"

"I already have one."

Bravic picked up the spear. "I have a feeling that down here we should have as many weapons as possible." He pushed the bones around with his boot and saw a leather pouch. He pulled on the leather straps and gasped when he saw the gold coins inside. "A small fortune." He sighed and held the coins out. "Take your share."

Dean shrugged. "It won't buy us a way out. Hold on to it, though."

The four walked quickly toward the darkened exit. It was a tunnel-like archway, and at its end stood a rectangular opening the size of a normal doorway. There was no door, but it looked as though there should be one.

Dean pointed to a dim glow far away. "There are lights farther down."

"Stay close to me and the wall," Bravic instructed. Once again he took the lead.

They had gone only twenty feet down the hallway when lights flared to reveal a long stone corridor with many openings on either side.

"It's a trap," Dean groaned. "I know it. It's going to be something like poisoned spears or a pit with huge stakes at the bottom."

"What do we do to avoid it?" Bravic asked, looking around nervously.

"We can always turn back," Han suggested.

Slam!

A large stone thumped down behind them, blocking their retreat.

"I should have known it." Dean laughed. "The old falling wall trap."

"You think this is funny?" Oieda shrieked.

"In a weird way."

"It is not funny." Oieda grabbed both the lapels of Dean's jacket and pulled him close so her face was right in his. "I want out."

"Okay, okay. We couldn't go back anyway. The cave entrance is smashed, and I doubt there's a fire exit. I'll go first. Han, keep me covered with the bow."

Oieda's hands were still clenching Dean's jacket tightly. She was breathing heavily. "I'm sorry," she muttered, looking at her feet.

"Look at me. Oieda?" Dean waited until she lifted her chin. "Two things. First, we'll get out of here, okay?" She nodded. "Second, in order to do that, you have to let go of me." She nodded again but still didn't let go.

Dean glanced at Bravic, who gave him an I-have-no-idea-what-to-do look.

"I'll be right back," Dean promised.

Oieda gritted her teeth and released her grip.

Han nocked an arrow. Dean silently crept down the hallway, stopped at the corner of the first side passage, and peered down it. Although the main hallway was clean, the side passage was filled with thick spider webs. At the end of it was a door.

"There's a door down there. It's closed," Dean whispered.

"Go by it," the three whispered as one.

Dean continued carefully down the corridor, peering down the side passages, all of which appeared the same. When he reached the end of the hallway, lights filled another huge cavern beyond. He flattened himself against the wall and peered out across the rock floor to the opposite end, nearly five hundred feet away. Stalagmites rose all across the floor. Dean waved the others forward and walked back to meet them halfway.

"What's up there?" Han asked.

"A really, really big cavern. There's a bunch of those stalag-somethings on the floor. This place is—" Dean stopped talking as the hairs on the back of his neck rose.

"We meet again, rabbit," boomed a voice from the beginning of the hallway.

"No way." Dean shivered. Standing in front of the slab that blocked their retreat was a man Dean thought he'd never see again. It was the hunter he and Han had faced at the beginning of their journey. That felt like a lifetime ago.

"Taviak?" Han cried in disbelief.

"The hunter you killed?" Oieda gasped.

"I see the rabbit has brought friends to my new home," Taviak said with a sneer.

"Are you surprised to see me here?" He walked forward. "When you killed me, you sent me to this prison of the dead. It seems like I've waited forever for you to join me. Dean, you look pale; don't you think I look good for being dead? My body has not yet started to decompose, you see." He laughed.

"You said he was dead," Han shrieked. "Remember? As a doornail? He doesn't have a head, he's dead?"

"Oh, I'm very dead, little one. And so will you all be. Please, welcomed guests, meet my new friends."

The hunter waved his hands, and the sound of grating metal filled the hallway. A foul stench arose. Taviak threw back his head and laughed a very evil laugh.

"Let's get out of here!" Dean screamed. He sprinted down the corridor with the others at his heels.

"Oh, a chase. I just live for a good chase." Taviak laughed. "Run, rabbit, run."

"Look out!" Oieda warned.

A skeleton in chain armor leaped from one of the side passages. As its rusted mace swung, Dean sliced its head clean off its shoulders. The skeleton fell to the floor.

"Got you," Dean snarled.

"No, you didn't!" Han yelped as the headless skeleton rose to its feet.

"Smash it!" Bravic's axe crashed down on the skeleton, crushing its bones.

More skeletal, armored figures had now appeared from all of the side doors.

"Run!" everyone called out.

The four turned and raced into the cavern. Screams of glee rose from behind them, and running footsteps echoed into the chamber. As the companions wove back and forth around the stalagmites, they got farther and farther apart.

"Die, creature!" Oieda cried as a dead warrior, with moldy leather armor and a rotting face, leaped before her.

Her spear pierced its chest and drove straight out its back. But the skeleton just drew back its sword, unfazed. Oieda swung the body as hard as she could into a stalagmite. It crashed into the rock with a cracking of bones. She swung it into the rock again, and several of its ribs broke off. With a snarl, Oieda yanked upward and her spear ripped through its shoulder. The skeleton fell backward and caught itself against the stone. Oieda spun her spear around and smashed the skeleton's head with the butt end. She bashed it repeatedly until it crumpled into a motionless pile.

Han's heart pounded in his ears as he heard footsteps

catching up to him. He stopped and turned. A skeleton with a broadsword rushed straight for him. Han drew back his bow. He let his breath out slowly and corrected his aim. The arrow whizzed through the air and sank deep into the skeleton's rotting chest, but it kept coming. Another arrow struck the skeleton in its eyeless socket. The skeleton merely rocked backward, then ran forward once more.

"Help! Help me! I can't kill this thing!"

Han darted behind a stalagmite and drew his little dagger. He fell to the side just as the skeleton's broadsword sliced through the air and crashed against the stone where his head had just been. Han slashed out with his knife as he scampered to his feet; the blade cut into the thing's rotted thigh.

The skeleton lifted the broadsword high over its head. Han ducked low and bounded under its legs. The weapon clanged against the ground.

Han's dagger jabbed into its back. Straining, Han pulled down, and a huge section of bone fell off the skeleton. The warrior fell forward. Han backed away. But once again, the skeleton rose to its feet.

"How do you make these things stay dead?" Han yelled.

Bravic appeared from nowhere and grabbed the skeleton. He picked it up over his head and threw it into a stalagmite. Then he picked it up again and slammed it to the ground with a cracking of bones.

"You smash them." Bravic grinned.

"Look out!"

A skeleton jumped on Bravic's back and grabbed his throat. With a snarl, the Dwarf seized the skeleton and flung it at his feet. His ax crashed down, and the creature soon lay in broken bits.

As Dean rounded a stalagmite, he realized he was alone. He was about to call out but stopped. Footsteps echoed around the stalagmite. Dean pressed his body against the stone. When he leaned forward, he came face to face with a skull. He screamed and jumped backward as he lashed out with his sword. The blade bit into bone, and the creature fell in two. Dean's stomach turned as the skeleton's upper body tried to rise. He smashed it until it lay still.

"You can do great things when you're dead. Don't you think so, rabbit?" laughed a voice from behind.

"Time to die again, tin-can man." Dean spun around, and his sword clashed with Taviak's.

"I'm going to make you suffer, boy," Taviak screamed. He kicked Dean in the chest and sent him flying backward.

As Dean landed, he rolled and came almost at once to his feet. He straightened and leveled his sword at Taviak's chest. "I killed you once, tin-can man. I didn't know you'd get recycled."

"You'll soon be joining me, boy." Taviak's sword sliced the air.

Dean lunged. His sword struck Taviak's armor, kicking off a shower of sparks. The hunter staggered backward.

"Nice move, boy." Taviak laughed.

Dean sprang forward again. This time Taviak parried, and they stood face to face with their swords pressed against each other. Taviak head-butted Dean and knocked him to the ground.

Taviak raised his sword, but Dean swept his legs out from under him. As Taviak pitched forward, Dean scrambled to his feet and ran.

"Stay and fight, rabbit!" Taviak bellowed.

Dean scanned the chamber, but he didn't see anyone else. He crouched down behind a stalagmite and heard footsteps on the other side. Staying crouched, he moved in the opposite direction, keeping the rock between them.

"Hey, boy," Taviak called from the other side of the stone. "Let us stop playing games and fight like men."

Dean took two long strides and saw Taviak's back. With a cry that sounded less than human, he jumped on Taviak's back and grabbed his helmet. His fingers locked on the visor, and he yanked backward. The helmet pulled free, Taviak spun, and Dean landed on his feet.

Dean gasped at the hunter's deathly white face, the slash around his throat, and his cold, unblinking eyes, now burning with hate.

"Scared, boy?" Taviak spat. He backhanded Dean with the hilt of his sword.

Dean staggered back. The hunter punched him in the face. Dean's lip cut on his teeth, and as he reeled back his sword fell from his hand. Taviak grabbed it and threw it as far as he could.

A smile formed on Taviak's cold lips. "Now it is my turn, rabbit. The hunt is over. Do you know what that means?"

"Hot cocoa back at the lodge?" Dean jeered.

Taviak howled in rage and burst forward. Dean set his feet. The hunter drew back his sword. The light flashed on his blade.

Dean lunged. His shoulder slammed into Taviak's armor, and he grabbed Taviak's legs and pulled.

Taviak slammed down; his arms were pinned beneath his back. Dean knelt on his chest. He pummeled Taviak's head with his fists, striking as hard and fast as he could.

Taviak wrenched his right hand free. His gauntleted fist smashed into Dean's head and knocked him sideways.

Dean's vision blurred. The lights in the cavern flashed and spun. His hands clawed at the ground as he desperately tried to get to his feet. He shook his head and felt blood fly from his lip, but at least the room stopped spinning. He stumbled toward the end of the cavern.

"There's nowhere to run now, rabbit," Taviak called.

Dean ran through the exit. Beyond it was not another cavern, but a large room. It was lit by flickering torches in sconces along the sides, though who had lit them, Dean didn't know. Ten feet from the door a pool stretched from wall to wall, and all the way across it, spaced about five feet apart, were two rows of clear pillars that rose just above the level of the water. The pillars were large enough to stand on, but one would have to leap from one to the other.

Dean was about to dive into the greenish water, but something about the water didn't look right. He picked up a chunk of rock and tossed it into the pool. It landed with a hiss, and the water bubbled and boiled all around it.

"Now you're trapped," Taviak said as he walked into the room. "No one leaves this hall. Time for you to die, rabbit. Kneel before me, and I will make your death quick."

"Yeah, right." Dean jumped and landed on the first pillar on the right. "Come and get me."

As Taviak leaped, Dean sprang to the next pillar.

"I didn't really mean that," Dean called back. He vaulted ahead three more pillars, but as he landed on the last one, he looked back toward Taviak and almost missed his mark.

Look where you're trying to land. Panadur's words echoed in his mind.

With a heave, Dean pushed off the edge of the pillar and landed on another one.

"Dean!" Oieda called. "My spear!"

Dean turned. Oieda tossed her spear to him. Dean grabbed it just before the weapon plunged into the pool.

"She cannot help you, rabbit," Taviak scoffed.

"She just did, stupid." Dean grinned as he hefted the spear. "I'm going to hit you right between the eyes."

"Don't tell him where you're going to hit him," Oieda yelled.

"Just like Panadur's stream," Dean whispered to himself.

Dean thrust the spear straight for Taviak's eyes.

Taviak grabbed the shaft. "You lose."

Taviak yanked the spear.

Dean let go.

Screaming, Taviak fell into the pool and disappeared into the bubbling liquid.

"You lost. No deposit, no refund, Tin-can Man," Dean said coldly.

"You told him on purpose?" Oieda stared in disbelief.

"My father taught me that move. I knew he'd grab the spear and try to pull me into the acid."

Dean jumped back the way he'd come. When he finally reached Oieda, she was grinning from ear to ear.

"I'm very glad to see you alive." She wrapped her arms around him. Her skin was warm and soft. Her breath tickled as her face pressed into his neck.

Oieda suddenly froze. She leaned back and stared at Dean for a moment with her eyes wide. She straightened up, clamped both her hands on his shoulders, and held him at arm's length. "Good . . . job. I thought you were—that was good."

She stepped back and muttered something, but Dean couldn't understand what she said.

"Thanks for the help." Dean rubbed the back of his head. "That was a nice throw."

"Dean," Han called as he and Bravic ran into the chamber. "I have your sword. We didn't know what had happened to you when we found it." He rushed forward and hugged Dean.

Dean took the weapon. "Thanks. Are there any more of those dead guys around?"

"I think we killed them all," Bravic reported.

"Bravic," Oieda said, "I'm in need of that spear you picked up earlier. Mine was boiled. I'll explain later."

14

DRAGON'S BREATH

The four jumped from pillar to pillar across the pool. Han had the hardest time, for it was a rather large bound for an Elvana, but they were all soon on the other side.

In the opposite wall were two towering iron doors with runes running across them.

"Can anyone read these?" Oieda peered at the runes. She placed her hand on one of the doors, and both doors swung silently inward.

"What're you doing?" Dean whispered. He and Bravic dove to one side, and Han grabbed Oieda and jumped to the other side of the door.

"I just touched it," Oieda said.

"We could have thought about it for a second," Bravic growled.

"I just lightly touched it." Oieda glared.

Han patted her shoulder. "Now you see how I feel."

"Don't worry, we were going to open them anyway," Dean said.

Beyond the doors was an enormous stonework chamber. It was bathed in a cold, dim light, though Dean couldn't see any source. The ceiling disappeared high above. On each side of the room lay a row of fallen pillars, as if one had fallen into another and caused a chain reaction. In the center of the chamber, a small staircase led up to a marble dais, and atop the dais sat an elaborate, black, high-backed chair.

Dean leaned back. "Creepville. This whole underground land of the dead is certifiably one hundred percent creepy."

"What should we do?" Oieda asked.

"There has to be a way through on the other side. When I count to three, Bravic and I will run and hide behind the pillars on the left. You guys run behind the ones on the right."

With a puzzled look, Han asked, "Why are we going to do that?"

"It's a trap. I guarantee it."

"If it's a trap, only one should go in," Oieda said. "I'll go."

"No way." Dean shook his head.

"It should be me." Bravic unslung his axe. "You three wait here."

"I said I was going first." Oieda moved in front of the door.

Bravic strutted forward. "Listen, missy—"

Oieda's nostrils flared. "What did you call me, mole?"

Bravic's knuckles turned white on his axe, and the veins on his neck stood out.

Han darted between them. "Both of you are acting like babies. I'll sneak in."

Dean rolled his eyes. "Like you can 'sneak' anywhere now that everyone's been shouting in the doorway. Listen, everyone chill out. This looks like the same deal as before: we go in, the doors slam shut behind us. I've seen it a hundred times."

"You've gone through a cursed hall a hundred times?" Oieda scoffed.

"Not gone through it. I've seen it in the movies."

"Movies? Why do you always sound crazy?" Oieda said.

Dean crossed his arms. "I don't sound crazy."

"You do sound crazy—quite often," Han said plainly. To Oieda he added, "He's from the Heavens, and it's very different there. Don't ask him to explain, or he'll just get frustrated and say, 'Oh, skip it.'"

"Can he explain how the four of us getting trapped in there is a good plan?" Oieda asked Han.

Dean held up a hand. "Don't talk about me like I'm not standing right here."

"She's got a point," Bravic muttered. "I don't see how all of us getting trapped is going to help."

"Look," Dean said. "Say one guy goes in. Oieda."

"I'm a girl."

"Fine. One gal."

"I want to be—" Bravic started.

"I don't care who goes in," Dean yelled. "It could be a monkey for all I care. Let's pretend a monkey goes in."

Han held up his hand.

"What?"

"Where do we get a monkey?"

Dean groaned. "Seriously. Everyone shut up, or I will go crazy. We send Han in." Han's mouth closed with a clap as Dean glared at him. "Han goes in the room, and the door closes. It's a trap. Now Han is on that side of the door, and the three of us are out here. The door opens. Han's dead. What then?"

"I'm dead?" Han gulped.

"I'm just—" Dean shook his head. "You know what? Just trust me, okay? We're all going to go in on three. Bravic and me to the left, Oieda and Han to the right. One. Two. Three."

The four sprinted into the room and dashed behind the pillars. As Dean expected, the doors behind them slammed closed.

"Welcome to the Kingdom of Night," a voice proclaimed. Dean peered over the column and saw a skeleton with a golden crown, dressed in long red robes, standing before the black chair on the dais.

"You were right," Han called out from behind his pillar.

Bravic groaned.

"At least we can fight it together," Dean said. He gave Bravic a wink.

"Those who come into my kingdom must pay me homage or be destroyed," the skeleton declared.

Dean stood up. "Hello," he said. "We're just passing through. We'd gladly pay you any type of homage you want if you just point us to the nearest exit."

"Who are you to walk before a king?"

"Your majesty." Dean bowed low. "I humbly ask how to get out —"

"Only those of royal birth may stand before King Lorious!"

Dean's eyebrows rose. He knew the name Lorious, but he couldn't remember where he had heard it.

"Do you know who stands before you, oh King Lorious?" Han asked, darting out from his own hiding place. "Dean Theradine, son of Panadur Theradine, stands before you."

Only then did Dean remember where he'd heard the name Lorious. "Lorious is the evil wizard guy Panadur killed," he muttered to Han.

Lorious's scream of rage filled the hall, and a ball of fire streaked from his hands.

"MOVE!" Dean ran at Han and pushed him over the fallen pillars. The spot where they had stood burst into flames.

"Panadur's son?" Lorious bellowed.

Bravic slipped out of his spot and ran to join his friends on the other side of the hall. As he raced, another ball of fire streaked through the air at him. He dove over the pillars and the ball burst into flame on the stone.

"Great, we almost had fried Dwarf," Han muttered. "So what're we going to do now?"

"We have to fight him," Oieda said.

"Now you sound crazy," said Dean. "It took Panadur,

Carimus, and Volsur to kill this guy, and you want to do it with just us four? I'm up for running away."

Han peered through the cracks in the stone. "There's an open passage at the end of the chamber."

"I'll create a diversion," Dean said. "This guy hates me more than anything. I'll meet you guys in the next room."

"No. We all go," Bravic said sternly.

"We're all going to go. But if I don't get that human flamethrower distracted, we're all going to die," Dean said. "Besides, it was my plan that got us into this."

"Each of us agreed to go," Oieda said.

Bravic handed Dean the small shield. "Take this."

"Son of Panadur, show yourself," Lorious demanded.

"Show yourself first. I'm bashful," Dean jeered.

"Why, you—"

Dean scrambled over the pillars and sped across the floor to the other side of the hall. Lorious twisted both his hands, and a fan of flames streaked from his fingertips. Dean fell on his stomach and let the flames pass over his head. Then he hopped over the pillars on the other side and crouched down again.

"Panadur told me you were a lousy shot," he shouted. "That's how he killed you so easily. He did you justice—you really stink!"

"I see your plan now, son of Panadur," Lorious spat. "You try to distract me so your friends can run free. How terribly noble of you. But I think it will end differently."

Lorious began chanting and held his hands above his head. He clapped his hands together, and a steel cage appeared, hovering in the air above the dais—with Bravic, Han, and Oieda inside it.

"Yes, young Theradine, it will be quite different," Lorious said smugly.

"Let them go, worm bait. If you want me, you can fight me."

Dean ran to stand in the middle of the floor.

"Did Panadur not tell you anything of me?" Lorious asked.

Dean shrugged. "You want to know the truth? I fell asleep during that stupid story."

Han laughed.

Lorious stomped forward. "Let me tell you something. I don't fight—let alone fight fair."

He tossed a small cube at the foot of the stairs. The cube hissed and smoked, and the floor seemed to melt around it. A wide pool formed, and the cube sank right into the floor. The hall shook, slowly at first, then more violently.

And a creature rose from the pool.

Its body was dark red. Its head was shaped like a wolf's, with coal-black cat eyes and six-inch black horns. Its arms were grossly large and twisted, ending in bird-like talons. Its legs resembled the hind legs of a large cat. It stood as tall as two grown men.

Once its whole body had risen, the floor beneath it solidified once more. Its black eyes lowered to Dean.

"Dean, run!" Oieda screamed.

The beast sprang forward. Dean fell flat on his stomach. Snarling, the beast flew over him and slammed into the doors behind him. They groaned at the impact.

Dean got to his feet and raised his sword. His weapon suddenly seemed pitifully small. "Come and get me," he taunted.

The beast howled and leapt after its prey. Dean dodged and ran for the doors through which they'd entered the room.

"I'm over here, ugly," Dean sneered.

The beast snarled and, with two great loping strides, sprang at him. Dean rolled to the side, but the creature's talons ripped across his back and cut through his leather jacket. Again, the creature crashed into the doors and they cracked from the impact.

Dean rose. He whipped his jacket off and held it out to the side. "Toro! Toro!" he called as he waved his coat.

The creature spun around and ran at Dean. Dean dodged the talons this time, but the creature's arm slammed into him and knocked him hard onto his back. The creature reared over him, its talons flashing in the light and its eyes burning with hate.

Suddenly, an arrow, an ax, and a spear slammed into the creature's back. Dean scrambled beneath its legs and slashed it across its stomach with his sword.

As the creature turned, Dean was already running back to the doors.

"Come on, break the dumb doors," Dean snarled.

Dean turned just in time to see the creature fly through the air at him. This time as he dove forward he thrust his sword up; he heard the beast howl in pain as it flew past—and smashed the doors to bits.

Dean vaulted to his feet and raced past the creature through the broken doors.

"Here, demon-kitty! I'm over here and all juicy," he cried as he ran to the acid pool and leapt onto the first pillar.

The beast ran after him and lunged, heedless of the pool. Dean pushed himself sideways and leaped two pillars away. His legs stretched out and his sneakers just caught the edge of the pillar. His stomach muscles burned as he struggled to maintain his balance and not fall to a grisly death.

The beast was not so lucky. It screeched in agony as it crashed down into the pool.

"Crud!" Dean screamed as a wave of acid crested in his direction.

He sprang from pillar to pillar, threw himself back to the edge of the pool, and landed in a heap on the stone. Behind him he could hear the screams of the creature and the hissing of the acid.

"Your turn now, Lorious," Dean snarled as he walked toward the broken doors. "Time for you and me, Skull-face."

"You are a simpleton, boy," Lorious sneered. "As I said before, I don't fight." He waved his hand, and the broken doors moved back together.

Dean jumped through just before the doors slammed shut. "Nice try, Lorious. Now I don't think you have a choice. Let my companions go," he ordered.

"Do you think I'm powerless, Theradine?" He waved his hands, and six blue flaming spheres surrounded him. "I am power," he screamed and thrust his right hand forward.

The six spheres streaked straight for Dean.

For a split second, Dean froze. There was nowhere for him to jump. Then he twisted his wrist, the shield sprang out, and Dean ducked behind it.

The shield held against the fireballs, but the impact blew him off his feet. Dean hit the ground hard; pain shot through his body.

In spite of the pain, he got up. "Nice shooting, Lorious. Too bad you hit like a baby." His arm hurt so badly he didn't know whether he could raise it, but he managed to twist his wrist, and the shield closed back down to its small size. "This is your last chance."

Dean ran forward—but before he was halfway to Lorious, chains sprang from the floor and wrapped around him. With a snap, they drew tight.

"Theradine, son and nephew of my murderers," Lorious howled. He tightened his fist, and the chains pulled tighter around Dean. "I'll have my creatures tear you apart limb by limb for the next thousand years."

"You have some serious psychological problems," Dean groaned as he struggled in his bonds.

Lorious squeezed his fist. Dean howled in pain as the chains constricted around his body.

"Leave him alone!" Oieda yelled.

"Let your suffering begin," Lorious proclaimed. He took another little cube from his cloak.

But before he could toss it, Han squeezed through the bars of the cage and dropped right down on Lorious's shoulders. The cube tumbled from Lorious's hand and landed at his feet.

Lorious reached back over his shoulder, grabbed Han by the shirt, and smashed the Elvana onto the floor. Han cried out in pain. Lorious bent down. His skeletal hand closed around Han's little throat.

"You insect," Lorious growled.

Han grabbed the smoking cube.

Lorious yanked Han up. "You dare to touch a king?"

"I dare," Han gasped. "Eat this."

He shoved the smoking cube into Lorious's chest.

Lorious screamed and dropped Han, who scooted away.

Lorious's ribs were filling with the growing mass. Bones cracked and then broke. He howled in pain—and then his body blew apart. Pieces flew all over the room, but his head and torso with arms fell next to the throne.

The chains around Dean vanished. The smoking cube vanished as well.

Then the cage disappeared and Bravic and Oieda fell. Oieda landed on her feet, but Bravic landed on his side. Dean ran over and helped him up. He took the shield off his wrist and handed it back to Bravic. "Thanks. That thing is awesome."

"I did it! I killed Lorious." He jumped in the air.

Dean went to pick up his jacket off the floor. "Way to go, buddy." He held his hand out in a fist, but Han just raised an eyebrow. "It's called a knuckle bump. Put your fist up."

Han raised his fist. Dean tapped his fist to it, then opened his hand.

"Boom." Dean grinned as he wiggled his fingers. "That's how you do it. Then you say, 'Blowing it up.'"

Han grinned. "Neat." Han raised his hand toward Oieda. When she raised her fist, Han tapped it and shouted, "Boom!"

The whole room shook.

"I didn't do that," Han squeaked.

Dean looked back at the throne.

Lorious's upper body was moving. His fingers clawed at the floor, picked up his fallen crown, and placed it back on his head. "You may have defeated me, son of Panadur, but this room will be your tomb now."

Lorious smashed his hand down.

Huge cracks appeared in the floor, and pieces of rock began to fall all around. Dean just jumped out of the way as an enormous section of the ceiling crushed Lorious beneath it.

"Let's get out of here before that happens to us!" Dean yelled.

They ran to the opening behind the dais, the room crumbling behind them. As they dashed into a dark, rough tunnel, the world seemed to shake all around them. The passage sloped upward, and their legs burned, but the rumbling ground ensured they kept running.

The passage ended in a solid stone wall. "What a poorly worked secret door," Bravic spat. "This is some of the worst workmanship I've ever seen. Notice that—"

"Just open the door!" all three cried.

Bravic reached up and pressed an unremarkable spot on the wall. With a grinding of stone, a door slid aside. The four rushed through into a small cave. The gray outdoors was visible just ahead.

"We made it!" Dean gasped.

They staggered forward to the cave opening. It looked out over a long, barren valley between two cliffs. At the edge of the valley were scraggly bushes and trees, and beyond that they could see the peaks of three mountains. The one in the middle rose much higher than the others, disappearing into the dark clouds that swirled above it.

The rumbling had at last stopped, and they collapsed, relieved to once again feel fresh air on their faces. Dean was ready to fall asleep right then and there, but Bravic nudged him.

"The Mountain of Despair." Bravic pointed to the tallest peak.

"It's where Ahulata said Carimus is kept." Dean sat up straight.

"Are we going to get him out?" Han asked.

Oieda gently put her hand on Han's shoulder. "Time is short. If we try to save Carimus, it might be too late to save anything else."

"The Elf's right, Dean," Bravic said. "We can't risk it. Not with just us."

As Dean bowed his head in thought, Han blurted out, "But if we do get Carimus, he could help. He could fight Volsur with us."

"Han's right," Dean agreed after a moment. "If we can get Carimus out, then maybe he can help us. And even if he can't, it'll let people see they can fight Volsur."

"It's too risky, and it will take too much time," Oieda said.

Dean turned to Bravic. "You said the only way through the mountains was through the Mountain of Hope, right?"

Bravic nodded. "It will take two weeks to go around."

"I don't think we have that much time anymore. I just feel it."

"Feel it?" Oieda rolled her eyes.

"You want to tell me you don't go by feelings?" Dean's jaw clenched.

"A leader uses wisdom to make decisions."

Dean stared out over the valley. His shoulders slumped, and he hung his head. "I never said I knew what to do. I don't. Yeah, I'm flying by the seat of my pants, and I'm going with my gut. Panadur told me I knew what I should do in here." He touched his chest. "Believe me, I wish I knew it up here"—he tapped his head—"but I don't. I know it doesn't make sense, but in here"—he touched his chest again—"that's what I think we need to do. We need to try."

"But what if we fail?" Oieda asked.

A stillness followed her words.

"If we fail, we die," Bravic said. "Once he makes up his mind, that's it. We'd only stay up half the night arguing about it, so let's just get some sleep."

Oieda stood to look out on the valley. The others lay down to try to get what little sleep they could.

***

Dean hadn't even gotten comfortable yet when he was startled by a gentle vibration. At first, it was soft and slow—then it grew more violent. The cave is collapsing.

"Out of the cave!" Dean ordered.

Everyone jumped to their feet and ran out.

Almost immediately, mere feet in front of them, a geyser erupted, shooting a hundred feet into the air.

"Back in the cave!" Dean screamed.

The pillar of super-heated water collapsed back upon itself, and a ring of steam blasted outward. The steam nearly burned them as they raced back to the safety of the cave.

Again and again, geysers erupted in a line across the valley, moving toward the far end. But within minutes, it was over. Steam rose from the valley floor and filled it with a cloud that slowly settled back into the ground.

"The Dragon's Breath," Bravic said in awe. "I never thought I would see it."

"Dragon's Breath? The name fits," Dean said.

"My mother told me the story when I was a child," Bravic continued. "She said the geysers were really the breath of a sleeping dragon."

"It looks like it's awake to me," Han said with a little grin.

"The pressure builds like a wave," Bravic explained. "They start going off here and then all the way over there." He pointed toward the end of the valley.

Dean peered across the field. "How often do they go off?"

"I don't know. We can wait a while to see."

"I guess that's our only choice." Dean leaned against the wall. "We have to get across it to get out of here."

Han sighed and sat down. "I wouldn't want to try to run across that thing without knowing when it was going to breathe again."

"Neither would I, Han." Oieda laughed.

A short while later, as Dean fought the heaviness in his eyelids, the ground trembled again. The rumble soon grew into a roar, and then the steam hissed into the air again, nearly touching the tops of the high cliffs on either side.

"About fifteen minutes," Oieda said.

Dean nodded. "We can make it across there in fifteen minutes, no problem."

"We don't know if it's going to be fifteen minutes though," said Bravic. "They may not erupt at regular intervals."

Han gulped. "We could be cooked. I'd listen to him, Dean."

"I'm going to. We'll hang out a while. We need sleep anyway."

The four settled down and watched the silent valley. As Dean waited for the next eruption, a shadow drew his attention to the sky. A cluster of dark forms was circling beneath the gray clouds.

"Stupid Tarlugs," Dean growled. "We have to do something about those things."

"They'll never leave us alone," Han said.

"They won't unless we do something about them. Oieda, how much time do you think we have before the dragon breathes again?" Dean asked.

"About five minutes. Why?"

Bravic moved to stand in front of Dean. "What are you thinking?"

"Those things aren't going to get off our backs unless we get them off. We can't fight them because there are way too many of them. But right now, they're flying right over our heads. They're over the Dragon's Breath. If I can get them to come after me, and I time it right, they'll get fried in a major way."

"And if you time it wrong?" Oieda asked.

"Dean," Han said, "let me go. You're too valuable."

"Don't give me that. You're just as valuable as I am. Besides, I'm the fastest. Does anyone care to dispute the fact that speed is going to give whoever goes out there the best chance?" Dean asked. "Time's a-wastin'. I have to do it now."

"I'll go." Oieda started to unstrap her armor.

"No. There's no time." Dean swung his arms and stretched his legs.

"Then we'll just wait until the next cycle," Oieda begged.

"By then they might have spotted us here." Dean pointed his thumb at himself. "You guys want to see fast? I'm going to move at the speed of sound, Mach five."

Without looking back, Dean raced out of the cave. He waved his hands in the air and yelled, "Hey! You stupid Tarlugs! I want to invite you to my little cookout, you dumb flying Krulgs!" He broke into a little trot. "Come on!"

One Tarlug lifted its spear and pointed down at Dean.

The ground began to shake.

Oieda grabbed Bravic's arm. "It's too soon . . . it's breaking the cycle! Dean, come back!" she yelled.

Dean looked to his friends in the cave and then back at the sky. The Tarlugs were sweeping right down the face of the cliff above the cave, rushing to get to him.

"You'll never make it!" Bravic screamed.

Dean shook his head. He didn't know if he could run fast enough, but he knew if he didn't try, the Tarlugs wouldn't stop. And one of these times, they would kill one of his friends—or all of them.

He sprinted away from the cave.

The Tarlugs shrieked as they pursued him. The ground rumbled and groaned. Every muscle in Dean's body strained as he sped across the arid ground. The dust kicked up behind his feet.

"Run!" Oieda cried.

Dean's lungs flamed and his muscles burned. Thirty Tarlugs swept after him, but he only looked ahead as his feet pounded the ground in rhythm with his heart.

Back in the cave, three figures watched helplessly as a geyser of steam rose into the air and Dean and the Tarlugs disappeared in its cloud.

"Dean!" Oieda yelled. The heat seared her face and dried the tears in her eyes.

Dean heard the snarls of the Tarlugs behind him—the plan was working—but he couldn't look back. He pushed his body to its utmost and beyond. He heard the geysers blast into the air right behind him. Heat washed over his back, and his skin blistered. He screamed in pain.

Before the last geyser had stopped, Oieda raced out of the cave, with Bravic and Han just behind. They ran through the steam that still swirled across the valley floor. The bodies of the Tarlugs lay everywhere, dried and shriveled like burnt meat.

"Dean!" Oieda called. Then she saw his body lying in the dirt at the far end of the line of geysers.

She ran to him, pushing herself as hard as Dean had, and dropped to her knees beside him. Her hand trembled as she rolled Dean onto his back. Dirt caked the side of his face. He gasped for air, and his eyes fluttered open.

"I told you. Mach five." He gave a small, crooked grin. "But I think I blew out every muscle in my body doing it." He groaned and then passed out.

15

SKINS

Dean's eyes snapped open. His back stung, and his legs ached. They were camped in a small rocky outcrop. Bravic and Han lay sleeping nearby. Oieda sat twenty feet away, looking out into the night.

Dean tried not to groan as he got up and walked over to her. She didn't look at him as she handed him a leather water flask. He drank his fill and sat down next to her.

"Thanks." He wiped the back of his mouth.

"Are you well?" she asked. She still didn't look his way.

He nodded. "Sore, but I'm good."

She slapped him so hard in the face the blow knocked him over. She jumped up and glared at him with blazing emerald eyes.

"What the—?"

"Quiet. They need rest." She tilted her head toward Bravic and Han.

"Nice of you to think about them while you punch me in the face," Dean whispered harshly.

"It was not a punch. It was a slap. And it wasn't hard."

Dean rolled his eyes. "Whatever. Why'd you do it?"

"Because you are a fool."

"For coming over and talking to you?" Dean muttered.

"No. For being willing to throw us away." Oieda sat back down and glared out at the night.

"You say I never make sense. What are you talking about? I

didn't risk your lives; I risked mine."

"Do you remember my spear?" she asked.

"The one on your back?"

"No. The one I threw to you, and you killed Taviak with it."

"Yeah. I remember it."

"It was destroyed in the acid. I was glad you used it to kill Taviak. It fulfilled its role. Even though it was very special to me, I do not regret it being destroyed."

"It was special to you? I'm sorry I lost it."

"You didn't lose it. That's my point." Oieda turned to face him. "If you threw it away, I would be sad. Do you know what a weapon is?"

"What a weapon is?" Dean shrugged. "Something you use to kill something with."

"No." She sighed. "It's a tool. One of its uses is to kill. But its purpose is to protect the bearer. To save their life. That's why I'm not sad that the spear is gone. It protected you."

"Okay..." Dean still didn't understand.

"Only you can stop Volsur," Oieda said.

"You don't know that."

"I do. In my heart, I can feel it. You alone can kill Volsur, but time and again you risk your life by tossing your tools aside. I am a warrior. A warrior is a weapon. A weapon is a tool. That makes me a tool—to be used to protect your life."

Dean searched her eyes. They kept their hard edge. "I don't want to risk your life," he admitted.

"Then you throw my life away. Maybe none of us will live through this quest, but you are the leader. You must be willing to use us. We will all die for you. Do not throw our lives away."

Dean exhaled and looked out into the night. "I'll take watch."

Oieda stood and turned to go.

Dean reached out and grabbed her arm. "Wait. Why was that

spear special?"

"It was my great-grandfather's. It was passed from father to son. My father died with it in his hands."

"I'm sorry it's gone."

"I'm not," Oieda snapped. "It was a tool. It saved your life. It did what it was made to do."

She left Dean alone in the night.

***

At dawn they set off from the Valley of the Dragon's Breath. Just before noon the sky unleashed a torrent of rain. There was no shelter nearby, and they all agreed they'd rather be moving and cold than standing and frozen, so they hurried their pace. The downpour came in fierce bursts, crashing down and then retreating, only to regroup and come against them again. Even when the rain finally stopped, large black clouds continued to swirl overhead, ready to unleash another torrent at any time.

The companions spoke little as they walked over the saturated ground, always toward the mountain. They walked until what they believed was sunset, although the day darkened only a little from its previous gloom, and made a chilly, wet camp. They ate soggy berries Han and Oieda had scavenged along the way. After little debate they risked a small fire to try to dry their soaked clothes.

The next week was more of the same. The mountain drew nearer and the sky grew murkier. The storm stood watch over them like a vulture circling a lost man. It shifted and pulsed, and its stinging, chilled wind fought to freeze their hearts.

When at last they reached the mountain, the storm attacked wholeheartedly. Its thunderous battle cry rose to a fevered pitch, and the wind blew like a trumpet. The rain and sleet poured down on them in full force. The rocks underfoot turned slippery as they inched their way up the mountain pass, clutching its rock wall with whitening fingers. But they bent into the wind and pushed onward.

As evening approached, Bravic constantly peered forward through the wall of rain, hoping for some sign of shelter, but all he found was a small alcove large enough to hold only two. Dean and Bravic silently decided that Han and Oieda would spend the night in what little shelter there was, for both were worse for wear from the onslaught of the storm.

Through the night, the wind continued to drive the rain upon them in a constant assault. It pelted them with hail and tried to wrench them from the side of the mountain with sudden, brutal gusts. All four were numb with cold. Even the alcove gave little protection against the vicious storm.

But when morning came, the rain and wind stopped. Oieda and Han gathered what little wood they could find, and the four huddled around a tiny fire, desperate for the warmth.

Without breakfast, they started along the drying path that spiraled up the mountain. Their pace was slow. When they entered a ravine whose sides rose above their heads, they moved cautiously, scanning the slopes for any sign of peril.

As they came to the middle of the gorge, a rock skittered down the slope from up ahead, followed by a faint muttered curse. Dean leaped into the deep shadows, and Bravic and Oieda dove behind a massive rock, but Han stood with his feet apart in the middle of the path. His little hands clenched and unclenched in anger as he looked upward.

"Han, get down," Dean whispered.

"What? What now?" Han screamed at the sky, his patience at an end. "Show yourself, whatever you are!" he demanded.

In answer to his command, a line of silhouettes appeared ahead. They numbered fifty or more. "Hold or be slain," a voice called down to them. "Show yourselves!"

"No, you hold. Show yourselves!" Han stuck out his chin and shook his fist.

A hail of arrows sank into the ground in a circle about him. Even though Han never flinched, all the color drained from his face.

Dean jumped from the shadows and grabbed the motionless Elvana. Oieda and Bravic drew their weapons.

The voice called to them again. "Drop your weapons or die."

All three turned to Dean, who drew his sword and laid it at his feet. The others did the same, then raised their hands. Humans, raggedly dressed in dirty armor, walked forward.

"Who are you?" a man asked. He was thin with a rough beard. His armor was in poor condition, as was the armor of the others.

"We're travelers," Dean answered.

Another soldier, apparently the leader, pushed his way to the front. He looked the companions up and down, and a disgusted look crossed his face. "More refugees?" he sneered. A murmur ran through the men around them. "We have no room for more refugees."

"We're just passing through," Dean said.

One of the soldiers gathered the companions' weapons from the ground. But when he picked up Dean's sword, his eyes went wide. "Look!" He showed the sword to the leader.

"Where did you get this?" the leader asked. "This is the sword of Panadur the wizard."

The men around him took a step back. Some raised their weapons.

"It's my sword," Dean said calmly. "Panadur gave it to me."

"Where did you get this?" the soldier demanded again.

"It's his," Han interjected, ducking under Oieda's arm. "Panadur gave it to him. We're trying to stop Volsur. And let me tell you, I'm sick and tired of no one lifting a finger to help us."

"Panadur gave the sword to me before he died," Dean said.

The leader gasped, and the men around him murmured. "This is grave news. Carimus is a prisoner in our mountain, and now his brother Panadur is dead." He looked at Han. "Now nothing can stop Volsur."

Dean's words echoed in the silence that followed. "We can."

"You really intend to slay Volsur?" the leader asked.

"Yes, we do."

The man looked up the slope. "We've talked too long here. Follow us. Our camp is not far. Do not speak until we're there."

He raised his fist, and all but ten of his men slipped into the shadows. With another gesture, the remaining men headed in the direction the companions had been traveling.

Han's mouth opened to ask a question, but Bravic's poke in his ribs cut him off. They gathered their weapons and set off.

The ravine rose until they were walking on a mountain path. The gray of the day seemed little different in the shadow of the mountain. The path twisted, turned, and forked often, but the man in the lead never hesitated about the way to go. The companions followed silently, surrounded by men who scanned the mountainside as they walked.

At the side of a particularly steep cliff, the leader turned and seemingly walked right into the mountain.

When the companions reached the spot where the man had disappeared, they saw it was an opening that only one man could fit through at a time—sideways. They looked behind them one last time before slipping through.

On the other side, the narrow crack opened into a large cavern that extended some hundred feet in both directions. It was filled with the smell of fifty rough-looking men who eyed them curiously. The soldier who had escorted them this far walked over to a tall soldier with short dark hair. The two had a whispered conversation, and the first soldier handed the second one Panadur's sword.

The tall soldier strode over to Dean and the others. He grinned as he opened his hands. "Welcome to the remains of the warriors of Mount Hope," he said bitterly. "I'm Navarro, the leader of these men." With that, he bowed low. "Now, what can I do for those who wish to stop Volsur?"

"My companions and I would like to know about Carimus. We're going to set him free."

"Stop Volsur and free Carimus?" Navarro slapped his leg and laughed loudly. Some of the other men in the cavern joined in. "There were over two thousand men in Lord Tanaro's army in the mountain. Now there are less than a hundred, living like rats in these caves. We can't even get near the main castle anymore. Yet you four are not only going to stop Volsur, but you're going to free Carimus from a thousand Krulgs." His laughter echoed off the walls.

"We're going to try," Dean replied coldly.

Navarro's laughter chilled into an uneasy silence.

"Well, you'd better hurry," said another man, stepping away from the wall. His appearance was cleaner than the others. He was thin with a sullen expression, dark eyes, and hair falling about his shoulders. "Some Krulgs we caught this morning said they're taking Carimus to Volsur's tomorrow. Something wicked is in the works."

"How did you talk to the Krulgs?" Han asked. "I thought they only knew how to speak Krulg?"

"Some of us here have been around the foul creatures so long that we know some words. You wouldn't want to talk to them, though—horrible conversationalists." The man winked at Han.

"Stay out of this, Dalvin," Navarro growled. "I'm in charge now."

"No one made you king. Besides, Kala will make it back."

Navarro shook his head and spat. "I told Kala that raid was foolishness. Look what it got him. Look what it got us. Twenty more men lost, and I'm sure Kala was captured. He was taken to Naviak."

"That's not confirmed."

"Neither is his being alive. I think he's dead."

"Until there's confirmation Kala's dead, we leave decisions to a vote," Dalvin said. "That's what was agreed. Let's hear the boy out." He turned his steady gaze to Dean. "If you do have some plan to attack the castle, now would be the time. Reinforcements arrive tomorrow from Naviak, but they sent half their number to the front."

"Where, specifically, did the others go?" Oieda asked.

Dalvin's eyes locked on hers. "Kilacouqua."

Oieda squared her shoulders and nodded.

"Do you have a plan to attack the castle?" Dalvin asked. "Even with half their number, that's five hundred Krulgs. We can't risk a full assault."

"Nor will we risk any mission," snapped Navarro. "I'm not going to be part of an attack whose only result would be to stir the Krulgs into sweeping the mountain looking for us. They'll come with five hundred more tomorrow. It will be us who are the refugees next."

"Then we'll do it on our own." Dean's voice was calm as he leveled his stare at the seething man.

"And get me killed? I don't think so." Navarro drew his sword.

In a split second, Oieda's spear tip was pressed against Navarro's throat, Bravic's ax was in his hands as he stood back to back with Oieda, and Han's bow was taut. The men in the cave drew their weapons and rushed over. Some stood behind Navarro; most moved behind Dalvin.

"Let's everyone dial it back," Dean said.

Navarro's eyes swept over the cavern. Surely he recognized he was outnumbered. He glared at a few of the men who stood against him, but his eyes burned with hate when they fell on Dalvin.

"It's your death," Navarro spat as he sheathed his sword. He sneered first at Dean and then at Dalvin, then pushed his way to the opening of the cave. A small group of men followed him out.

"Forgive him." Dalvin shook his head. "He wasn't always like this."

Han lowered his bow. "Was he just a jerk before and now he's a complete and total—?"

Bravic hit him in the shoulder.

"Navarro's a good man. Living like this can break anyone," Dalvin said.

"Was a good man," Han mumbled.

Dean held up his hand and glared at Han. "You don't know what he's been through, Han. Anyone can break."

Dalvin reached out and shook Dean's hand. "I'll try to help in whatever way I can. What is your plan?"

Dean looked at Oieda. "Before we go over that, did anyone send word to the Kilacouquen?"

"No. We couldn't spare the men."

"It is not necessary," Oieda said. "Our scouts will see them. The Kilacouqua will be ready." She gazed stoically around the room. "Let us plan for Carimus."

Dean nodded. "Can you show us the layout of the castle?" he asked Dalvin.

Dalvin led them to the back of the cave. Someone had scratched a top-down view of the castle on the rear wall. "Our caves are here, outside the main mountain. The castle is in the mountain itself," he said.

"Inside the mountain?" Han's voice rose. "Like inside-inside?"

"It was the winter home of the king, right?" Dean asked.

Dalvin nodded. "Most of the men here are from the king's guard. When Aeriot fell, the king set out for here. The captain of the king's guard led the decoy convoy. Hestian, the commander of the army, led the convoy with the king."

"What happened?" Han asked.

Dalvin's throat tightened. "Volsur didn't fall for the deception. He attacked the real convoy with his entire army. They killed everyone. The king, his family, soldiers—even children."

"Yet you and your men still fight on," Oieda said. "That is honorable."

"We made it this far. We hid in these mountains. But now the captain of the king's guard has been captured—during a raid. I pray for his safety. Other than the king, I have not known a nobler man. And without him, our numbers are dwindling. Soon there will be none left."

"I'm sorry," said Dean.

Dalvin's back stiffened and he turned back to the markings on the wall. "There's one main gate on both the north and south sides," he explained. "The south gate is the least guarded. A wide road leads up to the castle."

"How many are on the road?" Dean asked.

"Only a few. Krulgs don't patrol. They're undisciplined. Most stay at the castle. But they'll probably be drunk. They have some kind of down day when they rotate out. That would be tonight."

"Why would half leave before the reinforcements come?" Bravic asked.

"As I said, they're undisciplined. But we tried to take the castle back."

"What happened?" Han asked.

Dalvin frowned. "They aren't the brightest monsters, but

they know how to fight. They still outnumbered us three to one. We failed."

"Do you know where they're keeping Carimus?" Dean asked.

"In the main tower."

Dean studied the map.

Dalvin leaned against the wall. "If you could find a way through the main gate and stick to the side streets, you might make it. But how do you plan on getting through the main gate?"

Dean searched his mind for some scrap of an idea. "We're going to sneak in," he said. "The way we're going to do it is . . ." He looked around, and his eyes fell on some dried Krulg skins hanging on the wall. He had an idea, though it made his stomach turn. "Those skins! We're going to hide in the skins."

"Ewww. What?" Han made a face.

"We'll sew them on. You could tell up close we aren't Krulgs, but if we keep a good distance I bet they'll be fooled," Dean explained.

"Is there any other way in?" Bravic asked.

Dalvin shook his head. "The mountain fortress was made by your people, Dwarf. The only way in is through the main gate. We had to collapse the secret passageways as we fled from the attack."

"It couldn't hurt to try Dean's idea." Han shrugged.

"Couldn't hurt? It could get us all killed," Dean grumbled.

Han's hands went up. "Do you want me to go along with you or not?"

Oieda spoke up. "I think it could work."

Dean smiled.

"It's settled then," said Han. "Dean, we'll probably have to add some padding to you to get you to fill out one of these skins, but Bravic won't need any because . . ." He smiled.

Bravic raised a bushy Dwarf eyebrow.

Oieda lifted a skin from the wall and held it up. "It still smells like Krulg. That is good. Krulgs have a keen sense of smell. And yes, we will need some padding."

"I'll see what I can find," said Dalvin. "As you can see, our supplies don't flow too freely."

***

Dean stood with his arms out as Oieda finished with the last stitches around his waist. He moved and stretched, and the Krulg skin flexed with him. "This looks way better than I thought," he said. "It moves with me."

"It stretches." Han pulled on it. "If it wasn't for the stink, I would say it's amazing."

Dean still felt uncomfortable with the smelly skin all around his body. It even covered his face, which was now smeared with black soot to cover any exposed areas.

Dalvin came over with a cup and spread a greasy substance on Dean's new Krulg skin. Dean gagged at the odor, but Oieda nodded approvingly.

"Whatever that grease is," she said, "it gives life to the skin."

"Yeah," Han agreed. "He really looks like a slimy Krulg. What is that stuff?"

"Rat fat." Dalvin wrinkled his nose.

"How do I look?" Dean asked and turned around.

Bravic's lips curled. "If these Krulgs are as blind as they are stupid and drunk, we may have a chance."

"Good. Now you three have to get in yours."

Soon Han and Bravic were sewn into hides as well. Han made all sorts of ghoulish noises once he was in his Krulg skin. He would have run all around if Dean had not forced him to stand still.

"Is he too small?" Dean asked. "Do they have super-short Krulgs?"

"They do," said Oieda, chuckling, "but he'd be the shortest I've seen. The boots help. Try to stand up taller."

Dalvin took the heavy needle and coarse thread from the Elf's hands. "I will sew you in, Oieda."

"I am not getting in one." Oieda stepped back, and the color drained from her face.

"You have to, Oieda. It's the only way we can get in," Dean said. "You'll be okay."

"I cannot ..." Oieda said, backing up. "I don't like enclosed spaces ..." She turned and bolted toward the exit. Han grabbed her legs, and they both landed in a heap.

"Oieda, you have to," Han begged. "There's nothing to be afraid of."

Oieda stiffened. "I am not afraid."

"Then you'll get in the skin?" Han prodded.

"No." She got up.

Dean stormed over, took her by the arm, and pulled her to the side. "Listen, this plan is crazy and has about zero chance of working. I don't want you to go."

"Then why do you push me?" She crossed her arms.

"Because I know you. If you don't go, you'll never forgive yourself."

"I just ... if we were going straight at an army of Tarlugs, I would have no fear. But this ..." Her neck muscles tensed. "Trapped inside skin. I do not know how to defeat this fear."

"I do."

"How?"

"Suck it up, buttercup." Dean smirked.

There was murder in her green eyes. "I open my feelings to you, and you taunt me?"

Dean's eyebrows rounded. "I'm serious. You have to dig down deep, and suck it up. The situation blows, but what choice do you have? Sometimes you just have to take the crap. Look, part of me doesn't want you to go. I want you safe. But I know you. If Bravic, Han, and I go in there and you don't, no matter what happens, you'll beat yourself up over it."

Her eyelids clenched shut. Her nostrils flared as she breathed deeply. "I will ... suck it up," she replied grimly.

She looked pale, but her jaw was set as she stomped over to the hide. And as Dalvin sewed her into the skin, she stared quietly straight ahead, though sweat ran down her face.

***

"My men will take you close to the entrance," Dalvin said. "The entrance to the mountain is not heavily guarded. The Krulgs are now careless with their watches, as boredom has worn them down. I've gone over the layout with Bravic, and the Dwarf has mastered the way." Dalvin gave a broad grin, and Bravic nodded. "Whatever other help I can be to you, I don't know. Our supplies are limited, and Navarro will be against any other type of aid."

"Thank you for everything you've done already. It's getting late; I think we'd better get going." Dean tried to scratch his back beneath the skin.

The four companions, led by five men and Dalvin, left the cave. They crept in silence along the paths and were soon sweating profusely in the heavy skins. The walk would have been difficult unencumbered, but with the weight and clumsiness of the skins, they were constantly slipped and stumbling.

When they came to a small bluff, Dalvin stopped and pointed up the path. He clasped Dean's hand, and then he and his men silently faded back down the path into the shadows.

16

HAIR TODAY, GONE TOMORROW

Dean almost laughed at the sight of Bravic's scowl and Han trying to look fierce. But the look of controlled panic in Oieda's eyes made his laughter turn to worry. She looked as if she'd bolt any minute.

He gritted his teeth and walked up the path. The mouth of the mountain loomed above them. Sweat poured from their faces as they came closer to the main gate leading into the tunnel. Three Krulgs stood before the entrance, talking in varying volumes, obviously arguing about something.

The companions walked forward with their faces cast downward. As they approached, the Krulgs kept talking, but their gruff voices rose even louder. Dean's heart pounded in his ears so loudly he couldn't understand how the others didn't hear it. And then they passed the three Krulgs, went through the entrance, and before them a wide cobbled road stretched right into the rock. Sconces placed periodically along the wall lit the way.

Well, that was easier than I expected, Dean thought.

"Gunak. Gunak!" a coarse voice bellowed behind them.

They turned. One of the Krulgs was pointing at them with its barbed spear.

Dean's heart leapt into his throat. Bravic's scowl turned into a snarl of hate. But the Dwarf didn't lash out. Instead, he walked over toward the Krulg, keeping his eyes downcast.

"Gunak. Tarlurgan unbuldik wunur," the Krulg said. It motioned to a pile of sacks against the wall. The two other Krulgs stepped up beside the third.

Bravic walked over to the sacks and his companions followed.

"Gunak," Han said in a growl as he passed the Krulg. Dean's heart froze. "Gun—" Han was cut off as Bravic slammed a large sack on the Elvana's shoulder. Han bent nearly in half under the weight.

Dean and Oieda picked up the remaining sacks. Bravic started back up the road, and they followed him in a straight line. The Krulgs cackled in glee as they walked away.

As they trudged along the tunnel, a foul stench rose from the sacks—it smelled like rotting meat.

"What's in these things?" Han whispered with obvious distaste.

"Shut up, or you'll be," Bravic snapped.

"But I can hardly carry mine. You didn't have to give me the heaviest one." Han tried to shift the weight of the burdensome sack and nearly toppled over.

"If you say another word—" Bravic began.

"He's right." Dean slung the sack off his shoulder. "These things are too heavy and smelly to lug around."

With a sigh, the rest lowered their sacks. Dean and Bravic tucked them off to the side, and they continued on their way. As they walked, they occasionally passed other Krulgs coming their way. But they kept their eyes downcast, and no one paid them any close attention.

Finally, they reached the gates of the walled keep—or what used to be the gates. They had been smashed open and now lay broken on the ground. And through the broken gaps, they could see the burned and demolished buildings of a once-beautiful underground city.

Their eyes swept over the damage to one tower that stood in the middle. Carimus must be in that tower, Dean thought as they passed into the shadows of the mangled gates.

The streets were in darkness except for a few torches mounted periodically or carried by the Krulgs who scurried about. But lights illuminated the windows of the buildings.

They made their way through the twisting streets. After a short while, they all cast their eyes at the ground as a group of three Krulgs walked toward them.

"Vavick," one spat, pushing Dean as it passed.

Dean gritted his teeth and remained silent. The Krulg laughed, stopped, and turned as the four continued to walk.

"Palairg." It ran back in front of the group and stopped before Dean. "Palairg. Farlow jurgr . . ."

As the creature reached out and grabbed Dean by the chin, Dean's fist shot forward and smashed into its jaw. He punched it in the stomach and pounded it on the back with both his hands. The Krulg fell to the cobblestones and lay unmoving. Another Krulg swung at Dean, but Oieda grabbed its arm and swung it headfirst into the side of a building. Bravic growled and threw himself into the last Krulg. His arms circled its chest. Then a rock bounced off the Krulg's head, and the creature went limp in Bravic's arms.

Bravic cast the Krulg to the side and looked at Han, who stood with another rock in his hands.

"Well, there wasn't one for me," Han said as he cast the rock aside.

"What should we do with these guys?" Dean said.

"Leave them. If they're found, they'll think it was another group of Krulgs that attacked them," Bravic answered.

Oieda's hand reached up to her face. She started shaking.

"It's okay." Dean rushed over and grabbed her arm. "You're doing great," he whispered.

"Do not ever call me a flower again," she snarled.

"What?"

"This 'buttercup.' I am doing this because of your whole suck it up, buttercup talk. It is a flower."

"It's just an expression, but you're doing great."

"I am not your buttercup or baby. Like in your song. I am a warrior." She panted and closed her eyes.

"You are. You're very brave. I wouldn't call you my baby."

"Why not?" she snapped.

Bravic moved behind her so she couldn't see him. He started shaking his head at Dean and waving his hands.

Dean nodded. "Um, nothing. Everything is good. You're doing great, Oieda. We should get going."

"Walk. Now," Oieda said.

The four again moved closer to the tower. As they rounded a corner, they saw a large group of Krulg guards standing before the main gate of the castle. They quickly hurried into the shadows of a side street.

"Just our luck. How can we get around the guards at the gate?" Dean asked. "These guys seem to be paying attention to their duties."

Before anyone could answer, footsteps came from the other end of the side street, and a dozen Krulgs, sacks on their shoulders, approached through the gloom.

Oieda leaned close to Dean. "We could use them."

"How?"

"Trust me," she said, but her eyes still looked wild.

Dean grabbed her arm. "Are you sure you're okay?"

"I'm fine." She stepped in front of the Krulgs. "Gunak," she snarled in a voice that sounded just like a Krulg's. "Turlargan unbuldik wunur." She pointed at the first Krulg with her spear.

"Not only can she talk to animals, but she can sound like a Krulg too," Han whispered.

The Krulgs nodded and turned toward the castle; Oieda followed. Han skipped forward ahead of Bravic and Dean. As they followed the other Krulgs through the gate, the guards didn't even look up from their conversation. The Krulgskin suits were working.

The gates led to a wide courtyard, and as the real Krulgs turned to the right, Oieda headed straight toward a large building in the center. The others followed her. They crossed through a smashed door into a hallway littered with filth. A few Krulgs were there, either lying drunkenly on the floor or engaged in snarling arguments. The hallway was so wide you could drive two carts down it side by side.

Here, Bravic once again took the lead. He kept close to the wall as they made their way toward a door at the far end. But as they reached the middle of the hallway, two nearby Krulgs started pushing each other. One of them grabbed the other and pushed the Krulg into Oieda.

Both Oieda and the Krulg crashed to the floor. The Krulg's eyes widened as it stared into Oieda's face; its mouth formed a scream. Dean kicked the Krulg in the head, and it fell limp on top of Oieda.

She rolled the creature off her and got up hurriedly.

A deep, rough voice called from behind them. "Trugak. Vakin Larkork nugak."

They turned to see a massive Varlug motioning to them.

"Oieda, tell it to get lost," Dean whispered.

"I do not know how to speak Krulg," she whispered back. "I can only repeat what they have said. I do not know how to tell it to get lost."

"I'll tell it," Han offered, but Dean grabbed Han by the neck. "Just keep going," Dean muttered.

"Tarugak. Tarugak!" the Varlug bellowed.

Dean and his companions just kept on walking down the

hallway as if they hadn't heard a thing.

The Varlug roared, "Vaturack!" and charged after them.

Dean was about to burst into a sprint when the door at the end of the corridor opened, and another Varlug and a group of Krulgs walked out.

"Crud." Dean opened the nearest door and ordered, "In here!"

They sprinted inside, and Dean slammed and locked the door behind them.

Dean peered over his shoulder to see, to his horror, that they had entered some sort of dining hall where a hundred Krulgs were in the middle of a meal. The hall was lined with tables topped with food that spilled onto the floor. On the far wall, a life-sized carving of a dragon, ready to spring, spanned from end to end.

"I think we took a wrong turn, guys," Dean whispered.

Suddenly, the sound of steel upon steel filled the air. The evil creatures howled in glee and raced over to a corner of the room to witness some sort of fight. And as the crowd shifted, Dean spotted a shadowy sphere in the back of the hall.

"Stick to the wall. Move to the back," Dean said.

They hurried forward, keeping as far away from the real Krulgs as they could. When they reached the sphere, they saw the silhouette of a man suspended in its core.

Han gasped. "He must be Carimus!"

At that moment, the main doors to the hall burst open, and the Varlug that had pursued them earlier appeared. When its eyes came to rest upon the companions, it screamed in rage and drew its huge spear. With squeals of glee, the Krulgs parted to let the Varlug march forward.

"Well, I guess we don't need these disguises any longer," said Dean.

Han quickly unsheathed his dagger, Dean withdrew his

sword, and Bravic and Oieda freed their axe and spear. Then, as one, they thrust their weapons through the hides covering them, slicing them open from neck to belly. As the Krulgs in the hall watched in disbelief, they tore the skins right off.

"Stand aside!" Dean shouted.

His sword flashed brightly, swinging straight toward the gleaming sphere. With a blinding flash, it struck the red orb, and shafts of light engulfed the room. The sphere shimmered and then vanished. The old man suspended inside fell forward.

Bravic leaped ahead, low to the ground, and Carimus fell into his arms. "I got him!" Bravic yelled.

Dean's heart sank. He had expected Carimus to help them, but the old man lay unconscious in Bravic's arms. He looked across the room filled with Krulgs and felt as if he'd been kicked in the stomach.

"I've gotten us all killed," he said. "I'll try to distract them. Run for the exit."

Han and Oieda moved to stand beside him.

Carimus's eyes opened. "Run," he said weakly.

"That's a little hard right now," Dean said. "We're surrounded."

"If you freed me, you've awakened it," Carimus muttered. "Run," he whispered—and then he passed out.

The Varlug marched right up to them and pointed its spear at Dean. The Krulgs in the hall clustered into a circle around the companions and the Varlug.

So, this is it, Dean thought.

Then one of the Krulgs shrieked. Dean didn't know what it was saying, but he could hear the terror in its voice.

Everyone in the hall turned to look at the life-sized carving of the stone dragon on the wall. The dragon's eyes now glowed with a wicked life of their own. The massive stone dragon's head slowly turned, and the beast stepped out from the wall onto the floor. Great billowing swirls of smoke rose from its nostrils as its rock mouth snarled, spewing a great blast of flame straight at the crowd gathered around the companions. Those closest to the dragon were instantly burned.

The Varlug threw its spear not at Dean, but at the dragon. The weapon shattered against the stone.

Chaos erupted in the room.

"Run!" Dean yelled.

Bravic slung Carimus over his broad shoulders and the companions raced for the exit. The Krulgs had no interest in stopping them—they were interested only in their own escape—and a crush of bodies pressed through the doors. Another great wave of heat crashed over them, and the horrible cries of burned Krulgs filled the air.

Finally, they were out of the hall and racing down the hallway, fleeing right alongside terrified Krulgs. Behind them there was an enormous crash as the dragon drove its massive body through the doorway, no doubt destroying half the wall in the process. Its fiery breath moved ahead of it down the corridor, killing any unlucky stragglers.

Dean ran through the courtyard gates, into the shadows of the streets. The roads were filled with noisy confusion as some Krulgs ran to see what the commotion was while others ran to get away from it.

"That thing is coming after Carimus," Dean said. "Oieda, you couldn't . . . you know . . . talk to it?"

"What, are you crazy?" Oieda shrieked.

The dragon burst through the outer castle wall in a shower of rock and dust. With a tremendous thrust of its long wings, it soared up into the huge cavern that contained the underground city. Its breath fell like fiery rain upon the buildings below.

The companions ran once again, darting through the winding city streets and then down the long road leading to the exit from the mountain. Any Krulg who thought to stand in their way was struck down by bow, spear, or sword. Bravic shifted Carimus on his back and pushed on with greater speed.

Finally, they burst into the outside air. Dead Krulgs lay all around, arrows sticking from their chests. Dean smiled when he looked up and saw Dalvin's men at the ready all along the cliffs. Then he and the others threw themselves on their stomachs as a volley of arrows sped over their heads to strike down a group of Krulgs who were running from the opening behind them.

"Hold fire! Hold fire!" Dalvin ordered. "Dean! You're alive. And with Carimus!" Dalvin broke into a bewildered, delighted grin. "What's going on in there?"

"A stone dragon is free!" Han shouted.

"Well, that explains the panic," said Dalvin. "We'll deal with the dragon after we've dealt with the Krulgs. Come on, let's get you out of the line of fire."

Dalvin escorted them to safety along the cliffs. Two of his men took the unconscious body of Carimus from Bravic's shoulders and carried him away. Krulgs continued to pour from the mountain for some time, and as they did, they were cut down by hails of arrows from Dalvin's men.

And then a deathly silence fell over the mountain. All eyes looked to the smoking gates. A hundred bowstrings pulled back as one.

A massive shadow filled the gateway.

The dragon.

Arrows flew. But when they hit the beast, they merely bounced off its rock hide. And when a burst of flame shot from the beast's mouth, men fell, screaming, from the cliffs.

Dean ran forward; Oieda and Bravic raced after him. Han fired his bow and struck the dragon in its eye, but apparently even the creature's eye was made of stone, as the arrow shattered like glass.

Dean's sword swept downward against the dragon's foreleg, and a shower of sparks rose. But the sword had only chipped the surface of the stone hide. Oieda darted underneath the beast's belly and thrust her spear upward, but it shattered in her hands.

Bravic's axe stopped at the peak of his swing. He stood at the side of the beast, motionlessly staring at the dragon. He lifted the ax high above his head, but again he stopped. The beast swung its massive tail. Bravic tried to leap above it, but the tail caught his boots and he flipped end over end before landing hard on his shoulder. His ax skidded across the cobblestones.

Oieda stared at Bravic for only a moment before turning back to the dragon and drawing her dagger. She thrust it at the dragon's leg. But it was no more useful than her spear, and the blade snapped at the hilt.

The dragon's focus was still on the archers; it breathed again, and more men screamed in flames.

Dean jumped at the dragon's neck and grabbed on with one hand. He started to climb, intending to get on the creature's back, but a mighty twist of the beast's neck shook him off, and he landed in a heap at the dragon's feet. His vision was blurry and he couldn't rise.

The beast looked down at Dean. It snarled and raised its massive head, revealing rows of gleaming stone teeth.

"If you want to eat something, why not eat me?" Bravic called out.

Oieda looked up. Bravic had leapt onto a rock and was waving his hands over his head.

"Don't eat him. He's too sour!" Han yelled, rushing to stand right in front of the dragon. "You want something tasty like me." He was trembling from head to toe as he looked over at Dean and Oieda. "Run," he mouthed.

Oieda tried to lift Dean off the cobblestones, but he was too heavy. So Oieda ran away from Dean, shouting, "He's too small for you. You need someone bigger."

"I'm the plumpest, dragon," Bravic bellowed as he jumped up and down. "And my people have killed more dragons than anyone."

The dragon roared in rage. Its massive jaws opened, and its head swept down at the Dwarf.

Dean shook his head, and everything came back into focus. He was lying on the cobblestones. Oieda and Han were jumping up and down, screaming something, and Dean's heart nearly stopped when he saw the sheer terror on Han's face. Dean followed Han's gaze.

The dragon was about to eat Bravic.

"Bravic!" Dean screamed.

The Dwarf leaped upward, and the dragon's jaws snapped closed over him.

"No!" Han howled.

The dragon turned and threw back its head. Its jaws opened and great billows of smoke poured from its mouth. It swung its head from side to side, and its massive tail beat the ground.

Oieda raced over and grabbed Dean's arm. "Run!" she screamed, half dragging him toward the cliffs and away from the thrashing beast.

Han stood frozen in place. Tears poured down his face as he stared at the dragon.

Suddenly, a great crack appeared in the dragon's neck. It lifted its head, and the crack ripped open to its belly. Molten rock flowed down to its clawed feet, and its red jeweled eyes shattered. Its massive head fell forward and slammed to the ground. Black smoke poured from its open mouth.

It was dead.

Dean looked at the dragon, and tears flowed down his soot-covered face. Silence had once again fallen over the mountain. No one moved. No one spoke. The warriors stood with lowered heads. Not even the wind stirred.

A hero had died.

Then one long horn call split the air. Everyone turned to look at Han as the Elvana lowered the battle horn from his trembling lips.

"Volesunga!" Oieda screamed. She raised her fist in salute, and the call and tribute was answered by all Dalvin's warriors.

Han walked to the dragon's mouth and sank to his knees. Dean and Oieda knelt beside him. Dean bowed his head and closed his eyes.

A second later, his eyes snapped open. From somewhere in the dragon's mouth, he heard a grumble. And then, from the dragon's mouth, a pair of boots emerged. With a cry of hope, Dean sprang forward. He, Han, and Oieda grabbed hold of the boots and pulled a slightly charred Dwarf from the mouth.

As they turned Bravic over, he coughed.

"He's alive!" Dean announced, and a hail of cheers rose throughout the mountainside.

"Of course I'm alive." Bravic grimaced as he sat up. He turned his wrist, and the small shield on his arm snapped open. "This little shield stops everything." He grinned and then shrank the shield back to its small size. "Now what're you staring at?" He glared at his smiling companions. When he touched his face, his eyes went wide. "Don't tell me," he cried in despair.

Han's little arms clasped halfway around Bravic's chest as tears ran down his face. "Don't worry, Bravic. Your beard will grow back."

17

GOLDEN ARMOR

Dean looked to the sky and stretched his arms. It was hard for him to think that Bravic had killed the dragon only two days earlier.

"Dalvin said farewell again," Han reported as he and the others approached, smiling. "He's getting the men organized to search for more Krulgs while Navarro takes the credit for everything."

"Are the Krulg reinforcements still camping in the valley?" Dean asked.

"No." Han smiled and danced a little jig. "They didn't head back to Naviak either. They scattered."

Oieda laughed. "The cowards were too scared to come here and too afraid to go back to Volsur, so they ran!" She set her new spear on her back and grinned broadly.

"That leaves even fewer troops in Naviak." Dean looked north. "Any news on Carimus?"

Han frowned. "Carimus is still unconscious. He might be out for days."

Dean had hoped that somehow Carimus would help them. Now time was running out, and there was no way of telling how long they'd have to wait for Carimus to awaken, let alone be strong enough to help.

"Our horses are ready," Oieda said. "They may not be the finest, but they're the best Dalvin could offer. It's not far now."

Oieda's last words seemed to strike Dean somewhere deep in his chest.

***

As they rode away from the mountain city, the early morning fog clung to the ground and swirled around the horses' hooves. The sun was hidden behind thick black clouds that hung motionless in the air. Dean's horse pranced and skittered, straying off the path, and he struggled to bring it under control.

"I don't like what's happening to the horses," Oieda said after they'd been journeying a while.

"What do you mean, happening to them?" Han asked.

"This change in their mood. None speak to me now, but they whisper among themselves."

"What do they say?" Han now regarded the horses suspiciously.

"I only catch parts, but what I hear is not good. We should watch them. They want to run."

"As if we didn't have enough to worry about," Bravic grumbled, "now we have to guard our own mounts."

They traveled for three days before they finally left the mountain behind. The skies were overcast, and the nights were without stars or moon. But on the fourth day the sun at last broke through the clouds, shining on a beautiful grove of golden trees in a clearing below them. As they rode closer, they could make out old stone benches in the shade of the trees.

"I say we take a break and have some lunch," Han suggested.

"And I agree with that." Bravic smiled.

They galloped down and slid off their horses onto the thick, green grass.

"Why are these benches here?" Dean asked.

"For sitting for lunch." Han grinned as he began to ready a

cold lunch for everyone.

"Or for napping," Bravic added with a large yawn as he stretched out on a bench.

"We're just going to eat, then we're getting out of here," Dean said. Something about this spot made him uneasy.

They ate a small meal and talked. Their spirits were high with the sun shining down on them for the first time in days. Soon they were all stretched out on the benches and talking lazily as they gazed up at the blue sky.

One by one, they fell asleep.

***

Dean sat bolt upright as thunder ripped the sky open. He jumped to his feet and gawked at the storm that raged overhead. He spun around. The other benches were empty.

"Oieda? Bravic? Han?" He screamed to be heard over the howl of the wind, but there was no reply. "Where are you guys?" he called.

Suddenly, the wind stopped, and the air became deathly quiet.

"Crud." Dean drew his sword. "Something bad is going to happen."

"Are you scared, warrior?" a voice sneered from behind him.

Dean raised his sword as he spun around. Standing before him was a thin man dressed in black robes. His hair was the color of coal, and his face was thin and pale. His black eyes locked on Dean's, and Dean felt as if an evil hand clutched at his heart.

"So you're the one my brother chose to defeat me." The man's mouth twisted into a sarcastic smile.

"Volsur?" Dean cried in disbelief.

"I hope he prepared you to die, fool," Volsur growled as he walked forward.

"Where are my friends?" Dean demanded, leveling his sword at Volsur's chest.

"They're dead." Volsur grinned.

With a cry of rage Dean thrust his sword at Volsur, but Volsur vanished when the blade touched his chest.

"Fool," Volsur said coldly from behind him.

Dean spun around. Volsur's hand shot out and wrapped around Dean's throat. With a snarl, Volsur lifted Dean into the air, and his other hand clamped down on Dean's sword arm.

Volsur smiled. "You have failed."

Dean tried to struggle but couldn't move. His lungs cried for air, and his heart pounded in his ears.

Then Dean heard a voice call to him as if from very far away. "Butterflies," it said. He could only just make it out.

Volsur's hand squeezed tighter around his throat.

"Butterflies," came the voice again.

Suddenly, Volsur vanished in a swirl of smoke, and Dean found himself back on his feet, hundreds of colorful butterflies all around him. The green grass was back, the sky was blue, and the sun was shining. He laughed.

Oieda rushed up to him. She was wearing a light-brown dress with white trim. Her green eyes sparkled as she took his hands. Dean opened his mouth, but no words came out.

As butterflies circled around them, Oieda leaned in, and her head tilted back. Dean pulled her close. Her breath was warm on his lips, and her hair smelled of lily of the valley. They kissed. Her lips were smooth and soft. His heart raced. She smiled, and a little dimple appeared on her cheek.

"Butterflies."

Dean's eyes snapped open. He was lying on his back and staring up at the gray sky. The trees above him were no longer the golden ones he had fallen asleep under, but dead, twisted trees whose skeletal branches clutched at the sky.

He sprang to his feet. Han, Oieda, and Bravic stared back at him, and they all looked very pale. Dean looked down and realized they had not been lying on benches; they had been lying on graves.

"Let's get out of here," Dean said, and all four turned and raced for their horses.

They galloped far away from the graveyard.

Once they were a good distance away, they slowed. "What happened back there?" Dean asked.

"Well," Han began, "I fell asleep and began to have a very bad nightmare. It felt so real. Anyway, I don't like nightmares, so I decided to think about something else. I thought about butterflies, and soon they were all around me. I tried to catch one, and I fell off the grave. That's when I saw we were in a graveyard. All of you were yelling and kicking in your sleep. I started to shake you, but you wouldn't wake up."

"Evil magic," Oieda spat.

"When I couldn't wake you, I thought about how I woke up. So I thought if you thought about something nice, you'd dream about that and wake up."

"Butterflies," Bravic grumbled. "You couldn't have said girls?"

Dean and Han laughed, while Oieda rolled her eyes.

***

They made camp very late that night, as none were too eager to sleep again. Bravic took first watch, and then woke Han to take over.

While Han sat watch, the shadows seemed to dance and swirl, and he jumped at every noise. His knuckles turned white as he grasped his little bow, and his eyes burned as he stared into the woods.

Something drew his eyes to the horses, which were tied to a tree. Their eyes shone in the night. Suddenly, all five burst forward as one and snapped the straps that held them to the tree. Four ran straight into the woods, but one ran straight for Han. He drew back an arrow, but as the horse raced toward him, the arrow stayed in his hand. The horse reared up; its legs rose over Han, preparing to crash down on him.

Oieda pulled him out of the way.

They tumbled to the ground, and the horse galloped off after the others. Bravic and Dean sprang to their feet and raced into the woods after the fleeing mounts.

"Thank you," Han said with a frown. "The horse didn't know what it was doing."

"Yes, it did." Oieda got up. "It made a choice."

"But this dark ... Volsur made the horse do it," Han said.

"No. There's a dark pull on the spirit, but in the end, the choice is still yours." Oieda stared into Han's eyes.

Han nodded.

After several minutes, Dean and Bravic came panting back into camp. "They got away," Dean said.

"Now what're we going to do?" Han asked.

"The horses are gone," said Oieda. "They will go to the plain, and we will never catch them."

"Then we go on foot," Dean said.

They gathered up what little they had and walked down the path in silence.

***

When next they camped again, none slept for a long time—and when sleep did come, they tossed and turned and woke frequently.

In the middle of the night, Dean woke with his heart racing

in his chest. Faint noises came from the shadows. His eyes scanned the woods, but the night was still. Then Han sat straight up and screamed madly as his eyes flew open. An eerie silence swept down upon them, broken only by Han's labored breathing.

"Couldn't sleep, either?" Dean whispered, moving closer to Han.

"You don't have to whisper." Bravic turned over. "If I wasn't already awake and staring like a cornered rabbit at the dark, that scream would have woken me up."

Oieda shivered. "I do not like the feel of the woods now."

"Can we get going early today?" Han looked around nervously, all sleep now gone from his eyes.

"It's the middle of the night. I don't think we should trample around these pitch-black woods at midnight," Dean said.

Han's head turned, and the others looked to where he now stared. They heard a sound, as if someone was laughing, but it was so soft they weren't sure.

"Midnight or not, I want to go." Han backed away from the sound, and everyone silently agreed.

They moved at a quick pace, looking over their shoulders as they walked. They felt as if a new, unseen, unknown enemy was at their heels. Han broke into a trot, and the others followed. The noises around them slowly grew louder. Oieda jumped when she saw two eyes appear and then vanish.

Then the woods abruptly ended, and they found themselves on an overgrown path. As if in silent agreement, they broke into a headlong run. Sticks slashed their faces and roots grabbed their feet as they surged onward. The route sloped down, and they slipped and tumbled, only to scramble to their feet and continue their plunge. As they reached the bottom of the slope, they raced across a valley with perspiration pouring down their faces.

Suddenly, Oieda stopped and screamed, "Wait!"

The others froze. All stood panting and staring at one another.

"I know the beasts that chase us," she gasped.

"Beasts? You mean there is more than one?" Han cried.

"They are Vereortu. They create fear and feed off it," she said grimly.

"Vereortu?" Dean said. "Those are the things Norouk ruled."

Han turned to run, but Bravic's hand came down upon his shoulder. "We don't know how many there are or if Norouk still rules them. It's been many years since Norouk."

"But Volsur was around then." Han struggled against Bravic's hold. "And Carimus. And Ranadin. They're alive. Why wouldn't Norouk be?"

"Whether he is or isn't," Dean said, "we can't just run until we die of exhaustion."

"You want to stay here?" Han asked.

"It's almost morning. We've run half the night. We can't run any farther. I say we stay and see." Dean's eyes searched the faces of the others.

Oieda leaned close to Han and whispered something in his ear.

"I'll stay," Han grumbled. He kicked a white stone at his feet.

They paced, peering into the darkness. After another anxious hour, Dean offered to take watch so the others could lie down and rest—or at least try. As the night sky began to lighten, Oieda came over and sat down beside him.

"Hey." Dean smiled.

"It is almost first light."

"Thanks for calming Han down," Dean said.

She smiled.

"What did you say to him?"

She shrugged and shook her head, her ponytail bouncing

back and forth. "Nothing."

Dean noticed her cheeks flush. "What? Come on. I know you said something."

Oieda's eyes danced, and she blushed more. "I told him he had to be brave so you would not get scared."

"Me?" Dean exhaled. "Yeah, I'm a big scaredy-cat."

"I was trying to make him feel better." She grinned. "You are mostly brave."

Dean raised an eyebrow. "Mostly? I've never freaked out and gotten all girly scared."

Her smile vanished. "What is that supposed to mean?"

"Sorry. It's just an expression." He held up a hand. "A bad expression. I meant I haven't like ... gone all screaming and throwing my hands in the air."

"What about with the skeletons?"

"Okay, the first time I saw a dead guy go back together, I was freaked out. You get a point for that."

"The dragon?" Her dimple popped.

"It was a huge stone dragon walking out of a wall. Everyone freaked out."

She leaned her head to the side and raised an eyebrow.

"Two points for you," Dean muttered.

"What about—?"

"Enough." Dean shook his head. "I get a little wigged out when something totally Twilight Zone wacky happens. But other than that, I'm a rock."

"A rock?" Her lips pressed together.

"You're smiling." Dean leaned forward.

"I am not."

"You are too! I can see it."

"I am not!" She rolled her eyes, and her dimple popped out again.

"You are too. Your dimple shows when you smile."

Her hand went to her face, and she looked away.

"What did I say now? I didn't mean that in a bad way. It's cute."

Oieda froze.

"I mean ... I think ... don't freak out, okay?" Dean rubbed his forehead.

A ray of sunlight swept down, streaked across the ground, and passed over them. Dean looked around the valley floor and felt as though someone had squeezed his heart and stopped it from beating. Mixed with the sand were thousands of bleached-white human bones.

Dean exhaled and tried to keep his voice steady. "I think I know what valley we're in."

Han sat bolt upright. "We're in Grenadil!" he screamed.

They all leapt to their feet.

All around them dark shapes appeared, silhouetted in the faint light, their forms bent and twisted. Somehow Dean knew—he felt it—that these were the Vereortu, the creatures who had driven them here last night. Hundreds of high, cackling voices united into one twisted, evil laugh as they jumped from side to side. Then, from their midst, a figure appeared, sunlight shimmering on his golden armor. The wicked beasts stopped their advance and quivered with excitement as the golden-armored man walked through their ranks and stopped a hundred feet from Dean.

"Norouk," Dean spat, his hand gripping the hilt of his sword.

"Welcome to the Valley of Death," Norouk shouted. A grin crossed his gnarled face. "Four vagabonds. I wish you were more of a challenge for me. Be afraid. Before you stands the mighty Norouk!" He raised his sword.

Dean noticed Oieda had moved to their packs. He didn't know what she was doing, but he was sure she was up to something. "Mighty Norouk?" Dean scoffed. "Whenever I've heard the name Norouk, the word mighty was never before it. It was more like 'that traitor Norouk' or 'that dog Norouk.' Mostly, it was 'that coward Norouk.'" Dean laughed.

Oieda rushed back to Dean's side. "Do you always have to enrage your enemies?" she whispered.

Dean's smirk vanished. "Get ready to run. I'll catch up to you guys."

"Do you intend to fight them all?" Oieda grabbed his arm.

"I'll stall and give you guys a head start. I'm fastest, remember? I'll run for the front of the valley and try to get them to come after me."

"Come forward," Norouk called out. "Kneel at my feet and surrender."

Dean smiled. "Sure. Let's keep this between you and me. Maybe we can work this out."

Oieda grabbed his arm. "Dean, wait." Her body pressed against his.

Dean looked down into her green eyes, which were filled with concern. His gaze traveled down to her lips. He tilted his head and leaned in to kiss her.

"What are you doing?" she asked. She pressed Graylen's shield against his hand. "Ranadin believed this shield would avenge the Wardevars' deaths."

Dean cleared his throat. "I thought you were going to ki— Uh, thanks." He grabbed the shield and rolled his shoulders.

"Come forward," Norouk bellowed. "Or are you afraid?"

"You're a big, tough guy with a hundred guys backing you up. I bet you're too cowardly to fight without your little twitchy friends," Dean said, keeping the shield behind his back. Dean glanced at Oieda and whispered, "Get ready to run."

"You dare taunt me, boy?" Norouk screamed in rage, and the Vereortu cackled in glee. "You think you're man enough to fight a warrior such as me?" The veins in his neck bulged.

"Man enough? I wouldn't ask a dog to lower himself to fight you." Dean held his hands out to the side, his sword pointed down and Graylen's shield facing backward. "I think you're all talk. If it wasn't for your fear freaks, you'd be sucking your thumb and running away. I bet you're wearing a diaper under that armor. That's why it's so yellow."

Han laughed.

The Vereortu lifted their hands and clicked their claws together.

Dean's blood ran cold, and his stomach twisted.

"Hold your ground," Oieda snarled. "They cause this fear. Fight it."

Dean glanced back at his companions. They were pale, but they had their weapons drawn. "Just me and him," Dean insisted.

"Stay back," Norouk ordered the Vereortu. "This is my fight."

"You're fighting your own battles?" Dean said. "Well, I guess there's a first time for everything." Dean walked forward and Norouk stomped out to meet him.

"It's a pity that Volsur wants you all alive," Norouk said. "But he didn't say I had to bring your friends back with all of their limbs."

Dean's chest tightened. Only ten feet separated them. "Your fight is with me."

"You come to fight me, and you don't even know how to hold a shield," Norouk sneered.

"You want to see my shield?" Dean asked with a cold smirk. Dean spun the shield around and held it before him.

Nothing happened.

Norouk laughed.

Dean looked down at the shield. He had expected ... something. Wasn't that what Ranadin had said? Wasn't this shield supposed to give the Wardevars' their vengeance against Norouk?

"Look out!" Oieda screamed.

Norouk swung his sword at Dean's head. Dean raised the shield just in time. The blow rang off the metal, and Dean stumbled backward.

"Nothing happened!" Dean yelled to Bravic. "Did I do something wrong?"

Norouk swung again, and Dean danced out of the way.

"Repeat the words!" Bravic shouted.

"What words?" Dean shouted back.

"The dying Wardevar's last words!"

"I don't remember them! What are they?"

Bravic looked abashed. "I don't remember them either!"

Dean groaned and dodged another attack.

"Shake the shield around!" Oieda yelled.

"Shake it?" Dean rolled his eyes. "Like that will help."

"Well, you could at least try!" Oieda threw her hands up.

"You're in the wrong spot!" Han yelled. "The words included something about being 'on this spot'! The spot where he was killed!"

Dean blocked another blow with his shield and staggered to the side.

"You're no match for me," Norouk sneered.

"What spot should I be in?" Dean shouted, raising his shield again. His bicep throbbed, and the heavy shield was quickly tiring him.

"Up on that rock!" Han was jumping up and down and pointing at a rock more than fifty yards away and twenty feet tall. A stone slope ran from the valley floor to a wide flat area on top. "That's the spot where he killed Graylen!"

At the mention of the name, Norouk turned to glare at the Elvana. "How do you know that name?" he demanded, taking a step forward.

As soon as Norouk turned his back on Dean, Dean lowered his shield, took three huge strides, and smashed into him.

Norouk flew backward and crashed to the ground.

Dean looked at the Vereortu, which formed a circle around them. "Bravic," he shouted. "I need to get to that rock."

"Then you will," Bravic roared, charging forward. "Follow me!"

Bravic swung his ax in a huge arc, and the Vereortu darted out of the way. Dean moved behind him, and Han darted behind Dean, firing arrow after arrow in front of them. Oieda brought up the rear, her spear flashing out. The Vereortu shrieked, but they stayed back from the Elven warrior with the blazing green eyes.

"Get them! Do not kill them, but stop them!" Norouk commanded as he rose to his feet.

The Vereortu shrieked and rushed at Bravic. Two jumped on his back. "RUN!" he bellowed. He leaned forward and charged, dragging the Vereortu with him before collapsing to the ground.

Oieda jumped in front of Dean, and Han shifted to protect the rear. The three of them continued to move toward the rock. Dean's sword and Han's bow cut down the Vereortu while Oieda's spear swept them out of their way.

Then Han shot one creature at point-blank range. The beast's body crashed into his, and Han stumbled back. Another creature lunged forward and knocked Han's bow from his hand.

"Don't worry about me!" Han said as he drew his dagger. "Get to the spot!" His little blade sliced the Vereortu.

Oieda's spear drove through another Vereortu and stuck fast. She set her foot against its chest and ripped her spear free.

"Duck!" Dean yelled as a Vereortu leaped at her.

Oieda crouched, and Dean's sword hacked the Vereortu, which collapsed to the ground.

They were now only ten yards from the rock.

"Stop them!" Norouk ordered, pushing Vereortu out of his way. "They have Graylen's shield!"

A Vereortu clutched at Oieda's spear, and she sank her dagger into its chest. "Keep going!" she screamed at Dean.

Dean ran past her. Two Vereortu blocked his way. He smashed one aside with his shield and cut down the other with his sword.

His heart caught in his throat as he heard Oieda scream behind him. Even as he ran, he couldn't stop himself from glancing back.

The horde of Vereortu had dragged down his three companions. Bravic struggled to rise. Han's little hands tried to cover his head as the beasts stomped him. One creature held Oieda's ponytail and punched her in the face. But her eyes locked on Dean's. "RUN!"

Dean sprinted up the slope. Halfway up, a Vereortu grabbed at his legs. Dean tumbled to the ground. Several more Vereortu rushed him. He kicked one and sent it screaming off the side. Clawed hands seized his legs and reached for his arms. He smashed one with the shield. Another one pinned his sword arm to the ground.

Dean looked at the top of the rock, still ten yards away.

Two more Vereortu jumped on his legs. He couldn't escape them. He wouldn't escape them.

He had only one option left.

Dean threw the shield.

It was as if the battle stopped. Everyone paused to watch Graylen's shield sail through the air. The metal clanged as it bounced off the rock twice. Then it rolled a few feet into a sandy area and fell flat.

The valley was silent as everyone waited.

Nothing happened.

Norouk rushed up the ramp, racing right past Dean. Dean could see the fear in his eyes. Atop the rock, Norouk stopped, bent at the waist, and peered down at the shield like it was a snake, coiled to spring.

Then he turned back to Dean and exhaled.

"It is, indeed, Graylen's shield," he mumbled as he pushed it with his boot. "But it's just a piece of metal." He chuckled.

A murmur ran through the ranks of the Vereortu.

Norouk tipped his head back and laughed. His laughter rang off the walls of the valley. The Vereortu joined in, their wicked chirps and shrieks growing so loud that Dean would have covered his ears if his arms weren't pinned down by the creatures.

Then the shield began to glow.

At first Dean couldn't see it from where he was down the slope, but he saw its reflection in Norouk's eyes—and he saw the fear on Norouk's face. Then the glow grew until it seemed to fill the valley with a radiance that shifted and pulsed.

Norouk screamed.

In response, a deafening cheer rose from a thousand human voices. Dean's mouth fell open as he looked around at an army of warriors filling the valley. One, standing just above Dean, looked down at him.

"Thank you." The silver-haired man gave a sweeping bow. "This fight is no longer yours. It's ours." The man drew a silver sword and strode up the slope to face Norouk.

"Graylen?" Norouk said with horror and disbelief. "Coren?"

A young man moved to stand beside Graylen. His armor was dented and battered, but he had a regal bearing.

"Norouk." Coren raised his hand, and the men behind him drew their swords.

"Coren, wait," Norouk pleaded. "Let me explain. I let Graylen have his last words. Give me mine. Let me explain."

Coren stepped forward. "Traitors don't deserve last words." His sword drove straight through Norouk's breast.

As Norouk slumped to the ground, a deafening roar came from the warriors. They raised their swords and attacked their murderers. The four companions turned their eyes from the carnage as the warriors of Wardevar crushed every last Vereortu in only a few gruesome minutes.

When the last of the Vereortu had fallen, the warriors let loose a triumphant cheer that swelled into a gust. The warriors stamped their feet and cried louder. The gust turned into a gale that swept about the companions and blinded them with flying sand, and the swirling wind's shriek grew so loud that Dean pressed his hands over his ears and tucked his chin against his chest.

And then, as suddenly as the wind started, it stopped. The valley floor had been swept smooth, with no trace of Norouk, the Vereortu, or the Wardevar.

And then a faint sound came from the end of the valley. A voice, singing. They couldn't make out the words of the song, but they rose beautifully into the air. Slowly, the singing faded away, and only the last lingering notes echoed softly through the valley.

18

THE LION MAN

Dean awoke with a start. It was midday, and he'd only slept for a couple of hours, but the events of the morning seemed to have taken place long before. As he looked up at the sky, he saw it was again filled with black clouds, only now they seemed nearer and darker. He looked to the north, over the woods that stretched before them. Soon they would be at Naviak.

The others were soon ready to move, though they were still weary. As they looked at Dean, he straightened up. He didn't have a plan yet, but he didn't want to tell them that.

They decided to travel through the woods and not on the main road. Oieda led the way as they silently slipped between the trees like shadows wrapped around the trunks. The days were cheerless, for they spoke little, whether because of the foul, cold weather or their thoughts about what would soon happen. The nights were pitch black; no stars shined, and no wind stirred the trees. The woods were filled with invisible creatures that moved and chattered in the darkness. They chanced no fire and slept little.

Late on the sixth day, the woods thinned. As the shadows lengthened, they could see the lights of the city ahead. They stopped to camp and to plan.

Dean drew a circle in the dirt with a stick. He drew a gate with a stick figure next to it. "This is Naviak. Dalvin said the city itself is guarded by humans."

"Filthy traitors." Oieda spat on the stick figure.

"That's kinda gross, but funny." Han grinned. "Why does Volsur have humans watch the city?"

"Because Krulgs would kill the slaves too often," Bravic said.

"Slaves?" Dean asked.

"Under Volsur's rule, there are two options: soldier or slave," Bravic explained.

"Great," Dean said. "Anyway, inside the city Dalvin said it should be almost all humans. That means we can blend in. You know, when in Rome . . ."

"Rome?" Han asked.

"It's a city in my world ... oh, skip it. We have to act like them. Blend in. Instead of skins, now we have to wear masks."

"That means you keep your big mouth closed." Bravic pointed at Han.

Han sat up straighter but pressed his lips together.

"Good work already." Oieda patted Han on the back, and Han smirked at Bravic.

"The castle's a different story," Dean said. "Dalvin said it's guarded by Krulgs and Varlugs. He doesn't know how many, but I don't think it will be a lot."

"Why? It's Volsur's castle. Wouldn't he surround himself with an army?" Bravic asked.

"This is Volsur we're talking about," Dean said. "He's prideful. I bet he thinks he doesn't need an army around himself."

"It still will not be easy," Oieda said.

Dean nodded. "There's another thing, and I have to say this. Tomorrow we'll be in Naviak. I don't have a plan for how to get in besides just walking through the gate. I also don't have a plan for how to get out. What I'm saying is ... if we do make it to Volsur, I don't see any of us making it back out."

"We know," Oieda said.

"What I'm saying is ... we might die. I might get you all killed, and I really don't know if it's fair for me to ask that of you."

Han leapt to his feet. "You never asked me. I said I was coming."

"And I told you I was coming," Bravic growled. "I'll tell you again, too, if you have any crazy notion of trying to leave me behind."

"Dean," said Oieda. "We all came with you because we chose to. If we must die to defeat Volsur, then we must die."

"Then we'll all go?"

The three nodded.

***

They woke to a morning almost as black as the night. A thick fog seemed to press into them. They ate nothing, as their supplies were exhausted. So it was with heavy hearts and light stomachs that they started on their way toward Naviak.

In a few miles, they came to a dirt road where people moved toward the city. Their clothes were tattered and worn, and their forlorn faces were downcast. Although their carts were light with what little belongings they had, they pushed them as if they were heavily loaded.

The wall around the city rose as they approached. Over the enormous bulwark, they could see buildings of stone and wood outlined in the gray fog. At the immense open iron gates, a group of bleary-eyed human soldiers stood leaning against the wall. Their armor was as dirty as their unshaven faces.

As the companions crossed through the gate, the world seemed to get darker; the fog became thicker and blacker.

Coming toward the center of the city, the streets opened to a large marketplace filled with people. Booths that sold all types of material—none of it appearing clean or well-made—were scattered about as haphazardly as the people who shopped at them. And in the center of the market a small crowd had gathered around a makeshift wooden stage, where a thin man dressed in rich blue robes shouted something down to the crowd.

At a motion from the blue-robed man, three burly men led onto the stage a figure that appeared to be part lion and part man. At least seven feet tall, the Lion-Man wore only leather pants, as his upper body was covered with golden hair, and the mane of a lion surrounded his human face. He was bound with a thick collar, and leather straps around his neck led down to his hands and ankles.

The blue-robed man's voice boomed. "What am I bid for this rare commodity? Half-man, half-beast. Strong as a bear and unique as a Penilique."

"Seventy-five," a grizzled man called.

"One hundred and twenty-five," bellowed a dirty soldier who pushed his way to the front.

"Five hundred," offered a man dressed in rich red robes.

"Five hundred? Now that's more like it for a Leomane," said the blue-robed man, apparently an auctioneer. "They're rarer than rare on this side of the sea."

"Five fifty," the grizzled soldier snarled.

"Seven fifty," the red-robed man replied.

"One thousand," the soldier barked. He glared at the red-robed man and placed his hand on the hilt of his sword.

A silence descended upon the crowd, and a curled grin came to the auctioneer's fat face. Dean felt inside his jacket pockets. His lighter was all he found. He'd forgotten he had it. The real-world money he'd gotten from Panadur had long since been lost, not that it would have done him any good here.

"Do you have any money?" Dean asked.

"You can't be thinking what I think you're thinking," Bravic muttered. "Look at that soldier's insignia: crossed swords on red. It matches all the other soldiers', and they're all paying attention."

"They're bidding on a slave," Dean said. "This isn't right."

"Neither is getting us all killed," Oieda whispered.

"One thousand. Going once?" boomed the auctioneer as he looked greedily over the audience.

"What are you buying him for?" the red-robed man asked the soldier. "I have a collection of oddities I display; we could split the ticket."

"No dice." The soldier shook his head. "I want him for the fights."

Dean turned to Bravic. "Did you hear that? I have to do this."

"It's a small fortune," Bravic said.

"Going twice?" the auctioneer squealed, and the soldier smiled.

"Bravic, please?"

Bravic looked at Dean for a second, then dove into his pack and pulled out the gold pouch they'd recovered from beneath the Hall of Warriors.

"I bid this!" Dean held up two handfuls of gold coins.

A gasp came from the crowd.

The auctioneer stared speechlessly. He opened and closed his mouth with no sound coming out. "Sold!" he finally squealed.

As Dean crossed to the platform, the soldier's eyes bulged, and he looked ready to explode with anger. Dean tossed the gold to the auctioneer with a look of distaste. All the color left the auctioneer's face as he gasped at his treasure.

Dean approached the Lion-Man and took the chain that a guard held out to him. As he walked down the platform, he whispered, "Don't worry." He hoped the Leomane could understand him.

"Just out of curiosity," Han asked Bravic, "how much money was that?"

"One thousand, four hundred and sixty-three gold," Bravic grumbled. "But who's counting?"

"It wouldn't do us any good anyway. By tomorrow, we're all going to be dead," Oieda said with a lopsided smile.

Bravic chuckled, and Han gulped.

"Thank you, all," Dean said to the others as he rejoined them, leading the Leomane. He looked back at the soldier, who stared blackly at him. "Let's go somewhere to talk."

The five walked to a tavern around the corner, its worn sign too faded to read. The interior was only slightly lighter than the gloom outside, and dark clouds of smoke swirled around the ceiling. The many tables were mostly deserted, but a few men were slumped at a grimy bar along the wall.

Following Bravic, the others headed to a table in the corner. As they sat down, the Leomane remained standing.

"Sit." Dean indicated the wooden bench, but the Leomane stood, unmoving. "Please, sit?"

The Leomane stared straight ahead.

"Can you understand me?" Dean asked. "Sit," he said, motioning to the bench.

The Leomane moved so quickly Dean didn't even see him coming. He grabbed Dean by the throat and snarled, "I'm not an animal."

Oieda's dagger pressed against the Leomane's side. "Then don't act like one," she growled. "Let him go."

The Leomane's hand opened.

Dean took a step back and exhaled. "Just sit down for a second, okay?"

As they all sat back down, the Leomane slowly lowered himself onto the bench. A thin, hawk-nosed man in a stained apron swaggered up to their table.

"What do you want?" he rasped to no one in particular.

Dean cast a glance around the table, and Oieda felt her small purse. "Five breakfasts."

"We don't serve slaves." The man cocked his head at the Leomane.

"One can't be too cautious when one eats in strange places," Dean said coldly. "The slave eats first."

The man nodded his head approvingly and walked away.

"I didn't mean that," Dean said quickly. "What's your name?"

"Kala Panteoth," the Lion-Man said curtly.

"I'm Dean. And this is Han."

"Nice to meet you," the Elvana said with a broad smile and quick bow.

"Bravic." Bravic nodded.

"And you've met Oieda," Dean said.

Oieda smiled awkwardly.

"We'll get food," Dean whispered, "and once we're sure the soldiers aren't watching, we'll let you go free."

Kala frowned. "You expect me to believe that you paid a fortune to feed me breakfast and let me go?"

"I don't believe it myself," Bravic grumbled. "But it's true."

"Once we eat—" Dean began, but Oieda's foot kicking him beneath the table cut him off.

"I don't think we're going to be able to eat," Han whined. He tilted his head to the doorway.

Several soldiers had just walked into the room. They immediately moved toward the companions' table.

"Their insignias—crossed swords on red—they're the same as the man you outbid for Kala," Oieda pointed out.

Dean pressed his dagger against Kala's wrist.

"You buy me to kill me?" Kala snarled.

"He's setting you free, stupid," Bravic snapped as Dean cut Kala's straps.

"Why?" Kala asked with a mixture of mistrust and disbelief. "So I can die fighting while you escape?"

"No!" Han blurted, now upset. "That's just the way he is. He was going to set you free the whole time."

Kala scanned Dean's face. Dean shrugged.

As the soldiers walked forward, Bravic started to pass his ax to Kala, but Kala pushed it back. "Thank you," he said, "but you keep it. I'm sure you can use it better than I, and I need a slightly bigger weapon." Kala leapt to his feet and cast his bonds aside. He ripped the collar from his neck and roared.

The soldiers stopped in their tracks. Kala picked up the long wooden bench and swung it into the first two soldiers, sending them halfway across the room.

Two other soldiers turned to run, then stopped as several more ran in, including the soldier Dean had outbid.

The companions readied their weapons and moved back against the wall, prepared for an onslaught. Kala tossed the broken bench aside and snapped a thick leg off the table.

"Go," Kala said. "I can hold them off." He smiled grimly.

"We go together." Dean drew his sword.

Han pulled on the handle of the back door, but it wouldn't budge. "This door's locked. The only other one is past them. If only Carimus were here. He'd have some spell with smoke and fire."

Smoke and fire, huh? That gave Dean an idea. He thrust his hand into his pocket, pulled out his lighter, and held it above his head. Waving his hands in the air and trying his best to sound ominous, Dean chanted:

"Yabba-dabba-doo
I curse you.

May this Bic do the trick
And your mothers all get sick.
May this spell fry your tails
And turn you all into snails!"

He lit the lighter and turned up the flame.

"He's a wizard!" one soldier shrieked.

The rest of the soldiers practically trampled one another as they fled through the door.

"Move!" Kala exclaimed.

He turned and kicked at the back door. Wood and splinters flew into the air as the door flew off its hinges, opening to an alley. The companions dashed out and raced down alleys that twisted and turned until they were sure they were well away from the tavern.

When they finally slowed to a stop, Han turned to Oieda. With a grin that went from pointed ear to pointed ear, he panted, "I told you he's from the Heavens."

19

VOLSUR

"You believe you can stop Volsur?" Kala asked after Dean explained their intent. "I admit you have powerful magic, but there are only four of you."

"Don't worry about us," growled Bravic. "We've gotten this far."

Kala considered. "I'll go with you," he announced. "I know a safe way into the castle. It's through a service courtyard. We'll have to get through the main gates, though."

"How do you know the way?" Dean asked.

"I guarded the castle before it fell. I know every inch," Kala said.

"Thank you," Dean said, "but I can't let you."

"What?" Han's hands shot up. "The big guy could be helpful."

"You still don't trust me?" Kala asked.

"We could use—" Bravic started to say, but Dean held up his hands to cut him off.

"Hold on," Dean said. "We don't think we're going to be coming back out of there. I can't ask you to die."

Kala's large eyes stared at each of the companions in turn. After a minute, he rolled his huge shoulders and straightened. "Volsur must be stopped. As I said, it was my job to guard the castle, and I failed. I have to try."

Dean looked down at the ground and clenched his jaw.

Han slid up next to Dean. "We could use him, and he said he wants to go."

Oieda grabbed Dean's arm and dragged him around the corner of the alley. She spun him about and got right in his face. "He knows the way. He knows the risk. The only debate is your fear."

"You're not helping," Dean muttered. "I'm no leader. It feels like yesterday I was sleeping under a bridge and praying for a hamburger. Now I'm trying to figure out how to stop a wizard, and I could get you all killed. I don't know what to do."

Oieda squared her shoulders and set her jaw. Then her dimple appeared. "Suck it up, buttercup." She smirked.

Now it was Dean's turn to glare.

She put her hand on his shoulder. "Sometimes you need to dig deep. You can't bear everyone's pain. A warrior knows when they need help. Use your tools. Don't throw us away. This is your time. Be a leader. Seize the moment."

Dean grabbed her around the waist and kissed her. Her arms flew out and her eyes went wide. He held her until he felt her relax. She kissed him back, and his chest swelled.

Dean pulled away and said, "Don't hit me. I had to do that."

Oieda swallowed and nodded. "When I told you to seize the moment, that wasn't what I meant."

"I know. I—"

"Hello?" Han stepped around the corner and tossed his hands up in frustration. "This is supposed to be a group discussion."

Oieda raised her hand. "One minute."

Han's lips pressed together, and he stomped away.

Oieda turned back to Dean and he slowly shook his head. "I'm sorry. I shouldn't have just grabbed you and—"

She grabbed Dean's leather jacket and yanked him against her. Her left hand wrapped around his waist and her right ran up his back and through his hair. Her lips pressed hard against his.

Now it was Dean's turn for his hands to flop awkwardly at his sides. He had kissed girls before, but none had ever come close to Oieda's ferocity. His heart raced. Oieda pinned him against the wall, and her mouth claimed his.

When she finally broke away, Dean stood blinking.

Oieda spun on her heel and walked to the corner.

Dean exhaled. She looked even more beautiful than before.

"Let's go, buttercup." She grinned.

Dean rolled his eyes but hurried after her.

When they rejoined their companions, Dean went up to Kala and held out his hand. Kala clasped Dean's wrist. Dean grabbed Kala's wrist, and they shook.

"So, what can you tell us about the castle?" Dean asked.

***

They stayed in the alley for hours, waiting for darkness. The stench from the garbage made the wait seem all the longer. Kala explained the route they would take over and over and described every turn in detail.

Finally, night came. The five walked toward the castle. It stood even blacker than the sky, its towers silhouetted against the starless heavens. Only two guards stood at the gates, and their chins rested on their chests. Bravic motioned to Kala, and the two crept into the shadows. Bravic and Kala swooped forward, and moments later, the guards slumped to the ground.

Bravic motioned to the others. They snuck through the enormous gates into the courtyard, and Kala led them along the wall. They stopped twice when they heard the sound of footsteps on the ramparts above, but soon they arrived at a narrow wooden door.

Kala opened the door a crack. The only thing greeting them

was silence and the dim light from a torch down a stone hallway. They slipped inside quietly.

They padded down several passageways, up a staircase, and to the immense doors of a huge hall. As Dean peered cautiously inside, he asked, "Are you sure this is the fastest way to go?"

Kala nodded. "We go through the hall and out to the king's courtyard. Just past that is the king's hall. Volsur will be there."

"Sounds good to me," Han whispered. "He knows what he's doing; so far, this has been easy."

Bravic poked him. "You don't talk."

Han scowled, but Bravic winked.

"It's way too easy," Dean muttered.

Kala slipped into the hall, and the others followed. But when they reached the middle of the hall, Oieda held up a hand. All five drew their weapons and scanned the silent room. Nothing moved except the flicker of the flames from the torches on the walls. They continued toward the double doors at the opposite end.

Crack!

"Watch out!" Bravic screamed as he leapt in front of Dean. A barbed arrowhead burst through his armor just below his shoulder. He stumbled and fell to one knee.

They all spun. Behind them, in the doorway through which they had entered, a Tearog with a long bow in his hand was mounted on a Ravinulk. A dozen armored Krulgs poured through the door around him, their curved swords flickering in the torchlight.

The Tearog fired again.

This time Bravic's shield flew open, and the arrow shattered against it. With a groan, Bravic snapped off the barbed head of the arrow in his shoulder and, snarling in pain, he pulled the shaft out. "Run," he growled, his face now ashen.

The Krulgs howled in glee and surged forward.

The companions ran to the doors. Kala lifted the crossbeam that kept them closed and swung them open. Kala and Han rushed through, but Bravic and Oieda did not. Dean stopped in the doorway.

"Go on," Bravic gasped, "I'll hold them off here. I'll stay for this battle, Han." A faint smile crossed his pained lips, and he hefted his massive battle-axe in one hand.

Dean shook his head. "No—"

"Dean," Bravic cut him off, his voice strangely soft, "get going. I'll catch up."

Dean's hand tightened around his sword, and he nodded.

Oieda stood beside Dean in the doorway. She kissed him quickly. "Remember the spear," she said. Then she shoved him backward through the doorway, stepped back into the hall with Bravic, and slammed the door closed.

"No!" Dean screamed.

He heard the crossbar fall into place.

Dean crashed into the door. "No!" he screamed again.

Kala grabbed his arm. "We'll never get back in."

Dean's fist pounded the door, but he knew Kala was right. He tore himself away and followed Kala and Han as they sprinted onward.

Kala led them down two more hallways, then a door opened into a colossal courtyard where a stone-covered path led to a massive stone in the center. Dean's eyes went wide. He'd seen the stone before. It was the same as the one in Panadur's field: a Middle Stone.

But Kala continued past it to a pitch-black gateway on the opposite side of the courtyard. The stones crunched underfoot as they ran.

Han suddenly howled, and a gigantic wing knocked Dean to the ground. Dean looked up to see Han's shoulders in the taloned clutches of a flying beast well over nine feet tall, with the body of a rat and leathery bat-like wings. The creature began to fly away with Han struggling in its grip, but Kala sped after it. With a mighty leap, Kala sprang into the air and grasped Han by his legs.

"Release him, Daehtar," Kala snarled.

"Let go, Kala! Leave me! Help Dean!" Han screamed as the creature rose with a powerful beating of its gargantuan wings.

Dean ran after them, but the bird-thing flew over the roof of the building and disappeared.

Dean stared into the night where his friends had just been. Tears burned in his eyes and fire swept through his heart. He screamed at the sky as burning hate spread through his body.

Then he looked to the doorway where Kala had been leading them. It was dark, completely devoid of light. He knew that through that opening he'd find the one responsible for all this pain. Volsur.

Gritting his teeth, Dean stormed through the opening—and immediately plunged into complete darkness. Blinded, he stumbled forward, feeling with his feet and swinging his sword ahead of him. Gradually, the void lightened. He could make out massive pillars towering above him, rising out of sight. Then distant walls appeared, and he entered a spacious hall that was bathed in a kind of twilight. At the opposite end of the hall was a golden flicker. Dean moved toward it.

A golden-armored figure stepped from the shadows.

"Norouk?" Dean said in disbelief.

***

As the Krulgs raced toward Bravic and Oieda, Bravic groaned and raised his shield, pain flaring through his body. Oieda ran the first Krulg through with her spear while Bravic's axe crashed into the neck of another. They fought side by side:

Oieda on the left, Bravic on the right. Spear and axe cut down the Krulgs that lashed at them, and bodies fell at their feet.

The Krulgs backed up to regroup, leaving half their number behind, dead on the stone floor. Bravic leaned heavily on his axe, never taking his eyes from his foe. Oieda's spear was covered in thick, dark blood. The two moved back toward the doors to get out of the slippery pool of blood.

"They're coming again, Bravic," said Oieda. She had a worried frown.

Six Krulgs surged forward like a wave. Two of them launched themselves into the air, snarling as they sprang. Bravic raised his shield. His arm felt as if it was being torn from his body when the Krulg landed on the shield, but he flung the creature sideways, and his axe cleaved it in two.

Oieda thrust at the other leaping Krulg, and her spear ran the creature through. The weight of the Krulg slamming into her drove her back, and she fell to the blood-soaked floor.

Bravic moved in front of her as the four others sprang forward. His axe crashed into one's head and sent it screaming backward. Another grabbed his shield in its clawed hands and pulled. Pain seared in Bravic's shoulder. As he tried to yank his shield free from the Krulg's grasp, another Krulg with a black sword sliced upward at Bravic's side. The Dwarf's armor split, and the Krulg's sword cut deeply into his flesh.

Bravic stumbled backward; his axe tumbled from his hand.

Oieda rolled the Krulg from atop her and saw Bravic drop to his knees. She jumped to her feet, but a sword ripped into her thigh as she impaled a Krulg with her spear. She had to grab the wall for support.

The other two Krulgs raised their weapons. Oieda lunged with her spear and drove it into one Krulg's chest. The other Krulg swung at Bravic's head, but Oieda's hand snapped out, and her dagger flew. It sank to the hilt in the Krulg's throat.

Bravic's face was pale. "Nice throw."

She winked.

The Tearog raised a massive ivory sword and pulled on the reins of the Ravinulk. The beast let loose a guttural howl and surged forward.

Oieda limped in front of Bravic. Blood splattered her armor. Her heart raced. She looked down at the leather band around her arm, and an image of her father's kind face flashed into her mind. She gipped her spear tighter. She cast one quick look over her shoulder at the barred doors. "We have to buy them more time."

"We will." Bravic picked up his axe.

The Ravinulk's claws clicked on the tile as it stopped before them.

Hobbling on one good leg, Oieda thrust with her spear. But the Tearog's sword swung right through her spear, snapping it in half. She tossed the broken shaft aside and drew her last remaining dagger. Pain washed over her, but she attacked. The Tearog easily knocked aside her blow. Then its bony, death-like hand grasped her by the throat.

Bravic swung his mighty two-headed axe. The Ravinulk's taloned feet knocked Bravic's axe to the side. Its massive mouth closed on Bravic's head, knocked him down, and pinned him to the floor.

Oieda stared down at Bravic, his head partly visible in the mouth of the beast. One pointed tooth was under his jaw, and the top row of teeth clamped down on his forehead. She turned her eyes back to the Tearog as its hand tightened on her throat. The Tearog's deathly eyes stared into hers and flared malevolently.

Bravic felt the blood run down his face. His hand fell to his side and landed on the broken shaft of Oieda's spear. The beast clamped down harder on his face, and Bravic's jaw made a snapping sound. Pain shot through Bravic's head, but his hand firmly grasped the spear shaft. This was one fight he was determined he wouldn't lose. He wouldn't be defeated.

With one final, powerful thrust, he stabbed upward.

The Ravinulk's jaw opened and Bravic fell back to the floor. The Ravinulk fell onto its side, sending the Tearog and Oieda crashing onto the tile.

Oieda scrambled over to pick up Bravic's axe. Gripping it in both hands, she swung with all her strength and screamed a battle cry that filled the hall.

The Tearog raised its sword.

The axe shattered the blade and drove deep into the Tearog's chest.

The Tearog crumpled to the floor.

Oieda sank to her knees. Her hands shook. She drew a ragged breath and looked down at Bravic, who lay unconscious.

Then pain ripped through her side. She looked down to see that an arrow had pierced her leather armor. The blow knocked her onto her back, and her vision blurred. She struggled to sit up but fell back down.

The last thing she saw was another group of Krulgs streaming into the room.

***

Kala's grip tightened around Han's legs as the Daehtar flew skyward. Han gritted his teeth; the weight of the Leomane hanging from him only increased the pain of the talons digging into his shoulders.

The Daehtar began to dive hard toward a rooftop, no doubt planning to knock loose its unwanted passenger. Kala groaned as his body slammed against the wood. Splinters flew, and the cracking of bone pierced the air. But Kala seized the opportunity. He thrust one hand upward and grabbed the Daehtar by its waist.

The beast rose again—and released its grip on Han. The Elvana fell.

Kala reached out for Han, but his hand found only air. Then he felt Han's hands catch hold of his right boot. Now it was Han who dangled from him, and not the other way around.

The Daehtar zigzagged mightily, trying to shake them loose. Han screamed as they spun wildly through the air. Again the Daehtar dove toward a rooftop, this time slamming Han against it. Han howled in pain and his grip loosened, but Kala grabbed Han's arm and pulled him up. Han scrambled onto Kala's back and wrapped his arms around the Lion-Man's thick neck.

They rose once again. As the cold wind swirled around them, the city fell away. Higher and higher they went. The creature's face twisted into a wicked grin, and Kala realized what it had planned.

"It's going to try to shake us loose!" he cried. "Climb onto its back!"

Han climbed up Kala's shoulders and onto the Daehtar's back.

The Daehtar hovered high above the city. Its huge wings beat the air, and it kicked Kala in the face. Kala's head shot sideways, and his hands slid off the creature's waist and onto its leg. Again and again, the beast's talons ripped and struck the Leomane.

And then Kala's hands slipped.

He fell.

Han's dagger pressed against the Daehtar's throat. "Get him or die!" Han screamed as he pressed down on the blade, drawing blood.

The creature hesitated for only a moment before it folded back its wings and dove. Han tightened his grip on the creature's hair and kept the pressure on the knife. He could barely see as the wind rushed against them. The rooftops neared. Han pressed harder.

The beast's talons flashed as it grabbed Kala in midair.

Kala screamed in pain.

The Daehtar's wings beat furiously, trying to stop its descent, but they were diving too steeply to stop. The creature shrieked and let go of Kala, but Kala didn't let go of its legs. The beast tried to turn, but started to spin. It shrieked in terror now as the three plunged straight for a tall building.

"Hang on!" Han shouted, and then they smashed through a roof.

***

"Norouk?" Dean asked again in disbelief.

The golden-armored figure moved forward, and Dean saw it wasn't Norouk. "Navarro? What're you doing here?"

"Don't look so surprised, Dean. Volsur pays better." Navarro smiled. "I hope you've decided to give up that foolish quest. If not, I'm supposed to kill you right now."

Dean's anger burned. "You sold out for what? That stupid-looking armor?"

"For what?" Navarro laughed. "Look around. I was living like a rat. Cold, poor ... a loser. Just like you. Now look at me." He held his arms out. "You'll find life with Volsur a lot more appealing."

"Do you know what happened to the last guy Volsur gave golden armor to? Norouk betrayed his friends too. His reward was living for years in a valley with a bunch of twisted freak creatures until the guys he betrayed came back and ripped him into little pieces. What a bargain he made! I don't know how you're going to end up, but if you side with Volsur, it's not going to end well."

Navarro drew his sword. "I won't be like Norouk. Volsur needs me."

Now it was Dean's turn to laugh. "Volsur needs you? For what? Your friends needed you. You betrayed them. Now you have nothing left to give Volsur. He used you."

Navarro rushed at Dean and swung his sword. Steel clashed against steel. Dean's anger finally burst and swept through his body like fire. His sword was a blur as he rained blow after blow down on Navarro.

Navarro backed up, the smile on his face replaced by a panicked scowl. Navarro parried again and again, but Dean's strikes flew fast and hard.

Then Dean swept Navarro's sword aside. Navarro lunged in and grabbed Dean's sword arm. Dean punched him in the face.

Navarro fell backward and pulled Dean down on top of him. Dean ripped Navarro's helmet off, and his fists pummeled Navarro's face. Blood splattered across Navarro's golden armor, and Dean kept punching.

"I surrender!" Navarro gasped.

Dean hit him again.

"I surrender," Navarro said. "Mercy."

Dean's fists stopped.

"Mercy," Navarro mumbled.

Dean stood up. He wiped his bloody hands on his jeans. He retrieved his sword. "You don't deserve mercy."

He walked back to Navarro and pointed his sword at Navarro's chest.

Navarro held up a trembling hand. "Please?"

Taking a deep breath, Dean lowered his sword to his side.

Navarro's hand fell to the floor, and he started to weep.

A bitter cold crept over Dean's skin. The hairs on his neck rose, and he tightened the grip on his sword. From somewhere in the darkness came footsteps.

"Nice, very nice," a voice called from the shadows.

A man dressed in white and green pants and shirt, with an

emerald-colored cape across his broad shoulders, strode forward. His blond hair fell down to his shoulders, brushed back from his handsome, tanned face.

"Very nice, Dean," the man repeated in a deep voice.

There was something very familiar about the man, but Dean couldn't place it until he got closer. Dean gasped when he saw the man's steel-gray eyes. They looked just like Panadur's.

"Volsur?" Dean stammered as he raised his sword.

"Please. Don't be so quick to kill me." Volsur smiled, turned his hands outward, and opened them to show they were empty. "Letting Navarro live was very kind. But didn't my brother tell you? In this world, kind gets you killed."

"Your brother told me a lot. He told me you're the reason this world is so evil."

"Me?" Volsur laughed. It was the kind of laugh heard on a warm day, the kind of gentle laugh that made other people smile. "This world was evil long before me. You met Lorious. How kind was he? My brothers and I traveled all over our world, fighting to make it better, until I realized we were wrong. I was just like you. I showed kindness, and it got me nothing."

"Panadur seemed pretty happy."

"He was a fool. The three of us could have taken over this world with less killing, but instead of helping me, they turned against me."

"Shocker." Dean's mouth twisted into a smirk. "The good guys wanted to stop the crazy bad guy. They didn't kill you, though. They showed you mercy. Seems if they'd killed you, this world would have been better off."

"Exactly." Volsur's teeth gleamed bright-white as he smiled. "If they'd been strong enough to kill me, they would have gotten what they wanted. But they're weak, like you. You let Navarro live. He'll come back someday and repay your kindness with a dagger in your back. It's not too late though. Kill him, and I'll let you take his place as one of my men."

"Tell you what. I'll kick your butt too, and let you take his place on the floor." Dean walked forward. "I'll never be one of your men."

"You're just like my men," Volsur replied calmly.

"What are you talking about?"

"Pure of heart?" Volsur chuckled. "Please. Pure of heart. The little shoplifter? You're a common thief. You're a cheater and a liar." His laughter echoed down the hall. "Pure of heart— you're just like my men."

Dean shook his head. "Those things didn't happen here. They happened in my world."

"It doesn't matter," Volsur scoffed. "You're the same as me. You really believed my foolish brother, didn't you? Pure of heart! Did you really think you were going to kill me? You and your misfit band? A deserting Dwarf, a helpless Elvana, a female Elf, and a beast? How do you think you got in here? Did you think you could just walk into my castle? You're a fool. I brought you here. The whole way. Ever since you crashed through little Han's roof and smashed his bed, I've watched over you. I wanted you to come here."

"You didn't bring me here. I came to stop you." Dean raised his sword.

"Stop me? I brought you here to join me. It's one big family reunion." Volsur lifted a hand and pointed to the corner of the room. Torches flared to life, and Dean saw what had been hiding in the darkness: Carimus hung suspended in a black sphere. His eyes were filled with despair, and his blue robes and silver hair were dirty and disheveled. His aged face seemed to age even more as he gazed at Dean.

"Have you formally met your uncle?" Volsur asked.

"How ...?" Dean stammered.

Volsur shrugged. "What I want, I get. I just walked in and

took him. Our friend Navarro here wanted to help, so I brought him along. For you."

Dean's heart was ready to burst in his chest. He wanted to cry. He wanted to die.

"It's over. I've won. You've been a loser your whole life. Don't be one now. Join me. I can give you everything. Money, power, anything. Look at Carimus." He pointed. "Why does he not say anything? Because he knows I'm right. Look in your heart, Dean. You think about others and not yourself. Where has that gotten you? Nowhere. You had no place to go, so my brother took you in like a stray dog. Was he any different, Dean? He used you. He knew why you were running away. He knew why, but did he say or do anything to help? He could have. He's a wizard. Wasn't love a wonderful thing?" Volsur laughed. "You failed then, and you've failed now."

Dean lowered his sword.

"But you didn't fail because of you; it was because of others," Volsur continued. "Because you thought about them and not yourself. When you thought about yourself, you had power. Telling the truth brought you pain. Lying, stealing: that's when you gained. Do you really think my world is any different from yours? Panadur? Was he any different? Your life is a fantasy. He cared nothing for you." The Dark Lord's laughter echoed through the room. "But you don't need him. You need to make others need you. Make them fear you. When you control them, they can never hurt you. Be a ruler, not a fool."

Dean's tears seemed to freeze in his eyes and ice them over. His heart grew cold, and his hand tightened on his sword. "No. Panadur loved me."

"Did he? Then why did he send a boy to fight me? A boy to fight the most powerful wizard in the realm? You said it yourself: it's a suicide mission. He sent you to die. That's love? So tell me, why did he send you?"

Dean's mouth opened and closed.

"I'm sorry, but I didn't hear you." Volsur leaned toward Dean. "Do you not know? Well then ... why don't we ask him?" Volsur raised his right hand.

Torches flared at the side of the room—and there, suspended in a dark orb much like Carimus's, was Panadur. The old man's face was pale, but the corners of his mouth ticked up into a faint smile when he looked at Dean.

"Do you think I'd leave my dear brother to die in some forsaken world? Alone? Unloved?" Volsur clicked his tongue. "You misjudge me, Dean. I'm not the evil monster you think I am. You thought he was dead, but I came to your world and saved him. I brought him here and nursed him back to health. I'm not the wicked warlord my brother said I am. I'm a realist. People will take what they can. I just believe you need to take it first."

Dean took a step toward Panadur, and the old man shook his head. Dean stopped.

"What?" Volsur's hands went out. "No hug for your father?" He chuckled. "Think, Dean. Think. Why would Panadur send a boy to another world to try to stop someone as powerful as me?"

Dean stared at Panadur. The old man's eyes burned. Dean could see emotions flash across his face. Anger. Pain. Love. Doubt.

Dean closed his eyes. After a moment, he turned back to Volsur, and a smirk spread across Dean's face. "I'll answer your question, and then you answer mine."

Volsur raised an eyebrow. "Agreed. Why would your 'father' send you to fight a man as powerful as me?"

"He sent me here because he believed in me. He knows I can win."

"You dare mock me?" Volsur roared.

Dean held up his hand. "Don't flatter yourself; I mock

everybody. Now, it's time for you to answer my question. Why would you save your brother's life?"

Volsur shook his head. "My poor boy. That's right. I forgot. You've never had a family. You don't understand what real love is."

"No, I get it. The whole 'blood is thicker than water' thing. But you? You said mercy is for the weak. The way I see it, you need something from your brothers. You need them in order to access the Middle Stone." Dean was just guessing, but he did his best to mask that.

Volsur leveled his gaze at Dean. A smile spread across his face, and then he turned his head toward Panadur. "It seems you have selected a bright pupil, brother. Very good, Dean. But you're wrong about one thing."

"What would that be?"

"I need them to access the Middle Stones. Plural. There are many worlds I intend to conquer. I can access one—that's easy. Getting an army through, however ..." Volsur turned his hands out. "That's a little more difficult. But with three wizards"—he snapped his fingers—"it's a piece of cake."

Dean felt his body grow cold. "You have a bit of a power complex. You should talk to someone about that, because you sure sound crazy."

"Silence!" Volsur shouted.

The sound of metal on tile rang across the hall. Navarro had risen to his feet and picked up his sword. He glared at Dean. "I'll finish him, my lord."

Dean turned toward this new threat.

Navarro shook his head ever so slightly as he approached Dean.

Dean took a step back.

Volsur laughed. "Looks like I'm right, Dean. This is what mercy gets you. Kill him, Navarro."

Navarro yelled and charged at Dean. He raised his sword above his head and smashed it down. Dean easily blocked the blow with his own sword.

Navarro pressed down until his mouth was near Dean's ear. "Free Panadur," he whispered, then swung again.

Dean blocked and pressed forward, chest to chest with Navarro. "Go for Carimus," Dean whispered back.

Navarro shook his head slightly as he swung his sword. "No. Volsur," he hissed.

Dean leapt in front of Navarro and blocked his path. "You'll die."

Their swords clashed again. The sound of metal on metal rang through the room. Navarro pressed close to Dean. "I know."

Navarro seized Dean and shoved him toward Panadur. Dean ran straight for the sphere while Navarro spun and rushed at Volsur.

"Traitor!" Volsur shrieked.

"Not anymore," Navarro cried as he charged at the wizard.

Dean jumped for the red jewel that spun over Panadur's sphere. His sword shattered the gem. The sphere flickered and then vanished.

Panadur fell to his knees.

Volsur waved his hand, and a black bolt streaked straight at Navarro. The blast hit Navarro in the chest and blew him fifty feet backward. Navarro's body slammed into a column and crumpled to the floor. Dean was certain he was dead.

Volsur turned his glare to Dean.

Flames flew from Panadur's hand. But he didn't aim for Volsur; he aimed for the stone above the sphere that trapped his other brother. The gem shattered. Volsur screamed in rage.

Carimus's hands were already moving as he dropped to the floor.

Panadur's hands wove the same signs as his brother. "Strike now, Dean," Panadur panted. "We're keeping him from using his magic."

Dean charged.

Volsur drew his sword and sneered. "I don't need magic to kill your cub, brother."

Their swords slammed together, and Volsur swept Dean's blade aside.

Dean leapt back, and Volsur's blade sliced into his left arm.

Volsur swung for Dean's head. Dean ducked and thrust at Volsur's chest, but Volsur parried the blow and countered with his own strike toward Dean's heart. Dean barely dodged.

The clang of metal rang through the hall as Dean's sword shot out and Volsur's blade blocked. Dean's blade became a blur, but every time he thought he could strike Volsur, he found Volsur's sword pointed straight at his chest. He had to pull back or be run through himself by the wizard's sword.

A cry of pain from Panadur caused Dean's eyes to dart away from Volsur. Panadur coughed and sank down to one knee. His face was ashen and his hands trembled. Blood ran from the corner of his mouth.

"Give up," Volsur sneered. "Your father is still too weak to fight. If he goes much longer, not even I can save him."

"Leave him alone," Dean screamed as he struck wildly.

Volsur's sword slashed Dean's side.

Dean jumped back. He could feel the blood running down his ribs.

"And what about your uncle?" Volsur stood tall. "He's very weak now, too."

Dean glanced at Carimus, who stood with his arms outstretched, his face twisted in pain. Dean could see that neither man could continue to fight much longer.

He thought of his companions. They were all willing to die

to defeat Volsur. Then he remembered Oieda's spear.

Dean danced back and cast a quick sidelong look at Panadur. Their eyes locked. The old man's eyes widened.

"Dean, no!" Panadur cried, but it was too late.

Dean planted his rear foot. His sneaker pressed into the tile and his muscles fired. A feeling of power surged through him as he pushed off and lunged forward. Everything slowed. He flew straight at Volsur. Dean's sword tip lowered and pointed at Volsur's heart. Like a mirror image, Volsur's blade did the same. Volsur's snide, almost bored, smile disappeared when he saw that Dean didn't turn away this time.

Dean came straight in. Volsur's arm was longer than Dean's, and his sword struck Dean in the chest first. His blade pierced Dean's heart.

But Dean's momentum carried him forward. Dean's sword drove through Volsur's chest, too.

Dean heard Panadur scream. He wanted to turn his head and look at him, but his body wasn't doing anything he asked anymore—including breathing. Dean knew Volsur's sword was buried in his chest, but he felt no pain. He couldn't feel anything.

His hand slipped off the handle of his sword, and his legs gave out beneath him. He fell to his knees, then onto his side.

But his sword and Volsur stayed where they were. Dean's sword had driven straight through the evil wizard and pinned him to a column.

Volsur looked at Dean with pure evil in his eyes. He screamed in rage. And then he began to change. His hair turned the color of night; his gray eyes sank back into his head. His face became worn and scarred, and his robes turned to tatters. His body smoldered. Smoke spiraled around the pillar, etching immense evil runes wherever it touched. With a last cry of hate, Volsur's body burst into an ebony cloud that swept up the pillar and sank into its surface.

Panadur and Carimus rushed to Dean's side. As Panadur cradled Dean's head, Carimus pulled the sword from his chest.

"Carimus, please, help him," Panadur begged.

Dean wanted to say something, but he couldn't talk. He couldn't breathe. He couldn't feel.

Carimus placed his hand on Dean's chest and narrowed his eyes. Dean's vision blurred and darkened.

"Carimus!" Panadur shouted.

"He's not strong enough to survive. He'll die in agony if I try."

"Dead's dead. Try."

"There's too much damage. I'm not strong enough."

Panadur laid his hand on Dean's chest too. "Then I'll help. Do it."

"You're too weak." Carimus shook his head. "It could kill you."

"Brother, please."

Carimus's scowl softened. Looking down at Dean, he said, "This will hurt."

Dean knew it wouldn't. After all, he couldn't feel anything. Just then, a pain unlike any he had ever felt ripped through Dean's body. He closed his eyes and grit his teeth. His heels pressed down, and he arched his back so high only the back of his head touched the floor. White light exploded all around him, and he screamed until his voice was hoarse. It felt as if his body was slowly turning inside out while it burned.

Then the pain stopped. Dean fell back to the tile, gasping, and his eyes fluttered open. His mouth opened and closed like a fish out of water, but no sound came out.

Carimus lowered his face closer to Dean's. His bushy eyebrows were arched with concern, and his lips were pressed together. "He lived through the first part." He cast a worried glance at Panadur.

Panadur smiled weakly. "Keep going."

"It will be too much for you." Carimus pleaded.

Panadur shook his head. "Hang in there, Dean."

Dean wanted to shout at Panadur to stop. He wanted to scream that it would be too much for the old man, but he was helpless. He couldn't move.

"Dean, this next step is going to be really painful," said Carimus.

Dean's eyes widened. And that last pain wasn't?

A greenish-blue light glowed from Carimus's hands. He pressed them against Dean's chest. Dean's eyes rolled back in his head, and his world turned black.

20

THE NEW KING

Dean's eyes fluttered open, and he drew a ragged breath. The horrific pain was gone, but he struggled to sit up.

"Easy," Carimus said. Dean looked at the old wizard who sat beside him. A smile crossed his face. "You lived. I'm surprised."

"Where's ...?" Dean's voice trailed off when he saw Panadur lying on the tile floor.

"He's alive." Carimus put his hand on Dean's arm. "He's very weak. The strain was almost too much for him, but he will live. We should not move him."

"Oieda ... I have to go help my friends." Dean winced as he stood up.

"Too soon," Carimus mumbled. "You're still hurt. And I cannot help you." He lay down, resting his head on the floor.

"Stay still," Dean whispered. "I'll try to find help."

He limped over to the rune-covered pillar where Volsur had died. Grimacing, he pulled his sword out.

Before he left, he hobbled over to Navarro's body and looked down at him. "Thank you, Navarro. I'll tell everyone you died a hero's death."

The end of the hall was no longer obscured by Volsur's magic. Light streamed in through the open doors, and Dean stepped out into a sunlit courtyard.

In the middle of the walkway, he saw Han's worn little shoe.

Tears rolled down his face as he picked it up and put it in his jacket pocket. He didn't know where Han and Kala had been taken, or if they were alive. But he knew where to find Bravic and Oieda.

Since the door would be barred, he took a different hallway, looking for a way around to the hall where he had left them. It was getting harder for him to breathe, but he pushed on. And then, up ahead, he saw stairs and a doorway he recognized. He was approaching the spot where Bravic and Oieda had made their last stand.

Dean stumbled into the hall. Bodies were everywhere. And next to the barred door in the back of the hall, lying side by side, were Bravic and Oieda, with more bodies all around them. Bravic lay face down, and Oieda was on her side.

Dean dropped to his knees beside her and laid his hand on her forehead. She was warm. As he rolled her onto her back, her eyes fluttered open. A faint smile came to her lips.

"You did it," she whispered.

"We did."

She smiled weakly and closed her eyes.

Dean turned to Bravic, who lay in a pool of blood. He turned the Dwarf over and gasped at the wounds all over his chest. Bravic drew a ragged breath and mumbled something. Dean held the Dwarf. His pulse felt weak.

Footsteps sounded behind him. With great effort, Dean forced himself to his feet.

"Hail!" a voice called as many armored men rushed into view. "Are you one of Volsur's?"

"Volsur's dead," Dean called out through gritted teeth. "I killed him."

A mighty cheer sprang from the mouths of the men. Two ran out of the hall shouting the news, and the others surged forward.

"My friends are hurt." Dean pointed to Bravic and Oieda. "And Panadur and Carimus need help in the King's Hall."

"Panadur and Carimus?" the armored man shouted. "They'll be cared for along with the others." He motioned to some men, who then ran out of the hall; others came to aid Bravic and Oieda.

Dean's vision blurred. "I've also lost two other friends. A Leomane and an Elvana."

"Yes, Kala and the little one," the man said. "We found them. They defeated a Daehtar."

"Are they alive?" Dean asked.

"They are indeed. They're in the captain's quarters."

Dean's sword slid from his hand and clattered to the ground. "Help them," Dean mumbled before he passed out.

***

The next time Dean awoke, it was to the sound of singing outside his window. Groaning, he sat up. His companions—Han, Bravic, Oieda, and Kala—all lay sleeping in the same room. Bravic snored loudly.

Dean slipped out of the bed and walked over to the window. He flung the shutters open and saw hundreds of people dancing in the sunlit streets.

"Dean," Han whispered, "you're awake. Carimus came by, but you were sleeping. He gave us all medicine then went back to the tower to take care of Panadur. He told us what happened with Volsur. I wish I'd been there, but Kala and I—ow!" Bravic bounced a pillow off his bandaged head. "Bravic's just mad because he can't talk," Han whispered.

Dean looked at Oieda. She rolled over and opened her green eyes. Her dimple popped as she smiled at him. Dean's knees went weak, but he wasn't sure if it was because of his recent brush with death or that dimple. He swallowed hard and sat on his bed.

"Breakfast is ready," a heavyset woman announced as she carried in trays stacked on top of each other. Soon all five were devouring eggs, bacon, ham, and toast. Han would have outeaten everyone, but Kala ate enough for four.

"Well, anyway, Dean," Han said as he pushed his plate aside, "when Kala and I were on that Daehtar thing, we smashed right through the roof of another building. Kala's arm snapped when he broke his fall on that thing's neck. The Daehtar died when we hit. I was lucky I landed on top."

"What happened with you, Oieda?" Dean asked.

"Bravic saved me from the Tearog." She smiled at the Dwarf, who nodded. "The Ravinulk broke Bravic's jaw, but Bravic still managed to kill it. I killed the Tearog, but then more Krulgs came into the hall. We wouldn't have been able to fight them. But when you killed Volsur ..." She pressed her hand against her chest and shrugged. "You could just feel it. The Krulgs must have sensed it too, because they turned and ran. You saved us all."

Dean looked from Oieda to Bravic. "And you saved me."

Han spoke up. "Carimus said it could be a few weeks before Bravic can speak again." He looked horrified at the thought of not talking for that long.

"Well, he'll have a lot of scars to be proud of now," Oieda said. "One across his ribs, that one on his shoulder, the scar under his chin, and the one running across the top of his head. Scars are marks of honor. The Kilacouquen think they're beautiful on a warrior."

"Then Bravic has to be one beautiful Dwarf now," Han giggled.

They all burst into laughter at the sight of Bravic scowling through clenched teeth while his cheeks turned bright red.

The five laughed and joked all morning and well past lunch. As supper approached, Kala motioned Dean over to his bed, careful not to disturb the others, who'd all lain down to rest.

"Dean, the people want you to be king," he whispered with a grin.

"Me? King?" Dean laughed. "Sorry, I'm no king."

"But the people need a leader." Kala rose onto his elbows. "I've watched you. You're brave. You did this with no thought of yourself. You should be king."

"Isn't there someone else you could get for the job? Like a real king?"

"The people want you. If you don't choose to be king, then you must choose someone else."

Dean wished there was some way out of making this choice. "They had a king before. Who's the next person in line?"

"The captain of the guards. But you should choose who you feel is right." Kala lay back down. "The people are hurting, and so is the land. They need someone who'll help heal them. Someone just and fair. You can be that man. There aren't many who are not corrupted by power and greed. The best king is a servant king. One who would place the needs of the people above his own."

As Dean looked at the Leomane, he felt a great respect for him. Dean knew Kala would do all the things he had just said a king should do. "Kala, do you know the captain of the guards?"

"My opinion does not matter." Kala raised his head. "The choice is yours."

"Everyone liked the last king, right?" Dean asked.

Kala nodded. "He was a great man."

"Did he pick the captain of the guard?"

Kala sighed. "He did. The king gave him a chance when many others would not have."

Dean frowned. "You know what? I think you know the

captain of the guards well. Every time I ask you about him, you duck the question."

Kala scowled. "I don't want to influence you."

"If this king, who everyone says was a good king, picked the captain of the guards, knowing he could possibly become king if something happened ... well, who am I to argue? Seriously, he picked the—"

A knock on the door cut him off. The door opened, and a young soldier stepped inside and saluted. "Excuse me, Captain, but the people are calling for their king."

"Captain? You're the captain of the guard!" Han yelled as he sat up in bed and pointed at Kala.

"You were leading the men on the Mountain of Hope," Oieda said.

"Then he should be king, Dean." Han clapped his hands together. "King Kala Panteoth!"

"It's settled, King." Dean laughed.

Kala glared at the soldier, who shrank before his look.

Then the Lion-Man burst out laughing, too.

The noise in the street continued, and the companions painfully slid out of bed. Dean hurried over to Oieda's bed and held out his hand. She smiled as she clasped his wrist and pulled herself up. Dean slipped his arm around her, and she leaned on his shoulder. Together they walked over to the balcony.

A great cheer erupted from the crowd in the streets. The applause rose to a roar as each of the companions came out onto the balcony and bowed. Dean made sure Kala came last. When Kala walked out, it was to a fanfare of trumpets. The other companions bowed to the new king, and the crowd went silent.

"People of Aeriot." Kala's voice rang through the streets. "Volsur is slain. His forces are scattered. Peace will once again come to the lands." Cheers rose after each sentence, and each time Kala had to hold his massive hand in the air and wait for the crowd's cheers to die down. "Riders must be sent out to all the lands to tell of Volsur's end and the tale of four brave warriors."

"Five!" Han yelled. "Long live the king. Let's feast!" he hollered.

The crowd erupted into cheers.

21

THE HEAVENS

Dean lay in the quiet room and listened to his companions sleeping. Oieda lay in the bed next to him. For the last hour, he had been gazing at her face. He didn't know why, but he couldn't bring himself to shut his eyes. He just lay there studying every detail about her. The curve of her lips. Her delicate features. The shades of brown in her hair as it draped over the pillow.

He finally rolled onto his back, stared at the ceiling just visible in the darkness, and sighed. His eyes had just started to close when the door opened and Carimus stepped inside.

"Carimus," Dean whispered. He slipped out of bed and walked over to the door. "How's Panadur?"

"He awoke for a moment." The old man smiled. "We have some things to talk about. Walk with me."

Dean hurriedly dressed. He took one last long look back at Oieda before quietly closing the door behind him.

Carimus led him to the castle and all the way to the king's courtyard—the courtyard with the Middle Stone. They stopped before it.

"Dean. You've done well. Volsur is slain. People are once again trying to rid this world of the evil that grew in his reign. It will take time, though. Volsur's power was strong, and under his rule many evil things came down from the Barren Lands. To hunt them all will take a long time. But now that does not concern you."

As Carimus said these last words, Dean felt as if he'd been struck.

"You are not from this world, Dean," Carimus continued. "All the thanks in this world could not repay you, and my gratitude is all I can give. This world owes you more than anyone can ever grasp. But now, it's time for you to return to your own world." He bowed. "Dean Theradine, my nephew, thank you and goodbye."

Dean wanted to protest, but he couldn't move.

Carimus walked over to him, closed his eyes, and bowed his head. When he raised his head and opened his eyes again, he gave Dean a smile. It was the kind of sad smile you see people give each other before they part for a long time.

Then Carimus pushed Dean through the Middle Stone.

***

"Hello? Are you okay?"

Dean heard the words as if someone was calling to him through a fog. Something pushed against his shoulder, and Dean scrambled to his feet. He looked around frantically and realized he was standing before the Middle Stone in Panadur's field back on Earth. The sun was setting behind the mountain.

Dean stood before a man wearing a large hiking backpack. Ten yards away, a woman with two children huddling at her legs called out, "Honey? Is he okay?"

The man held up his hand and took a step closer to Dean. "Are you okay?"

Dean stared down at his leather jacket. All the rips and cuts were gone. "No," Dean mumbled. "It happened. No!" Dean screamed at the sky, and the man jumped backward. "It wasn't a dream. Carimus!" Dean yelled at the stone. "Take me back! I helped you! I helped you! I killed Volsur!"

The man turned pale and stumbled backward, tripping over his own feet. Looking panicked, he hurried his wife and children down the path and away from this madman.

"No!" Dean yelled. He flung himself at the Middle Stone, only to crash against its surface and slide to the ground. Again and again he leapt at the rock, until his shoulder was bruised and tears ran down his face.

"Please. Please! I don't belong here. That's my home. Get Panadur. Get my father!" Dean sank to his knees before the stone and desperately cried, "Please!"

He knelt, sobbing, for a long time.

Finally, he opened his eyes and stared down at his hands. They were balled into fists. The leather jacket scratched his face as he dried his eyes. He stood. Taking one last look at the Middle Stone, he placed his hand against it, and then walked away.

The sky turned a brilliant gold, and a breeze swept across the field. Dean dug his hands into the pockets of his jacket. He stared past his faded jeans and worn sneakers as he started toward the trees.

Someone giggled behind him.

Dean spun around.

Han stood at the base of the Middle Stone with his mouth open and his eyes wide. "That was so neat!" Han exclaimed with a little jump. Then he saw Dean. "Dean! I woke up when Carimus came for you. I hope you don't mind, but I followed you. When Carimus sent you back, I ran and told Panadur. Wow, was he mad! He and Carimus had a huge argument, but Carimus finally agreed that you should come back. Panadur told me to hurry and get his son."

Dean ran over, picked up Han, and spun him around. "Thank you. Thank you."

When he set Han down, the Elvana continued to spin around

on his own. "Panadur also said he still has things for us to do. Do you know what that means?" Han held his arms against his chest, and his whole body vibrated.

"What?" Dean asked.

"More adventure!" Han leaned his head back and threw his arms out wide.

Dean laughed, grabbed Han, and jumped headlong into the Middle Stone. As they tumbled into the darkness, Dean heard Han call out, "So that's what the Heavens look like!"

THE END

IF YOU LIKED PURE OF HEART, YOU'LL LOVE JACK!

The Detective Jack Stratton Mystery-Thriller Series, authored by *Wall Street Journal* bestselling author Christopher Greyson, has over one million readers and counting. If you'd love to read another page-turning thriller with mystery, humor, and a dash of romance, pick up the next book in the highly acclaimed series today.

Novels featuring Jack Stratton in order:
AND THEN SHE WAS GONE
GIRL JACKED
JACK KNIFED
JACKS ARE WILD
JACK AND THE GIANT KILLER
DATA JACK
JACK OF HEARTS
JACK FROST

AND THEN SHE WAS GONE

A hometown hero with a heart of gold, Jack Stratton was raised in a whorehouse by his prostitute mother. Jack seemed destined to become another statistic, but now his life has taken a turn for the better. Determined to escape his past, he's headed for a career in law enforcement. When his foster mother asks him to look into a girl's disappearance, Jack quickly gets drawn into a baffling mystery. As Jack digs deeper, everyone becomes a suspect—including himself. Caught between the criminals and the cops, can Jack discover the truth in time to save the girl? Or will he become the next victim?

GIRL JACKED

Guilt has driven a wedge between Jack and the family he loves. When Jack, now a police officer, hears the news that his foster sister Michelle is missing, it cuts straight to his core. The police think she just took off, but Jack knows Michelle would never leave her loved ones behind—like he did. Forced to confront the demons from his past, Jack must take action, find Michelle, and bring her home... or die trying.

JACK KNIFED

Constant nightmares have forced Jack to seek answers about his rough childhood and the dark secrets hidden there. The mystery surrounding Jack's birth father leads Jack to investigate the twenty-seven-year-old murder case in Hope Falls.

JACKS ARE WILD

When Jack's sexy old flame disappears, no one thinks it's suspicious except Jack and one unbalanced witness. Jack feels in his gut that something is wrong. He knows that Marisa has a past, and if it ever caught up with her—it would be deadly. The trail leads him into all sorts of trouble—landing him smack in the middle of an all-out mob war between the Italian Mafia and the Japanese Yakuza.

JACK AND THE GIANT KILLER

Rogue hero Jack Stratton is back in another action-packed, thrilling adventure. While recovering from a gunshot wound, Jack gets a seemingly harmless private investigation job—locate the owner of a lost dog—Jack begrudgingly assists. Little does he know it will place him directly in the crosshairs of a merciless serial killer.

DATA JACK

In this digital age of hackers, spyware, and cyber terrorism—data is more valuable than gold. Thieves plan to steal the keys to the digital kingdom and with this much money at stake, they'll kill for it. Can Jack and Alice (aka Replacement) stop the pack of ruthless criminals before they can *Data Jack?*

JACK OF HEARTS

When his mother and the members of her neighborhood book club ask him to catch the "Orange Blossom Cove Bandit," a small-time thief who's stealing garden gnomes and peace of mind from their quiet retirement community, how can Jack refuse? The peculiar mystery proves to be more than it appears, and things take a deadly turn. Now, Jack finds it's up to him to stop a crazed killer, save his parents, and win the hand of the girl he loves—but if he survives, will it be Jack who ends up with a broken heart?

JACK FROST

Jack has a new assignment: to investigate the suspicious death of a soundman on the hit TV show *Planet Survival.* Jack goes undercover as a security agent where the show is filming on nearby Mount Minuit. Soon trapped on the treacherous peak by a blizzard, a mysterious killer continues to stalk the cast and crew of *Planet Survival.* What started out as a game is now a deadly competition for survival. As the temperature drops and the body count rises, what will get them first? The mountain or the killer?

ACKNOWLEDGMENTS

Thank you! Thank you for taking the time to read this book. I hope you loved reading it as much as I did writing it. Word-of-mouth is crucial for any author to succeed. If you enjoyed Pure of Heart, please consider leaving a review at Amazon, even if it is only a line or two; it would make all the difference and I would appreciate it very much.

I would also like to thank my wife Kathy. She's fabulous. She is an invaluable content editor and I could not do this without her! My thanks also go out to my family who have always been there for me. My fantastic editors: Karen Lawson and Janet Hitchcock of The Proof is in the Reading and Faith Williams of The Atwater Group. My fabulous consultant—Dianne Jones, the unbelievably helpful Beta readers, including Michael Muir and Melinda Rennie, and the two best kids in the world Laura and Christopher. My thanks to them for all of their help, jokes and love.

ABOUT THE AUTHOR

Since I was a little boy, I have dreamt of what mystery was around the next corner, or what quest lay over the hill. If I couldn't find an adventure, one usually found me, and now I weave those tales into my stories. I am blessed to have written the best-selling Jack Stratton mystery series. The collection includes And Then She Was GONE, Girl Jacked, Jack Knifed, Jacks Are Wild, Jack and the Giant Killer, Data Jack, Jack of Hearts and Jack Frost.

My love for tales of mystery and adventure began with my grandfather, a decorated World War I hero. I will never forget being introduced to his friend, a WWI pilot who flew across the skies at the same time as the feared, legendary Red Baron. My love of reading and storytelling eventually led me to write Pure of Heart, a young adult fantasy.

I love to hear from my readers. Please go to ChristopherGreyson.com and sign up for my mailing list to receive periodic updates on this and new book releases, plus be entered for prizes and free giveaways.

Thank you for reading my novels and I hope my stories have brightened your day.

Sincerely,

Made in the USA
Las Vegas, NV
15 September 2021

30351066R00163